Copyright © 2024 by Sophia Charles

This is a work of fiction. Names, characters, places, and incidents are the product of the author's imagination or are used fictitiously. Any resemblance to actual events, locales, or persons, living or dead, is entirely coincidental.

SHATTERED

secrets!

"Attention: This book contains explicit sexual content, strong language, and depictions of death and suicide. Reader discretion is strongly advised. The content explores mature themes, including intimate situations, explicit language, and mortality. Please be aware of the explicit nature of these elements and proceed only if you are comfortable with such content."

In the pursuit of truth, some secrets are best left buried.

Table Of Contents

CHAPTER 1

BRITTNEY

Jarred, get your lazy ass in here now, is what I wanted to say as I pressed the intercom. "Jarred, my office NOW."

Jarred came rushing into my office a few seconds later, tripping over his shoelace. I couldn't help but roll my eyes.

His disheveled appearance was a striking reflection of his disregard for personal grooming. His tousled hair fell in unruly strands as if untouched by a comb for days. His beard grew patchy and unkempt, suggesting a neglect for shaving or trimming. The wrinkles on his face appeared deep and weathered, etching a story of a man who paid little attention to skincare or self-care routines.

What irritated me the most was his choice of attire. He always chose suits that were several sizes too big for his frame. The ill-fitting garments seemed to hang on him like a costume, emphasizing his outsider status in the polished corporate world.

Despite his attempts to blend in, he stood out like a sore thumb, starkly contrasting the impeccably dressed executives surrounding him.

The first day he walked in here with shorts, I knew this pathetic man-child would not last; I don't care who his father is.

After taking a few deep breaths, I stood up from behind my desk, eyes locked on a nervous assistant. I strode towards him, coming only inches away from his face.

I stood five feet eight, but with the stilettos, I was almost, if not six feet tall. I'm glad I chose to wear them today; they will drive my point.

"Where is the Ricci file?"

Shaking like a leaf, he uttered,

"I'm sorry. I will get to it as soon as I can."

As soon as I can? I've put in countless hours and effort to achieve my position as the youngest legal director in this law firm. My goal of becoming a partner by age 30 drives me forward, and I won't let setbacks like this slow me down.

In this cutthroat world, it's survival of the fittest, and if you can't keep up, you won't last in this office.

I fixed my gaze on him, my eyes narrowed, and my lips sealed tight for a full fifteen seconds. If I were to terminate his employment, it would undoubtedly cause an uproar with Marla, my boss. She values loyalty and second chances, often giving people more opportunities to prove themselves. But with Jarred, it's different. I've given him ample chances to improve and meet the expectations of this demanding job. Yet, time and time again, he falls short.

His lack of professionalism, disregard for punctuality, and constant excuses have pushed me to the edge. I cannot continue to tolerate his incompetence, as it reflects poorly on both me and this firm's reputation. It's time to make a tough decision, even if it means facing the consequences from her.

"You're fired; pack your shit and get out."

I pivoted on my heel before he could utter a word, striding purposefully back to my desk. Just as I was about to settle into my seat, I realized Jarred hadn't budged an inch; his eyes fixed on me.

A fleeting sense of hope fluttered within me as I watched him, expecting him to finally stand up for himself (did he finally find his balls?). But my hope was short-lived as he turned and walked away without a word.

Disappointment washed over me, heavy and stifling, as I realized Jarred's lack of determination remained unchanged. It was clear that he lacked courage or ambition.

My decision to part ways with him had become even more justified, even if it meant dealing with the consequences that would surely follow.

I took pride in myself, and some might say I have OCD. My office was always spotless. The walls were pure white, and the floors were shiny marble. Everything had its place, and I ensured everything was clean and organized.

Having a clean and orderly space helped me focus and work efficiently. When everything was in its proper place, I felt calm and ready to tackle any task that came my way.

The neatness of my surroundings reflected the precision and attention to detail I brought to my work.

With my demanding schedule, finding time for hobbies was a luxury I couldn't afford. The long hours I devoted to my work often consumed my days and nights. However, amidst the chaos, one thing brought a sense of tranquility and normalcy to my life— plants.

My office and home were adorned with an array of greenery. Lush ferns, vibrant flowers, and cascading vines breathed life into my surroundings. Their presence provided a respite from the sterile corporate environment, infusing it with a touch of nature's beauty.

Taking care of my plants became a therapeutic ritual. Watering, tending to their needs, and watching them thrive brought me a sense of fulfillment. This simple act connected me to the natural world, reminding me of the cycles of growth and rejuvenation.

Amid my demanding career, the sight of my plants offered peace. Their vibrant hues and delicate fragrances created a calming ambiance, even during hectic days. They reminded me to slow down, breathe, and appreciate the beauty that existed beyond the confines of my office walls.

I had a crystal-clear vision of my future path from a young age. Even at the tender age of 10, I knew with unwavering certainty that I was destined to become a lawyer. It was a calling that resonated deep within me, a purpose that ignited a fire in my soul.

While other children were engrossed in games and toys, I found comfort in books and legal dramas. The pursuit of justice fascinated me, and the power of the law to shape and protect society captivated my young mind. It was as if the legal profession had chosen me, whispering its secrets and possibilities into my eager ears.

As I grew older, my passion for the law only intensified. I devoured books on constitutional rights, criminal justice, and civil liberties. I immersed myself in debates and mock trials, honing my persuasive skills and sharpening my intellect.

I was determined to equip myself with the knowledge and skills necessary to advocate for those who needed a voice.

I earned my law degree through countless hours of studying, researching, and relentless dedication.

Stepping into the courtroom for the first time, the weight of my calling settled upon my shoulders. The responsibility to uphold justice, to defend the innocent, and to fight for what is right became my guiding principle.

Now, as a seasoned lawyer, I continue to walk this path. Each case I take on is not just a job but an opportunity to make a difference to ensure that justice prevails. The road is not always easy, and the challenges can be daunting, but my passion and purpose propel me forward.

My journey as a lawyer is more than just a profession; it is a lifelong commitment to the pursuit of justice. I am dedicated to standing up for what is right and using the law as a force for good.

From that young, determined 10-year-old to the experienced advocate I am today, my calling as a lawyer remains an integral part of who I am.

While my father was absent from my life, my mother played a significant role in raising me. She dedicated herself to providing for our small family, and despite the challenges we faced, she did her best to ensure I had a fulfilling childhood.

I often wished I had siblings to share my journey with, but I understood that it would have placed a heavier burden on my mother's shoulders.

Although we didn't experience financial hardship, there was a time when my mother's presence was scarce in my life.

It was during my favorite uncle Marcello's illness. His insurance didn't cover the necessary medication, and my mother stepped up by taking on extra shifts and working tirelessly to contribute to his medical expenses.

Despite being the youngest among her siblings, she exhibited a nurturing nature and a commitment to caring for her brother.

I vividly recall a period when my mother's dedication to supporting Marcello consumed her time and energy. She worked long hours, often undertaking doubles or even triple shifts, to provide for his needs.

Witnessing her relentless efforts only fueled my determination to create a better life for both her and me.

When Marcello eventually passed away during my fifteenth year, it marked a challenging period in my life.

It wasn't solely his death that impacted me, but rather the grief that engulfed my mother.

Marcello had played a paternal role in our lives, walking my mother down the aisle and never missing a birthday celebration or any celebration for that matter. Losing him had a devastating effect on her well-being.

During that time, my mother's emotional and physical state deteriorated. She became weak from lack of nourishment, and it fell upon me to take care of her daily needs.

I would wash her, dress her, and ensure she was fed. I slept by her side every night for nearly a year, providing her the support and comfort she needed during that challenging period.

Surprisingly, her siblings seemed absent during this trying time, and it became evident that it was just her and me against the world.

While the passage of time did not entirely heal the wounds of losing Marcello, it did provide a sense of solace and the strength to bear the pain. My mother gradually regained her usual self, demonstrating resilience and an indomitable spirit.

During this transformative experience, I recognized our unbreakable bond as we faced life's trials together.

The sacrifices and unconditional love my mother showed me shaped my character and instilled a fierce determination to pursue my dreams.

I carried the weight of her sacrifices and aspirations, knowing I was responsible for giving her a better life.

As I pursued my path toward becoming a lawyer, I did so knowing that my mother's support and my uncle's spirit would guide me. Through their love and the challenges we overcame, I gained a deep appreciation for the importance of family and the strength that can be found in adversity.

My mother and I faced the world, hand in hand, a symbol of the enduring power of love and the unbreakable bond between a mother and her child.

A knock on my door startled me, snapping me out of my thoughts and bringing me back to the present moment.

"Come in."

Susan, a paralegal, came strolling into my office with a file in hand.

"Were you looking for these?"

Susan may have been vertically challenged, but her feisty personality made up for it. Standing at a solid 5 feet (in heels), she was a force to be reckoned with.

Her fashion sense was on point, even if her body resembled a teenage boy's. But hey, she rocked those form-fitting outfits with confidence and style.

As Susan placed the file on my desk, excitement washed over me. It was the Ricci file, and I couldn't be happier.

Susan had only been with Charles' LLP for two years, but her brilliance and professionalism were unparalleled. She consistently delivered exceptional work; I couldn't imagine navigating my caseload without her. She was a true asset to the team, and I was grateful to have her by my side.

With a smirk, I responded, "Yes, I was, thanks."

Susan's eyes darted to where my former assistant was clumsily stuffing his belongings into a cardboard box, his face now red as a tomato. It was clear that the news of his termination had spread like wildfire through the office grapevine.

I leaned back in my chair, trying my best to stifle a laugh,

"Let's just say he had a talent for turning simple tasks into complicated messes. I finally had to cut the cord before he tangled us all in a web of inefficiency."

Susan couldn't help but giggle at my choice of words.

"Well, you've saved us from a sticky situation. I'll send a memo informing the team about the change."

"Perrrfect,"

I replied with a mischievous grin.

"And if anyone asks, tell them I'm sharpening my firing skills for the next round."

We both burst into laughter.

Susan gave me a playful wink before exiting, leaving me to revel in the satisfaction of a well-executed firing and a workplace lightened of dead weight.

I dove into the case, feeling a surge of focus and determination.

The courtroom was my arena, and I thrived in the high-pressure environment. Each piece of evidence I reviewed and every legal argument I crafted gave me a sense of purpose.

A sense of direction.

A sense of fulfillment.

As I delved deeper into the details, I reminded myself of the two fundamental rules I lived by: trust no one and trust no one.

In the world of law, where deceit and manipulation can be commonplace, it is essential to remain cautious.

I had learned the hard way that even those who seemed trustworthy could have ulterior motives or hidden agendas.

I meticulously analyzed every angle of the case, leaving no stone unturned. I questioned witnesses, pored over documents, and sought out potential inconsistencies or loopholes.

My instincts served as my guide, guiding me through the labyrinth of legal intricacies.

Some might consider my approach overly cautious, but it has led to my impeccable track record. I had never lost a case and intended to keep it that way.

Trusting no one meant relying solely on my abilities and intuition. It meant being prepared for any surprises that might arise, ready to adapt and outmaneuver any opponent.

In the world of law, the stakes were high, and the consequences were real. I couldn't afford to let my guard down or put my faith mindlessly in others.

It was a strategy game where every move counted, and I was determined to come out on top.

So, with my trust reserved solely for myself, I continued to work tirelessly on the case, confident in my abilities and steadfast in my resolve.

CHAPTER 2

BRITTNEY

Even though my job no longer involved handling cases in court, I couldn't resist taking on this particular case. It wasn't just because Ricci and his wife were my friends; his case intrigued me professionally.

Ricci, a man of immense wealth and influence, is accused of double murder. It seemed like a plot straight out of a crime thriller.

As I delved deeper into the details, I couldn't help but feel something was amiss. The puzzle pieces didn't quite fit together. How could a man with such power and connections find himself behind bars? It was rare, like spotting a unicorn at a busy intersection.

However, I couldn't deny the allure of the challenge.As I flipped through the case files, I couldn't help but imagine Mr. Ricci's speed dial list, filled with the who's who of politics and high society. Perhaps he even had a direct line to the president, ready to be dialed in times of need. It was a world where money talked, and connections ruled, and yet, here he was, facing severe criminal charges.

It seemed that Karma had finally caught up with him. Justice was a tricky game; sometimes, even the most influential individuals could find themselves entangled in its web.

The satisfaction of seeing someone like Mr. Ricci held accountable for their actions was undeniable. But as I continued my investigation, I couldn't shake the feeling that there was more to the story.

The pieces of the puzzle were scattered, waiting to be assembled. It was up to me to uncover the truth and unravel the web of deception and intrigue surrounding the case.

Curious, I set out on a mission to dig deeper and unearth the hidden truths beneath the surface. I knew it wouldn't be easy, but I was ready to navigate the treacherous waters of power, money, and politics.

So, armed with my wit, legal expertise, and a healthy dose of skepticism, I delved further into the Ricci case enigma.

The truth was out there, waiting to be discovered, and I was determined to unveil it, no matter the consequences. It was time to turn the tables on the elite and show them justice would prevail despite seemingly insurmountable odds.

I let out a frustrated groan and quickly scrambled to gather my things. Paperwork scattered across my desk, forming a chaotic mess that mirrored my racing thoughts.

How could I have let time slip away from me again? Francine had been looking forward to our meet-up, and now I was about to be fashionably late in the most unfashionable way possible.

Frustrated with the never-ending paperwork, I muttered curses, blaming Jarred for his negligence. Seriously, how hard was it to send a simple fax on time? He could be such an idiot sometimes.

As I continued faxing the remaining documents, my thumbs swiftly tapped on my phone's screen, composing a text to Francine. With each keystroke, my annoyance at Jarred transferred to my message.

ME: HEY, SO SORRY I'M RUNNING LATE. BLAME JARRED AND HIS FAXING INCOMPETENCE. BUT I'M ON MY WAY NOW. I'LL BE THERE IN 30 MINUTES, AND HOPEFULLY, I WON'T BE ANY MORE FASHIONABLY LATE THAN I ALREADY AM. SEE YOU SOON!

Sending the text, I couldn't help but chuckle at my sarcastic tone.

Francine would understand my frustration; humor was the best way to lighten the mood. I imagined her reading the message, rolling her eyes playfully, and shaking her head at my perpetual work-related predicaments.

FRANNY: NO PROBLEM. I THOUGHT YOU'D STAND ME UP... ... . AGAIN.

As I read Francine's text, guilt washed over me.

She had a point— I had stood her up occasionally due to work-related commitments. It wasn't that I didn't value our friendship; it was just that my career demanded a significant portion of my time and attention.

Deep down, I knew Francine understood the demands of my profession, but I couldn't help but feel a twinge of remorse for occasionally neglecting our social plans.

She was always there for me, ready to let loose and enjoy life while I buried myself in stacks of paperwork.

Our personalities were like night and day. While Francine embraced the party scene and sought excitement, I found solace in a book's pages and the calmness of a quiet night. Netflix and chill were all I wanted to do after work every day.

Our contrasting preferences never affected our bond, though. In fact, they complemented each other, allowing us to experience different aspects of life together. But lately, it seemed that Francine's wild side grew stronger with age.

Every time we met, she had a new story about a random guy she hooked up with or a wild adventure she had embarked on. I couldn't help but wonder how she managed to juggle her social life and constant partying while still functioning.

Her ability to consume five drinks with grace and composure never ceased to amaze me. She could glide through the evening, maintaining her poise and articulate speech, while I, on the other hand, felt like a metamorphosed creature after a mere glass.

It was as if those sips triggered a strange alchemy within me, turning me into a sleepy koala bear, my eyelids drooping and limbs growing heavy. But before the drowsiness entirely took over, my true talent seemed to be making its grand entrance - the art of embarrassing myself.

It was uncanny how, in that inebriated state, I could navigate a minefield of awkward situations with astonishing precision. From misplaced jokes to overly enthusiastic storytelling, my mouth seemed to operate on a mischievous agenda, utterly detached from the filters of sobriety.

Glancing at the time on my phone once more, I realized I was running late. Without wasting another second, I hurried out of my office and raced down the elevator to the garage.

Francine's comment about thinking I'd stand her up again lingered, pushing me to quicken my pace. I didn't want to keep her waiting or give her any reason to doubt my reliability.

CHAPTER 3
BRITTNEY

In the dimly lit corridor of the building stood Oscar, whose presence commanded attention; Oscar is the head of security and has worked for the building forever.

His tall, athletic frame filled out the crisply pressed uniform, highlighting his muscular physique. With broad shoulders and a well-defined musculature, he conveyed an aura of both physical prowess and unwavering vigilance.

Underneath his neatly trimmed dark hair, streaks of silver gracefully added a touch of maturity, hinting at the wisdom gained over the years.

His grooming was impeccable, with a well-kept beard that framed his strong jawline, enhancing his masculine allure.

Something I appreciated.

His deep baritone voice resonated with authority and confidence, the kind that could calm turbulent situations with its soothing timbre.

He was more than just a security guard; he embodied the idea of a protector... ... ... a guardian.

His shift is usually from 8 pm to 8 am, and since I always leave work past eight and come to work before eight, we have developed a friendship.

"Brit, there you are, hold on, I'm coming."

Oscar, my trusty companion in the security team, had earned the privilege of calling me Brit.

It was a nickname that only he and Francine could use. They were the exceptions to my general disdain for anyone attempting to address me by that name. If anyone dared to cross that line, they would surely face the wrath of my car and my unyielding determination.

Oscar would be there every evening, waiting to walk me to my car. It didn't matter if he wasn't scheduled to work that day; he would arrange for another security guard to accompany me in his absence.

I had argued with him countless times, insisting that it wasn't necessary, but he had won that battle long ago.

So, now, I accepted his protectiveness.

There was a time when I resisted his overprotective nature, asserting my independence and insisting that I could take care of myself.

However, I understood and appreciated his genuine concern for my safety over the years. Having someone like Oscar by my side provided a sense of security and peace of mind in a world that could sometimes be unpredictable and dangerous.

Oscar approached me with his characteristic steady stride. As he reached my side, he extended his arm, offering it to me as a gesture of support.

I looked at him, appreciating the chivalry that had become second nature to him.

With a small smile, I looped my arm through his, feeling the firmness of his grip.

"How are Trevor and Taylor," I asked.

"Why do you want to babysit?"

I laughed.

"I can't even care for myself; how will I look after two babies?" I questioned.

"What do you mean, Brit? You'll make a great mom."

"Wooow, slow down bud, don't put that on me."

Shaking his head, "Damn, my bad." he said, laughing.

It was heartwarming to see Oscar embracing fatherhood with such pride and joy.

The arrival of his twins had brought a new light to his life, and his happiness radiated whenever he spoke about them.

His wife, Gigi, was thrilled to welcome their little ones into the world.

What struck me the most was the love and care Oscar extended to Darius, Gigi's son from her previous marriage. Despite not being his biological child, Oscar treated him as if he were his own. Their bond was a testament to Oscar's nurturing and compassionate nature.

It was evident that he saw Darius as a part of his family and embraced the role of father figure to him. Oscar's devotion to his children and stepson only reaffirmed my admiration for him.

His character and values make him an exceptional role model and guide for any future husband I have.

Oscar's ability to provide love, support, and understanding would be qualities I'd look for in a partner, knowing that he had set a high standard for being a dedicated husband and father.

As Oscar and I made our way to the garage, I couldn't help but admire the genuine joy on his face as he shared pictures of his precious twin boys.

"Trevor smiling... ... . Gigi bathing them... ... . last time we washed them both together, one of them shitted the tub, but we didn't know who; it was a mess," he said, shaking his head.

"Eww," I said, scrunching my nose.

"Look, they are holding hands."

"So adorable."

Evidently, he cherished every moment with them, and his excitement was infectious.

He would eagerly take back his phone, engrossed in the images as if he was seeing them for the first time, and I couldn't help but smile at his fatherly delight.

Once we reached my car, Oscar's chivalry shone through. He opened the door for me, a gesture that felt both comforting and old-fashioned in the best way. As I settled into the driver's seat, he closed the door behind me, ensuring my safety and well-being before bidding me farewell.

As I drove out of the underground garage, I glanced back to see Oscar standing there, waving goodbye with a warm smile.

His genuine care and attention reminded me that chivalry was alive and well.

In a world that often feels fast-paced and detached, it was comforting to have someone like Oscar, who embodied traditional values of respect and courtesy.

CHAPTER 4

BRITTNEY

Arriving at Chaos' Steakhouse just before nine, I quickly surveyed the room and spotted Francine sitting at the bar. With a smile, I walked over to join her, excited for a night of laughter and catching up with my dear friend.

Francine and I have been friends since college, and our connection runs deep. We were not just roommates; we were partners in crime, navigating the ups and downs of university life together.

From late-night study sessions to crazy dorm parties, we experienced it all side by side. We were like two peas in a pod, always supporting and challenging each other to be the best versions of ourselves. We shared laughter, tears, secrets, and dreams.

Our friendship was built on trust, understanding, and loyalty. Francine is the kind of friend who knows me better than I know myself. She's there to celebrate my successes and lift me up during challenging times.

Our shared history can't be replicated, and our friendship is a constant source of strength and joy in my life.

Francine stands about five feet six inches tall with long, dirty blond hair that reaches her lower back and smells like lavender. This woman is undeniably beautiful; her striking blue eyes hold a captivating allure. Her appearance is effortlessly enchanting, leaving a lasting impression on all who have the pleasure of seeing her.

She is always impeccably dressed, and her make-up is a masterpiece, flawlessly applied with meticulous precision.

Despite the differences in our physical appearances, I never let myself feel jealous of Francine's slim figure.

We had an unspoken agreement: she could handle the gym and counting calories, and I would handle devouring desserts and counting billable hours. While Francine diligently watched her diet and religiously attended fitness classes, I was the master of forgetting to eat and replacing meals with caffeine. It wasn't intentional, but somehow, my busy schedule always trumped my basic survival instincts. Who needs food when there are legal briefs to be drafted... .. right?

"Hi, sorry I'm late," I say, kissing her cheek.

She stands and hugs me tight, whispering,

"Not a problem."

I raised an eyebrow at Francine's unusual behavior. Her usually bubbly and carefree demeanor had been replaced by a sense of unease. Something was up, and I couldn't help but feel a knot forming in my stomach.

"What's wrong," I say, scanning her face.

"Let's get a table and some drinks first," she said, looking worried.

"OK" was all I could say at the time.

We settled into a table by the window, and I couldn't help but appreciate the restaurant's ambiance. The service was impeccable, and the aroma of sizzling steaks filled the air.

As I glanced outside, I marveled at the bustling city scene. Despite the late hour, the streets were still alive with people, and the traffic showed no signs of relenting. It was a stark contrast to the small-town life I had envisioned for myself. However, the allure of high-profile cases and the opportunities in New York made me change my plans and stay in the city. I opposed starting my law firm somewhere in the South.

We decided to treat ourselves to a bottle of Chateau Montrose, feeling all fancy and sophisticated. As we raised our glasses and took a sip, memories of our hilarious trip to visit Francine's parents in Italy came rushing back.

"Do you remember when we went to Italy and stayed with your parents?" I asked, a mischievous grin spreading across my face.

Francine's eyes lit up as she burst into laughter.

"Oh, how could I forget? That was the vacation of a lifetime! From my parents' colorful stories to the endless pasta and gelato, it was an adventure we'll never forget."

"And the wine!" I chimed in. "Remember when we stumbled upon that tiny vineyard in the countryside? They gave us a taste of their homemade wine, and we couldn't get enough. We felt like true connoisseurs, swirling our glasses and pretending to know what we were doing."

Francine giggled, recalling the moment.

"We must have looked ridiculous, but we enjoyed every drop. It's a good thing we didn't have any Port wine. That stuff would have given us a hangover just by looking at it!"

We both laughed at the mention of Taylor Port, remembering the days when we were less discerning with our wine choices. Those were the times when a cheap bottle seemed like a good idea until the next morning's regret kicked in. That cheap stuff caused me to have hangovers that lasted two days, and I was starting to worry about all my organs shutting down, not just my liver.

"Let's toast to the good times in Tuscany, where wine flowed freely, laughter was abundant, and hangovers were minimal," I proposed, raising my glass.

Francine raised hers, clinking it against mine.

"To the unforgettable moments and the lessons we've learned along the way. May we always have good wine, great company, and fewer encounters with questionable bottles!"

We clinked our glasses again and savored the rich flavors of the wine, relishing in the memories of our Italian escapades and the joy of sharing laughter, stories, and a good glass of wine with a cherished friend.

My stomach grumbled in anticipation as I perused the menu, desperately trying to decide what to order. I had skipped lunch, and my caffeine-fueled morning had worn off, leaving my stomach in a state of rebellion.

With a pang of hunger, I finally settled on a juicy filet mignon accompanied by creamy mashed potatoes and a salad for some semblance of health.

As I placed my order, a thought crossed my mind.

"Hey, Francine,"

I said, leaning across the table.

"Do you still eat Brussels sprouts? And do they still taste like a fart!"

Francine burst into laughter, covering her mouth as the nearby tables turned to see what was causing such amusement.

"Oh, come on, Brit! You're just not giving Brussels sprouts a fair chance. They're delicious when prepared right!"

I rolled my eyes dramatically.

"I don't care what anybody says, Francine. Brussels sprouts will forever be the villains of the vegetable kingdom. No amount of roasting or seasoning can mask their inherent fart-like essence!"

We continued to banter back and forth, debating the merits (or lack thereof) of Brussels sprouts, much to the amusement of our waiter, who discreetly chuckled as he took Francine's order for a mouthwatering lobster over roasted potatoes and Brussels sprouts.

As our dishes arrived, I couldn't resist teasing Francine once more.

"Enjoy your fart-flavored sprouts, my friend. I'll be here savoring my delightful filet mignon, away from the vegetable villain."

After attempting to lighten the mood, I gave Francine a meaningful look, silently hoping she would share what was on her mind without me prying.

Thankfully, she caught the hint, and just as she was about to speak, two men approached our table, interrupting our conversation.

"Good evening, ladies." Said the blonde head.

Seriously, this is not the time; all I wanted to do was tell them to fuck off. The tension in the air was palpable as Francine and I exchanged glances, silently communicating our mutual frustration with the situation.

"Ti sei perso?" (Did you lose your way?) she said.

"Quanto tempo pensi che impiegheranno per avere un indizio," (How long do you think it will take for them to get a clue.)

I said, looking between the two men, a mischievous grin spreading across my face.

They exchanged a glance, the brunette man nervously rubbing the back of his neck while his companion shook his head in resignation.

"Well, enjoy your evening,"

The brunette said with a hint of disappointment in his voice. The two men turned on their heels and walked away, making their way to another table where three women eagerly awaited their company.

Typical, I thought, rolling my eyes at the sight. Francine and I locked eyes, and laughter escaped our lips.

The aroma of the perfectly cooked steak enveloped me, tempting my senses and igniting a primal hunger as soon as the waiter placed it in front of me.

It took every ounce of self-restraint not to abandon all table manners and devour the succulent meat with my bare hands.

As I focused my attention on the piece of culinary perfection before me, Francine's voice reached my ears, but it was like distant background noise. I was in a carnivorous trance, savoring each bite, relishing the explosion of flavors in my mouth.

Finally, after three generous bites, I paused to sip wine, my taste buds rejoicing in the harmonious pairing.

It was then that I noticed Francine's watchful gaze fixed upon me, her eyes filled with amusement and disbelief.

Swallowing my mouthful of deliciousness, I mustered a response, my words somewhat muffled by the remnants of food.

"What?"

I asked, my voice betraying my unabashed enjoyment.

A playful smirk danced on Francine's lips as she retorted,

"One would think that you haven't eaten in years. You're devouring that steak like your last meal on Earth."

With a mischievous twinkle in my eyes, I responded to Francine while my mouth was still occupied with the heavenly flavors,

"Mmmphh, th're's always room f'r more!"

I managed to mumble, my words slightly muffled by the food.

In the haze of my long day, I savored the second glass, feeling lightheaded yet yearning for more. This wine was my refuge, and I contemplated ordering another bottle to prolong the feeling it offered.

"So, what's going on, Franny?"

I said, my mouth still partially full of food as I looked at her expectantly. She took a moment to gather her thoughts, then replied with a serious expression,

"Brit, there's something important I need to tell you."

I leaned in closer, my curiosity piqued.

"What is it?"

She hesitated momentarily as if debating how to phrase her words. Finally, she spoke, "My parents want me to move to Italy permanently to help with the legal aspect of their business,"

Franny revealed.

She spoke while intently looking at me, her eyes filled with apprehension.

We had been inseparable since Francine and I became friends in college. We went through law school together and shared an apartment, and even though she recently moved down the hall for some space, she was still my lifeline. Losing her now felt like a part of me being ripped away.

I tried to maintain a composed expression, but my appetite seemed to vanish. The thought of not having her by my side in this chaotic world made my heart sink. It was as if the vibrant colors of life were slowly fading into shades of gray.

But then, a mischievous smile played on Francine's lips, breaking the heavy silence.

"Don't worry, Brit. We may be miles apart, but we'll always find a way to keep our sanity. We will master the art of long-distance friendship. And who knows, maybe our adventures will become even more epic now that we have an excuse to explore new horizons!"

Her words injected hope into my heart, and I couldn't help but chuckle.

"You're right, Franny. No matter the distance, we'll always find a way to stay connected. And hey, think of the incredible stories we'll have to share when we reunite!"

"When are you leaving?" I asked, my voice tinged with a hint of sadness.

"In a few months," Francine replied, her gaze fixed on mine.

Those words hung in the air, reminding us of the impending separation, and knowing that our time together was limited, a bittersweet feeling washed over me.

"We still have some time left,"

I said, trying to infuse optimism into my tone.

"Let's make the most of it and create unforgettable memories before you embark on your Italian adventure."

Francine nodded, a small smile playing on her lips.

"Absolutely, Brit. We'll seize every moment, squeeze out every drop of fun and laughter so that our memories keep us connected even when we're far apart."

I chuckled to myself as I reflected on my limited social circle. I wasn't outgoing, and making new friends didn't come naturally. But that's what made Francine's presence in my life all the more precious.

Aside from Francine and my mother, the Chinese food delivery guy was a recurring character in my day-to-day interactions.

But Francine went above and beyond. She followed me to New York, sacrificing her desire to support me. We had an unspoken understanding; though she may never admit it, her actions spoke louder than words.

Instead of dwelling on the impending separation, we embraced our remaining few months together.

With her adventurous spirit, Francine coined the phrase "painting the town red" to describe our upcoming escapades.

And even though it wasn't my usual style, I was determined to step out of my comfort zone and make the most of our time together.

I raised an eyebrow in surprise as I realized I had unconsciously polished off the entire bottle of wine. Only then did I become aware of the slightly hazy feeling in my head and the warmth that spread throughout my body.

I couldn't help but chuckle at my indulgence.

"Well, that was weird," I muttered under my breath, a mixture of amusement and mild concern.

It seemed my long day and the weight of Francine's impending departure had driven me to seek refuge in the crimson elixir. I never considered myself a heavy drinker, but tonight, it seemed I had surpassed my expectations.

"I need to pee," I announced louder than intended, catching Francine's attention. She chuckled, clearly amused by my sudden declaration.

Standing up from the table proved to be a challenging endeavor, as the effects of the wine made themselves more apparent. I silently cursed myself for wearing stilettos, realizing that navigating in them would require extra focus and balance.

Contemplating whether it was worth enduring the discomfort of the heels, I briefly considered walking barefoot. However, the thought of encountering an unpleasant floor stench quickly extinguished that notion. Bare feet and restaurant floors were not a compatible combination.

With a determined sigh, I steadied myself and gingerly took each step towards the bathroom, my stilettos providing an unsteady soundtrack with every click-clack.

I couldn't help but hope the journey would be swift and uneventful, with no unexpected encounters or embarrassing slips.

CHAPTER 5

BRITTNEY

On my way back to the table, a faint noise emanating from a dimly lit hallway at the back of the restaurant caught my attention.

Ignoring it initially, I continued my stride, but the sound persisted, growing more distinct and resembling someone in distress. My curiosity got the best of me, fueled by the combination of nosiness and the influence of alcohol.

With an unsteady gait, I ventured into the dark hallway, my attempts to maintain a stealthy approach foiled by the uncooperative nature of my tipsy state. I unintentionally collided my stilettos with an unseen obstacle, prompting a hushed "shhh" from my lips, followed by an unexpected burst of laughter. The absurdity of my situation, stumbling around in the darkness, amplified by the effects of alcohol, was not lost on me.

Undeterred by my lack of grace or sanity, I continued my wobbly exploration, determined to uncover the source of the mysterious noise. My steps were unsteady; the uneven rhythm betrayed my intoxicated state.

Despite my best effort to maintain a quiet presence, the occasional misstep or clumsy collision with the surrounding objects echoed through the otherwise silent corridor, potentially drawing unwanted attention to my journey.

I finally arrived at a door to my left, hoping my journey was complete; I leaned my body against the door, struggling to maintain my balance as I attempted to eavesdrop.

My unsteady movements and muffled giggles risked giving my presence away, casting doubt on my ability to gather meaningful information, let alone save anyone discreetly.

As the door swung open, I nearly lost my footing and stumbled forward, caught off guard by the sudden movement.

In a hasty attempt to regain composure, I reached out for support, desperately grasping onto any nearby object to steady myself and crashing against an unexpected man.

The man swiftly reached out, his strong arms wrapping around me, steadying me. Embarrassment filled me as I stepped back.

Taking a deep breath, attempting to compose my words, and striving to sound coherent, I slowed my speech, enunciating carefully to minimize slurring.

"I'm...(swallow)... sorry, I heard ... (breath)... . a noise ... . (swallow) and though, someone was... trouble." (Nailed it)

The beautiful-bodied man had a striking combination of mesmerizing green eyes and luscious black hair. His emerald eyes sparked with vibrant intensity, drawing me into their depths with a magnetic allure. Framing his face, his locks cascaded in waves or were styled sleekly, adding to his overall appeal.

His well-toned physique was a testament to his dedication to fitness. The suit he wore, absent from its coat, was a refined masterpiece, impeccably tailored and excluding timeless elegance. Its sleek lines and luxurious fabric showcased sophistication. The sleeve rolled up to reveal intricate tattoos adorning his arms. I wanted to trace them with my tongue.

I tried to swallow but forgot how; I only hoped I wasn't drooling.

When I realized I had been standing awkwardly for minutes, eye fucking him, I cleared my throat and turned back the way I came.

He gently grabbed my elbow, sending a surge of unexpected electricity through my veins. My heart skipped a beat, and I couldn't help but feel a rush of warmth spreading through my entire being.

At that moment, it felt as if the mere touch of his hand could ignite a fire within me, threatening to make me spontaneously combust on the spot. I tried to maintain my composure, fighting against the overwhelming urge to melt into a puddle of goo right then and there.

My mind raced, desperately searching for something clever or witty to say, but all I could manage was a weak smile and a feeble attempt at coherent speech.

"You look familiar," he said, studying me intensively, moving closer, closing the space between us, straining my neck to look up at his eyes, which seemed to hold a world of secrets and depth. My eyes widened with surprise as I noticed his lip ring adorning his lower lip. It was an unexpected detail that stood out against his overall appearance, adding a touch of edginess.

His eyes darted to my mouth as I bit my lower lip, silently praying it was his lip I was biting. His hands pressed against the wall behind me, blocking any potential escape route.

He leaned in, pressing his mouth to my neck, and the voluntary movement of my neck, allowing him in, made him groan.

The sexiest groan I have ever heard.

As his warm breath touched my skin, I realized I wanted him more at that moment than my will to live. As his presence enveloped me, a distinct aroma filled the air, a captivating blend of musk and bergamot. It was a smell that I never thought I would enjoy, but the wetness building in my panties told me otherwise.

Finding myself in a situation where speaking became a challenge, my voice evading me... .

"What's the matter, cat got your tongue?" he said with a mischievous smirk, his eyes sparkling with a hint of amusement.

Feeling attracted to his playful comment, my mind raced to devise a clever response, but all I could manage was a sheepish grin.

I desperately searched for the right words. But the more I struggled, the more tangled my thoughts became.

"Um, ... frithgdsy," I uttered, my voice barely a whisper. (What! Was that even a word?) How do I keep embarrassing myself like this? I cringed inwardly, realizing the nonsensical nature of my utterance.

It was as if my tongue had a mind of its own, betraying me in the most crucial moments. My cheeks burned with the undeniable evidence of embarrassment, feeling hot and flushed from the string of stupid things I had said and done within the last ten seconds. I desperately wished for an eraser to rewind time and delete those awkward moments from existence.

Smiling, he looked at me, his lip ring glistening as he licked his lips.

How could someone look this irresistibly handsome? I couldn't help but wonder if the wine played tricks on my perception, conjuring up a dream-like scenario.

His thumb traced a slow, teasing path across my bottom lip, a delicate caress that sent an electrifying shiver cascading down my spine. The anticipation hung thick in the air as his lips inched closer, my heart quickening with every passing moment. Just when the space between us seemed to vanish entirely, he skillfully extended his tongue, barely grazing my lips, catching me off guard and sending a shockwave of excitement through me.

But the surprise didn't end there. Without warning, his hand asserted its dominance, seizing the back of my neck with a firm yet strangely exhilarating grip. It was a claim, a possessive gesture that left no room for resistance. Our lips met in a dance of longing and intensity. At first, the kiss unfolded with a gentle touch, a prelude to the storm of desire that was about to unleash.

As his tongue parted my mouth, the kiss transformed into an exploration, a journey of shared passion and unspoken desires. He took me with a magnetic force, possessive and powerful, leaving an indelible mark on the canvas of our connection. Our lips moved in tandem, each echoing our desire's growing rhythm.

I pulled him closer, my hands instinctively finding their place on his back, fingers entwined in the fabric of his shirt. The closeness intensified, and I could feel the warmth emanating from him, a magnetic pull that drew us together. As the kiss deepened, the pulsating energy seemed to bridge the physical and emotional realms, creating a powerful connection that transcended the mere meeting of lips.

Beneath the fabric of his pants, I could sense the growing tension, a tangible manifestation of the desire that pulsed between us. Pressing me firmly against the wall, he skillfully traced a path along my neck, a tantalizing mix of licks, kisses, and passionate bites that ignited a fiery response within me. Unable to contain my pleasure, a moan escaped my lips, a testament to the intensity of the sensations coursing through my body.

As he continued his exploration, I fought against the primal urge to reciprocate by sinking my teeth into his flesh.

Then, unexpectedly, he abruptly ended the kiss, leaving me bewildered and confused. Questions raced through my mind, and I wondered why he had stopped, unsure of what had prompted the sudden change.

Was it me?

Did I not kiss well enough, or was I too drunk to comprehend? I couldn't figure it out.

"You should get going, baby girl; you don't want to get yourself into trouble."

What! Yes, I want trouble. As the ache in my core started begging for release.

He stepped back, letting me go; a tinge of disappointment washed over me, attempting to conceal it with a subtle mask of composure, not wanting him to perceive my genuine emotions.

I turned and walked away disappointed, embarrassed, horny as hell and sober.

CHAPTER 6

BRITTNEY

I made it to my office at 6:30 am, balancing two cups of steaming hot coffee in my hand,

"Black, two sugars, just how you like it,"

I said, smiling at a very tired-looking Oscar.

"My angel," he said, reaching for his cup.

I made a point of bringing him coffee every morning since he insisted on walking me to my car in the evenings; this was the least I could do.

Working early in the morning, when the office was still devoid of other individuals, uniquely appealed to me. The serene ambiance allowed for uninterrupted focus and a sense of tranquility that was difficult to find during the bustling hours. But I got lost in my thoughts about what happened last night.

After making it back to the table, we ... ... I ordered another bottle.

Recounting my peculiar details of the strange encounter with Francine, she listened attentively, her smile getting wider and wider, eyes sparkling with genuine interest; she swallowed my words without interruption. The ending seemed to disappoint her more than it did me.

In the delicate dance of personal relationships, Francine emerged as the only one with a wealth of experience when it came to navigating the intricate landscape of connections with men. My life had been a narrative tightly woven around the fabric of work, a dedication that left little room for the capricious nature of romantic entanglements. Each encounter with men left me with a residual sense of letdown and frustration, prompting a subconscious reflex to keep them at a safe distance. Managing emotions and maintaining that arm's length had become a subtle art, a secondary skill almost as natural as breathing.

Despite the transient nature of a recent encounter, my thoughts quickly redirected themselves to the looming Ricci case, a complex legal puzzle demanding my undivided attention with a court appearance just days away. The intricacies of the law tugged at my focus, each detail requiring meticulous consideration as I delved into the preparation for the impending legal battle.

Amid this professional immersion, Marla abruptly barged into my office, her entrance shattering the tranquility that had settled within the walls. Fueled by frustration and a steadfast desire to maintain personal boundaries, I lifted my head, prepared to unleash a torrent of expletives at the audacious intruder. However, as my gaze met hers and I discerned the storm brewing within her, I chose a wiser course of action - silence.

The air in the room crackled with an unspoken tension as I braced myself for the verbal storm Marla seemed poised to unleash. Her agitated demeanor hinted at a brewing storm, and I adopted a defensive posture, ready for whatever cascade of emotions she was about to release.

I always looked up to Marla; in a world where opportunities seemed scarce, she extended a lifeline of hope when nobody else would. She was the only one who took a chance on me and gave me an internship position in this law firm six years ago. So, my loyalty remains steadfast, dedicated to her and her alone.

She was among the most beautiful women I have ever seen; she stood tall and poised, with a slender yet toned physique. Her flawless features captured attention effortlessly. She had perfectly curled brunette hair that was shoulder length and brown eyes, and I envied those perfect eyebrows. She was taller than me, which was very rare to see.

Her attire exuded an undeniable sense of perfection. Every garment she wore seemed carefully selected, tailored to fit flawlessly against her body. Hell, a plastic bag would look amazing on her.

If I had her looks, I would be on the runway in Dubai strutting a string bikini. (Note to self, join a damn gym.)

Her fondness for me allowed me to push her buttons, and she did the same.

A welcomed game we played.

"For the love of God, Brittney, why did you fire him?"

I knew exactly who she was referring to, but I loved seeing her combust,

"Whatever do you mean, Marla?" I said with puppy dog eyes, holding back a laugh.

"I swear to all things holy."

I see a throat vein pulse, and I don't want to be responsible for her heart attack or stroke.

"Yes, I fired him; he was pathetic, weak, and stupid; horrible combinations."

"Do you know who his father is? "

He was probably some pathetic old rich fart who wanted to get rid of him by paying the bosses so he could work here.

"No, even if his father were God, I would still have fired him."

She sat down, and I'm glad she did; I was worried she might faint. Marla rubbed her temples with her thumbs and sighed loudly.

"Does Edward Belfi ring a bell?"

Of course, I know Mr. Belfi, one of our top clients. His business made us over a hundred million dollars last year alone.

I was the one who reeled him in; it was a remarkable achievement that reverberated throughout the office, instantly elevating my status and reputation. I got a promotion and a hefty raise.

"Don't tell me dipshit is his son?"

"Yes, he is, and he is not too happy."

"I think McDonald's is hiring."

Marla's head whipped so fast in my direction that I thought it snapped. She got up and darted toward me, "I'm glad you find this amusing."

I did; I secretly wished I had installed cameras in my office to replay this moment.

"He knows his son is useless."

"Be that as it may, I must do damage control because of you. Stop firing assistants and hire a new one before the end of the week. I'm not fucking around Brittney."

Anger now surged through her veins like a roaring storm.

Jarred is the third assistant I have fired in five months; I had reached a level where I could confidently navigate my responsibilities and tasks independently.

Making myself self-reliant, but the way Marla's head looked like it had teetered on the edge of its axis, I held my breath, anticipating the possibility of a complete revolution, a visual manifestation of the swirling storm within her soul. This had me carefully watching my following words.

"All right, I'll go ahead and bring in an assistant, and I promise not to let them go... as long as they prove to be competent," I concluded, the last part escaping my lips in a hushed whisper.

A subtle smile played upon her lip, suggesting an awareness of my eagerness, while she raised an eyebrow, hinting at a challenge to delve deeper.

With a graceful turn, she skillfully broke the taut atmosphere, announcing, "Heads up, the bosses are here," a smirk playing on her lips as she strolled out of my office. The cryptic message left me in a moment of puzzlement. What did she mean by 'the bosses are here'? In her usual enigmatic fashion, Marla seemed to revel in the knowledge that such ambiguity would gnaw at me, a tactic she knew all too well.

As I pondered the implications, a wry acknowledgment formed within me: She had deftly orchestrated a move that would consume my thoughts, leaving me to navigate the impending visitation of the higher-ups with a lingering sense of uncertainty.

Touché, Marla.

CHAPTER 7

BRITTNEY

A bit after 6 pm, when most of the staff had gone home, someone knocked at my door. (I need to hire an assistant soon.) I thought, pissed at the sudden interruption.

"Come in," I said, hiding my irritation with my head still engulfed in my work.

An irresistible fragrance filled the air; a swirling mist of amber and vanilla enveloped me and my surroundings. Captivated by the smell, I eagerly looked up. At the threshold of my door stood a man, an enigma wrapped in unfamiliarity.

Dressed in a meticulously tailored three-piece suit, he exuded an aura of timeless elegance and refined charm. Every element of his attire was impeccably assembled, from the perfectly tailored jacket that accentuated his broad shoulders to the crisp shirt and silk tie that added a touch of sophistication.

The trousers perfectly hugged his trim form, while the waistcoat accentuated his slender waist. His attire complimented his chiseled jawline, striking cheekbones, and intensively striking blue eyes, which shimmered like pools of azure and sparkled with intelligence.

His meticulously styled jet-black hair framed his angular magnetic charm. The contrast between his piercing blue eyes and dark, lustrous locks created a captivating visual harmony that left an indelible impression.

He strode to my desk and extended his arm to greet me.I managed to hold it in together while I received his greeting. The contact made my heart skip a beat.

"I wanted to introduce myself, Leonardo Luca Charles."

Wait, Charles, as in Charles' LLP? He read my expression.

"Yes, I'm one of the partners."

Of course, he is.

He looked at me intensely, then his gaze descended to our intertwined hands, which remained connected in a delicate embrace. In a sudden flush of embarrassment, I hastily withdrew my hand, my cheeks tinting with a faint hue of pink.

"Brittney Wright," I said, desperately holding my composure.

He smiled at me and took a seat on the couch. He has fucking dimples; why can't my boss be an overweight, short bald guy? And what is it with these good-looking men? Two in less than 24 hours is insane.

"I have an important case that requires your immediate attention," he commanded, his voice laden with an urgency that cut through the ambient air of my office. I raised an eyebrow, acknowledging his words but withholding any immediate acquiescence.

"I require you to drop everything you're doing and sign an NDA before my assistant gives you all the information about the case," he continued, his gaze unwavering.

A surge of frustration coursed through my veins. Who did he think he was, issuing such demands without so much as a courteous preamble? Did he believe I could simply pivot my entire focus at his command? The audacity of his request grated against my sense of independence and autonomy.

At that moment, a glitter of defiance ignited within me, clenching my hand into a tight fist. I met his gaze with a steely resolve, ready to assert my position in this unexpected power play.

"I appreciate you considering, but I will not hand over a case I have worked on for months to anyone. This is mine, and I intend to see it through to the end," I declared, my tone firm.

The owners have yet to be seen by anyone. They are very secretive, and I stopped asking questions years ago. From what I heard, they lived on the West Coast. During meetings requiring attendance, they would voice call, and that's how all our sessions have been held. The fact that one of the partners was physically in the building made me suspicious.

Leonardo will have to learn how to speak to people... . to me.

"You don't trust your employees? ... Shame."

The words were spoken before I could think.

He stood from his seat, a towering figure that filled the room.

Then, he placed both hands on my desk (I never wanted to be a piece of wood so bad).

His gaze bore into me with an intensity that sent a shiver down my spine, and then a gentle curve formed on his lips, a smile that should be illegal; how does it feel to be God's favorite?

"No one has ever spoken to me like that."

"Glad I was your first."

My mouth spoke again before my brain. The words were out of my mouth, and I couldn't take them back, so I needed to show no remorse.

"If you weren't so good at what you do, I would... ."

"You would what... Fire me?"

He seemed shocked by those words; someone needs to show Mr. Charles that even though he owns the law firm, the building and a couple of hotels, maybe a yacht or two, a private island... . (Where was I going with this?) ... right... He does NOT own me.

Two law firms had expressed a strong desire for me to join them just this month alone, and I knew he would lose more if he "fired" me; tilting my head, I continued,

"Go ahead, Mr. Luca, finish your sentence."

He gave me the sexiest smile known to mankind, straightened himself, turned, and walked towards the door.

"Finish your case; then you're all mine."

I was almost done with the case; I needed this done tonight.

It was past 9:00 pm, and the office was bare. The only signs of life were the diligent cleaners.

Yawning, I rose from my desk and headed towards the break room, in dire need of caffeine. As the aroma of freshly brewed coffee filled the air, I instinctively began my search for my favorite mug.

The office kitchen was a treasure trove of ceramics and porcelain, but among the assortment of cups, one held a special place in my heart.

"Ahh, gotcha." The first sip of the hot elixir down my throat was phenomenal, making me moan.

Hearing someone clear their throat behind me surprised me, making me drop my coffee on the floor.

"Didn't mean to startle you."

His blue eyes met my gaze and dropped to the spilled coffee and broken mug around my shoes. I rushed to grab paper towels to clean up my mess, but he was by my side in seconds,

"The cleaners will get that. Why are you still here?"

"I prefer working late."

He studied my face and asked, "Are you hungry?"

Yes "No!" Of course, my stomach deceived me by growling loudly.

Smiling, "Pizza or Chinese?"

Pizza "I'm fine."

As if he heard my thoughts,

"I'll order us some pizza; meet me in my office in 30 minutes."

He turned and left.

Weariness settling in my bones, I should have gone home early - I thought to myself as I reached for the paper towel to clean up the mess I had inadvertently created, ignoring his request.

The liquid had pooled on the surface, threatening to spread further and leave an unsightly stain.

As I pressed the absorbent paper against the spill, the coffee was quickly soaked up, vanishing into the fibers. It was a small act of remediation, a momentary interruption in my day. Still, it served as a reminder that despite mishaps, there was always an opportunity to restore order and carry on.

On my way back to my office, I approached the diligent cleaners and requested their assistance in mopping the area, aware of the residue left by the spilled coffee.

Like Oscar, the cleaners and I have formed a friendship due to my late nights; as we conversed, I couldn't help but realize I checked my phone's time over three times in the past 5 minutes.

What was wrong with me?

With resolute determination, I decided not to meet him in his office; I would finish my work and go home. That was my plan.

Precisely 30 minutes after our encounter, my phone buzzed.

UNKNOWN: WHERE ARE YOU?

He can't be serious.

ME: WORKING

UNKNOWN: GET UP HERE NOW!

He must have lost his mind, and how the fuck did he get my number!

I ignored his last message, threw my phone on the table, and directed my attention back to the task at hand.

Fifteen minutes later, as I struggled to regain my concentration, I realized that my mind needed a break. Despite the tense atmosphere and the recent events, I boldly decided to overcome the discomfort and join Mr. Grumpy for a slice.

Taking my time, I walked to the elevator and pressed Grumpy's floor, one floor above mine. When I got to his door, I debated whether to stroll in or knock. I chose the latter.

"Come in," he said in what seemed to be an irritated tone, and I couldn't help but chuckle.

Casually strolling in his office, the first thing that I noticed was that his office was enormous.

Though mine was immense, his office exuded an air of grandeur and sophistication with its expansive dimensions and carefully curated design, highlighted by a large desk at its center.

Crafted from rich mahogany, the desk commanded attention with its imposing size, polished surface adorned with tasteful accessories, and neatly arranged assortments of documents.

Surrounding the desk, plush leather chairs beckoned visitors to sink into their comfort, offering a welcoming space for discussions and negotiations. The room boasted a high ceiling adorned with elegant chandeliers that caused a warm glow, illuminating the tastefully arranged bookshelf lining the walls.

A strategically placed sitting area, complete with cozy armchairs and a coffee table, is where the pizza rested- a separate zone for more casual conversation or moments of respite.

He was standing by the window back towards me with his hands in his pocket. He had removed his suit coat, and I had a great view of that tight ass; even his back looked edible.

(Stop it.)

Shaking my head vigorously, attempting to draw those evil thoughts out of my head.

He turned and gracefully walked towards me. His movements radiated a quiet confidence that filled the room.

His height was intimidating as he stepped into my personal space, forcing me to step back and hit the wall. He moved one hand from his pocket and barely grazed my arm.

Chills went up my spine, and he knew just what he was doing to me by the way he was smirking,

"I said 30 minutes. "

"I was busy."

"The food is cold."

"I like cold pizza."

He's such a baby; the pizza can't be that cold.

I pushed him off me and thank heavens he let me.

I walk into his private bathroom to wash my hands. When I returned to the room, it was filled with an aromatic bouquet of wine, adding a touch of sophistication and ambiance. (Not that kind of party, buddy.)

Sitting across from him, I positioned myself on a comfortable chair, mirroring his relaxed posture. His gaze remained fixed on me.

Unable to resist the temptation any longer, I reached out and delicately grasped a slice of pizza from the box before us. The aroma of freshly baked dough and savory toppings wafted through the air, whetting my appetite, and adding an element of comfort to the moment.

As I took a bite, savoring the flavors that danced on my palate, I moaned in satisfaction.

I couldn't help but notice his eyes following the motion of my hand, his gaze momentarily drawn to the act of indulgence.

His smile made my mouth water, but not for pizza anymore. He reached out and confidently grabbed a slice for himself. At that moment, we both indulged; a sense of camaraderie settled between us as we ate in silence.

 After finishing my slice and reaching my threshold for the lingering tension, I stood and headed towards the door.

"Thanks, I have to get back to work,"

I said as I reached the handle. His warm hand was on top of mine instantly, keeping the door shut.

(How'd he get to me so fast?)

He was so close that I felt the warmth of his breath brushing against my skin, and he smelled... ... . incredible. As I turned around, desperately trying to keep my composure, "We need to stop meeting like this,"

(Shut up, Brittney.)

Ignoring my stupid comment, he rubbed his nose on my throat, inhaling, "You smell fucking incredible."

In response to his electrifying touch, a subtle yet undeniable shiver rippled down my spine. My involuntary reaction manifested as a soft, breathy moan that escaped into the intimate space between us. As he deftly tilted my head, I was trapped by the intensity within his smoldering eyes. Simultaneously, his other hand embarked on a sensuous journey, grazing my arm with a feather-light touch before venturing down to the curve of my hips.

A pause hung in the air, pregnant with anticipation, as his fingers lingered at the juncture where the fabric of my dress met my knees. His penetrating and intent gaze bore into me, causing an exhilarating dance of emotions within. Unable to resist the magnetic pull of desire, I succumbed to the sensation, biting down on my bottom lip with a fervor that introduced a metallic taste to the tableau. His eyes, locked onto mine, sparkled with a knowing smirk that bespoke a silent understanding.

With calculated grace, his hand resumed its exploration, tracing the contours of my bare thighs as he artfully lifted the folds of my dress. A decisive grip on my thigh followed the gentle parting, evoking a magnetic tension. His stare remained on me.

Fervent.

Piercing.

When his finger grazed my panties, the intensity made my body involuntarily thrash forward; I closed my eyes, enjoying the moment until his finger movement stopped, "eyes on me, cupcake," my eyes ripped open, not wanting his actions to stop.

Our bodies were pressed together heatedly against the wall, breathing heavily as our lips connected, and at that moment, I thought I was going to pass out at the feeling of his thumb rubbing my clit and his palm by my entrance while his full lips devoured me.

Seeming like he felt my body letting go, his other arm grabbed my waist, holding me up while he moved my panties to the side,

Oh. My. God.

His finger rubbed my bare pussy.

"Fuck, Cupcake, you are so fucking wet."

My chest, now rising and falling expeditiously.

"You enjoy defying me, huh?"

He moved from my lips to my neck and bit me. He bit me so hard I thought he was going to rip my skin, but the pain of the bite made the pleasure even more profound.

"Answer me."

"Yes." I managed to scream out.

Chuckling, he sucked where he bit and did it repeatedly while his finger rubbed me gently, then more aggressively.

"You're so fucking beautiful," he said as I held him as tightly as I could, trying not to scream. The familiar buildup in my chest caused my movements to intensify as it made its way down to my stomach, making my eyes roll behind my head,

"I'm cu... ..." I only managed to say in his ear, shuddering violently with pleasure. He took my mouth, trying to conceal my screams; I hope that worked because I believe even Oscar heard me.

It took me a few minutes to come down from our height.

"Damn." He said as he removed his hand from my core and sucked his fingers. "You taste better than I imagined."

He rubbed the same finger on the bottom of my lips and kissed me, this time gently. Tasting myself on his lips, making me quiver.

He pulled my dress back down, attempting to restore my appearance. I chucked at his failed attempt.

The moment our eyes met again, there was an unmistakable flicker— an epiphany, a sudden dawning of realization that seemed to strike him with a thunderclap. It was as if all the puzzle pieces had fallen into place within the confines of his mind; the last clue found, the final code deciphered.

He recoiled slightly as though the weight of this newfound knowledge had physically impacted him, creating a distance that hadn't been there a moment before. His eyes, still locked with mine, now held a different light, a mixture of enlightenment and perhaps a shadow of regret.

"Thanks for the company," he said, stepping back, allowing me to open the door, and I left without saying a word.

CHAPTER 8
BRITTNEY

Sleep evaded me, slipping through my fingers like an elusive mist. After "dinner," I left the office and came straight home, conscious of the need to maintain a sense of normalcy and avoid arousing suspicion from Oscar; I made sure I fixed myself and sprayed some perfume on to remove his scent.

Oscar didn't look suspicious, and I thank my lucky stars for that.

As I lay in the solitude of my bed, my thoughts incessantly gravitated toward him, his smell, eyes, lips, fingers, and muscles.

Memories and glimpses of our interactions replayed like a recurring melody, each note carrying the weight of longing and curiosity. The mere thought of him stirred a whirlwind of emotions, intertwining desire and lust.

"Stop it," I said to myself, knowing I must conduct myself professionally next time I see him. Unlike 'restaurant guy,' I know I will probably see Leonardo again.

I rose out of my bed and headed to the bathroom, seeking a brief respite from the confines of my thoughts.

It was a few minutes after 3 am. The cool tiles beneath my feet offered a grounding sensation, momentarily distracting me from the whirlwind of emotions that had engulfed my mind.

But unfortunately, he was consuming my thoughts, and I acknowledged the stark reality that I knew nothing about him. All I knew was that he was my boss's boss, and what we did should never happen again.

"Right?" I questioned, almost seeking reassurance from my reflection in the bathroom mirror. "Right!" I responded aloud, realizing the absurdity of answering my musings.

I spent over an hour in the shower, ensuring I cleaned myself of the vile act I committed last night, hoping that would make me feel better.

Reaching out, I grabbed the shower handle, allowing the rush of water to envelop me, wishing it was his hands. The cascade of droplets danced upon my skin, creating a symphony of sensations that awakened my core.

Leading the handle to where my ache was forming, wishing it was his mouth. I held it still while imagining how he would feel inside me, soaking me with his warm cum while groaning in my ear. My other hand was rubbing my clit vigorously while I chased my high.

I moaned, my breath heavier than the last, "Leo," I screamed while imagining I was cumming on his dick.

Catching my breath, I exited the shower sighing, realizing that what I intended the shower to wash down the drain failed miserably.

I decided to forgo my habit of arriving early. I resolved to make it to work on time, strolling toward my office at 9 am with a latte in hand.

"Good morning."

A new assistant (I assumed) greeted me while rising from the seat Jarred sat a few days ago.

I could only assume Marla was behind the hire. Sometimes, she surprises even me. Despite my best intentions, I had overlooked an email she sent, maybe because I was busy getting finger fucked by my boss to read it.

However, I did glance through it; this must be Rebecca (or Raven) ... . Recognizing my oversight, I felt a sense of regret and the realization that I had missed out on an opportunity to stay informed. It reminded me of the importance of attentiveness and ensuring thoroughness in my professional responsibilities.

I shook my head and said, "Good morning, Rebecca, right?"

"Rachel"

"What?"

"My name is Rachel, not Rebecca."

Ignoring her... (I give her a month).

"Where is everybody?" I asked aloud, my voice slicing through the unusual hush that blanketed the office. The rows of empty desks seemed to echo back my confusion.

"At the meeting upstairs," came the reply, tinged with a hint of exasperation. "I left you three voice messages and sent you an email."

What meeting? The words ricocheted inside my head as adrenaline surged through me. Fuck. How had I missed that?

With a sense of urgency clawing at my chest, I quickened my pace, my shoes thudding against the carpeted floor as I made a beeline for the elevator. I jabbed the call button more times than necessary, each press fueled by a growing impatience and the hope that it would hasten the elevator's arrival.

The digital numbers above the elevator door seemed to descend in slow motion, heightening my anxiety. I tapped my foot, fingers drumming against my thigh, willing the doors to part.

Finally, with a soft ding, the elevator arrived. I slipped inside, pressing the button for the meeting floor with a thumb that still trembled slightly. The doors closed, and as the elevator began its ascent, I tried to compose myself, smoothing down my clothes and running a hand through my hair.

I hoped against hope that the meeting had started late or that my absence had gone unnoticed. As the elevator climbed, so did my resolve.

As I entered the board room, I could feel the weight of the room's collective attention upon me... great. I quickly found my seat, feeling embarrassed. I have never been late to a meeting. I am allowing these men to get into my head, and it needs to stop. I was determined to regain my composure and keep them at arm's length.

When I walked in, Marla was in the middle of an introduction, and I made a mental note to ask the present assistants for the meeting minutes later.

Leonardo rose a few minutes later, commanding the room's attention with his confident presence. Caught up in my rush to enter the meeting, I failed to notice him as I hastily found my seat. FUCK!!

Leonardo commanded attention in his all-black ensemble, the suit, shirt, and tie forming a seamless canvas that exuded an air of dangerous allure. The ebony hue not only lent him an unmistakably sexy edge but also served as a backdrop that accentuated the piercing brilliance of his blue eyes. His sartorial choice, a deliberate play between danger and sensuality, cast a magnetic spell that had every woman in the room watching him intently.

The impeccable fit of his suit elevated the overall effect, molding his body with precision. Each turn and movement seemed orchestrated, causing the fabric to scrunch and unfold in a dance that showcased his muscular physique to perfection. The result was a visual symphony, where the interplay of shadow and fabric accentuated every contour of his body, leaving an indelible impression.

It was undeniable that his attire, combined with his charismatic presence, drew the attention of every woman in the room. His magnetism went beyond mere words; it was an unspoken language of confidence, power, and undeniable sex appeal.

His voice conveyed authority and charisma as he addressed the gathered audience. Every word he spoke resonated with purpose and clarity, capturing the room's full attention; well, most of the room, all I could think about was where those lips were, where those strong arms were, how he made me cum on his fingers by just rubbing my clit... ... Shifting uncomfortably in my seat, I closed my eyes, determined to banish the provocative thoughts from my mind. The tension in the room was palpable, and I desperately hoped that my attempt at mental distraction would prevent any noticeable physical reactions. Whispering a mantra of "professional" to myself, I tried to regain control of the situation.

However, when I opened my eyes, I caught Leonardo's gaze shifting in my direction. His eyes showed undeniable awareness as if he knew the effect he had on me. That infuriating grin he flashed my way, a perfect cocktail of arrogance and amusement, felt like a silver bullet aimed straight at any resolve I had left.

Leonardo smoothly introduced the other two partners of the firm, each accompanied by a brief and impressive summary of their expertise and accomplishments. My curiosity was piqued, and I was eager to see if the other partners matched Leonardo's stature.

As the two additional partners strolled into the room, my eyes widened in surprise and realization. A shock reverberated through me as I recognized the second man walking in. His piercing green eyes, confident demeanor, and unmistakable lip ring all belonged to HIM - the man I had encountered before. Our paths had crossed once, and now, here he stood, a partner in this prestigious firm— my boss.

Memories of our previous encounter flashed through my mind, as did the intensity of his graze and the unexpected connection we shared. I was only hoping he didn't remember me.

His eyes finally found mine; seeing the realization on his face, he smirked, licking his lip ring, FUCK, he does remember me. (I wonder if Jarred can put in a good word for me at McDonald's?)

He introduced himself, speaking just like Leonardo. He took control and commanded the room with his voice, but his eyes never left mine, making me blush like a schoolgirl.

Finally, the third partner stepped forward to introduce himself. As he began to speak, it became apparent that he bore a striking resemblance to Leonardo, almost like a meticulously crafted photocopy. His eyes, a captivating shade of gray, sparkled like two mesmerizing gems, drawing you in with their depth and intensity. His hair, a rich shade of brown, added to the captivating allure that mirrored his counterpart.

What set him apart were the tattoos that subtly peeked out from beneath his crisp white collared shirt. Unlike Leonardo, whose canvas seemed untouched, this partner showcased inked artistry on his skin. The tattoos hinted at a story, adding an element of mystery to his otherwise polished appearance.

He, too, donned a suit like the other partners, but with a distinctive choice – he forwent the suit coat. This decision brought attention to his muscular arms, making their definition more pronounced. The contrast of the tattoos against the white shirt and the muscularity of his arms created a visual impact that set him apart, an individual expression within the collective elegance of their attire.

The meeting ended after what seemed like an eternity. I found paying attention throughout the session challenging between dodging looks and daydreaming. The discussion and presentation blurred together as my mind wandered to other matters occupying my thoughts.

The urge to be elsewhere, anywhere but there, became almost palpable, fueling an inner restlessness.

But just as I was mere steps away from the door, a familiar sound reached my ears: my name being called. Fuck me.

It stopped me in my tracks, causing me to pause and turn my attention back to the room. My escape, so close within reach, is now gone.

"May we speak to you?" Leonardo said.

I had an overwhelming desire to vanish into thin air, to escape the situation entirely and dissolve into the ether, but unfortunately, I wasn't Houdini... .

"Of course."

As the boardroom gradually emptied, I found myself seated next to Marla. Across from us, the three men maintained a stoic and silent presence, their eyes fixed on me with a palpable intensity. Determined to keep my composure, I silently repeated a calming mantra: "Stay calm, don't puke, breathe, don't puke, don't sweat, don't puke."

I continued this internal chant, desperately trying to ward off any signs of nervousness as the men observed my every move. The pressure in the room seemed to escalate with each passing second. My mantra became a lifeline, a mental exercise to stave off any potential embarrassment.

However, the fragile equilibrium was disrupted when a phone rang, shattering the tense silence. Marla answered the call, stating she had to take it, and abruptly left the room. Panic set in - a silent plea echoed in my mind: "No, not now."

Alone in the room with the three men, the weight of their collective focus bore down on me. I felt like a deer caught in the headlights, desperately clinging to my internal mantra to stave off an impending sense of nausea. The atmosphere thickened, and I made a silent pact with a higher power, desperately bargaining for an escape. At that moment, I promised myself, and perhaps a higher force, that if I could get through this unscathed, I would amend my ways and never curse again.

"I met you at the restaurant," The 'restaurant guy' said. I should have paid attention to their names when they introduced themselves earlier.

No, "Yes."

I was unwilling to offer more incriminating information, so I remained silent after my reply.

"Your pictures do not do you justice," Twin said, rubbing his chin. His eyes now turning a devilish black.

Puzzled, "What pictures?" I asked, silently hoping the back of the restaurant we were in did not have hidden cameras that took stills of my encounter with one of the gentlemen.

His eyes casually drifted to my chest, and I realized that I had my employee badge with my face on it, of course. How could I not seem to hold my composure with these men? My escape was now my main focus.

"Is there something you wanted to speak to me about?"

"I wanted to introduce you personally to my brothers," Leonardo said, smirking. "It seemed your mind was elsewhere during the meeting."

Fuck me,..... brothers.

"Nice to meet you."

I said, glancing between the two. The absence of words echoed loudly in the room, each passing second elongating the awkwardness that hung between the four of us.

Desperate to leave, "I'll see myself out," I eagerly said.

As I rose to leave, Leonardo threw an envelope on the table.

"We're leaving Monday at 8 pm."

Leaving? Going where? Why the fuck didn't I pay attention?

Reaching for the envelope, the restaurant guy extended his hand, landing on top of mine; a shiver ran through my body, and I hated myself for feeling this way.

"Don't be late, baby girl, and pack for a week."

What the actual fuck?

Swearing to myself, I made a silent vow to banish daydreaming from my thoughts. The illusions and fantasies that once occupied my mind would no longer find a place to dwell. I couldn't wait to get out of there to find out what I've volunteered for.

I pulled the file from under his hold, not letting him see what his touch was doing to me. As I exited, relief and trepidation washed over me; casually looking back over my shoulder, I found their eyes fixed with an intensity that ignited a spark within my soul. It was then that I realized; I was fucked.

CHAPTER 9

BRITTNEY

Thirty minutes stretched out like an eternity as the tension in the air grew thicker. Finally, a breakthrough emerged.

As the missing puzzle pieces fell into place, a wave of both relief and exasperation washed over me. It became apparent that I had unwittingly agreed to fly to California for a week to collaborate on a case with them. I recalled Leonardo coming into my office yesterday and discussing something about it. I assumed he had looked into it and knew I would be wrapping up Ricci's case before Monday. I could gather that the case involved their father, and the envelope they handed me contained a Non-Disclosure Agreement that I had to sign before the flight scheduled in a few days.

"Regina, hold all my calls."

I said as I pressed the intercom.

"And grab me a coffee" (ahh, the joys of having an assistant).

Five minutes later, coffee in hand, putting my last-minute touches on the Ricci file, I can't believe I am almost done. With many witnesses with testimonies pieced together meticulously, revealing a coherent and compelling narrative, their accounts were consistent, their memories vivid, and their credibility unquestionable.

It was only a matter of time before this case was dismissed. He should be home with his family by dinner tomorrow night.

Marla came crashing through my office door as I jolted from my seat.

"Brittney!"

She said with the saddest look, moving slowly towards me.

"Marla, what is it?"

"Ricci," she softly said, staring at me.

When I realized she was not going to say anything more,

"What is it?" I said again.

Seeming to notice my frustration,

"Ricci is dead."

"What!"

"He was found this morning; he committed suicide."

This can't be happening; I just spoke to him yesterday. He showed no signs of distress, but some people usually don't.

Jails are equipped with security measures to ensure the safety and control of the premises. Among these measures are regular rounds conducted by guards.

In addition, the guards patrol the jail, moving from one area to another, checking cells, monitoring activity, and maintaining order. So why did nobody see him hurting himself?

"How?" is all I could utter

"He hanged himself."

Bullshit, I find it hard to believe the information presented; he was confident in the strength of his case; why kill himself on the day before trial? I knew this case was fishy; his death was the nail in the coffin.

I stood there, my mind consumed by a whirlwind of thoughts as I repeatedly replayed my entire conversation with him. Every word, every gesture, every subtle nuance etched itself into my memory, dissected and analyzed in an attempt to decipher hidden meanings and understand the proper intentions.

Seeing my perplexity, Marla said, "Don't overthink it, Brittney; take the rest of the week off."

Maintaining a professional distance had always been my creed, a line I drew in the sand of my career that I was careful never to cross. Clients came and went, their cases a series of puzzles to solve, their lives a collection of facts and narratives that, while often compelling, were not mine to share. But Ricci was different.

As the case unfolded, so did the layers of his life. I met his wife, a woman of grace and resilience, her smile a warm yet weary beacon in the storm that had become their lives. Their children, too, became more than just names in a file. I saw their photos, heard their laughter echoing down the hallways during unexpected visits, their presence weaving a more personal thread through the tapestry of legalities and proceedings.

And now, Ricci was gone.

"Brittney," Marla said with concern in her eyes. "Do you need me to drive you home?"

"No, I'm fine, thanks." Her skeptical gaze pierced me as if searching for cracks in my story. A feeble smile escaped my lips, lacking the genuine warmth and confidence I wished to convey.

"I know you were close to the family; if you need to talk... ."

"I'm fine, Marla, thanks," cutting her off.

The expression on her face stirred a wave of remorse within me as I realized the impact of my words on her, but my mind was focused on Mrs. Ricci and the children.

She surprised me by stepping closer and wrapping her arms around me in a heartfelt embrace.

It was a gesture filled with understanding, forgiveness, and a genuine desire to mend our momentary rift. We had always been reserved in our relationship, seldom letting our emotions surface. We had an unspoken agreement to conceal our feelings, a silent understanding that vulnerability was risky.

But this moment was different.

After the embrace, she slowly released her grip and offered me a warm, genuine smile.

It was a bittersweet moment as I watched her walk away, leaving a lingering sense of connection and a tingle of longing that will probably never be repeated.

As my office door closed, a single tear silently escaped from the corner of my eye, tracing a light path down my cheek and allowing it to linger, glistening in the light, without attempting to wipe it away.

Feeling like I was in another world, another life, another planet, my eyes remained wide open, yet they seemed incapable of perceiving the world around me.

"Britney."

I heard something, but uncertainty clouded my mind as I questioned the origin of the sound.

"Britney."

There goes the voice again, like a whisper in the depths of a forgotten memory, its meaning just beyond my grasp.

"Cupcake."

As I blinked violently, my eyes fluttered open, my gaze refocusing on the present moment. Finally focused, I realized Leo was in my office, towering over me and holding my arms. His eyes were full of concern.

"Are you Okay?"

"No" is all I managed to say before tears rolled down my face.

He gently pulled me close, his arms enveloping me in a comforting embrace. I leaned into him, feeling the warmth of his presence against my trembling frame.

Tears streamed down my face, unchecked and unrestrained, as I found comfort in the sanctuary of his embrace.

He held me with a tenderness that spoke volumes, providing a haven for the weight of my emotions to be released. His steady presence became a safe harbor, allowing me the space to embrace vulnerability. At that moment, I didn't need to hold everything together; I could let go, knowing he was there to offer support and understanding.

"I'll drive you home," he finally said after what felt like an eternity.

"No, I'm fine," I insisted, attempting to maintain a façade of composure.

"No, you're not. I'll drive you home," he asserted, his concern evident.

Frustration welled within me, prompting me to push him away, practically screaming, "I'm fine." As the words left my mouth, a pang of regret hit me, realizing the harshness of my response. His eyes softened, reflecting an understanding of my reaction.

"I'm sorry," I apologized, softening my tone. "Francine, my friend, is coming to pick me up," I added, weaving a white lie to redirect his concern.

He looked at me, reminiscent of Marla's scrutinizing gaze, but refrained from questioning further.

"Okay, at least text me when you get home," he suggested, concern lingering in his eyes.

"Sure," I replied, attempting to mask my inner turmoil with a smile.

CHAPTER 10

BRITTNEY

As I left my office, the weight of the day's events clung to me like a heavy shroud. Thoughts of Ricci and the funeral lingered in my mind, and I couldn't help but feel the need to reach out to his family. I knew that offering my condolences to Rachel, his wife, and her children was right.

As I got into my car and started driving home, the streets seemed to blur before my eyes. The grief in my heart was palpable, and I felt a sense of responsibility to be there for Rachel and the children in their time of need.

Arriving at their house, I took a deep breath before ringing the doorbell. The weight of the moment felt surreal, and as the door opened, I faced the stark reality of their grief.

Rachel stood before me, her eyes swollen and red from crying. Witnessing her pain only intensified my sorrow. We embraced without exchanging words— a silent understanding transcending the usual robotic condolences. I didn't want to be just another person reciting the customary phrases of sympathy; I wanted my presence to convey genuine support.

Inside, the atmosphere was heavy with sadness, starkly contrasting to my last time there. Over the past year, Rachel and I have spent significant time together due to Ricci's case. While creating a friendship with her as her husband's lawyer might have been unconventional, our relationship extended beyond Ricci's legal matters.

Rachel never asked about the case, and I ensured our conversations were clear of any legal discussions related to her husband. She was ruled out from involvement in Ricci's case, and our connection was more about sharing moments and genuine friendship. Despite the professional boundaries and the complexities of the legal world, we enjoyed each other's company.

Her children, aged 12 and 9, added another layer to the somber atmosphere. They were the most brilliant pair of children I had ever met, often engaging me with trivia questions whenever I visited. I made it a point to learn some trivia to share with them during our interactions, fostering a bond.
I sat with Rachel in her living room, the aroma of coffee filling the air as she prepared a comforting beverage for both of us. As we sipped the warm drink, I provided a supportive presence, allowing her the space to express her feelings. My role was to offer a listening ear and a reassuring shoulder.

Amid sorrow, words felt inadequate, so I chose to speak sparingly. Small words of encouragement and comfort were offered, interspersed with shared silence. Sometimes, a gentle touch or a nod spoke volumes more than any carefully crafted phrase. The living room, once a backdrop for moments of friendship and shared trivia, now hosted a different kind of exchange— one marked by vulnerability and the rawness of grief.

As Rachel navigated the tumultuous waves of emotions, I remained a companion, recognizing the healing power of being present. The ritual of sipping coffee, a familiar and comforting gesture, became a subtle anchor in the storm of emotions. In those moments, our connection transcended the complexities of our past interactions.

As Rachel walked me to the door, she expressed gratitude for spending time with her and the children. She mentioned that everyone, including Belfi, had been kind that day and that they had spoken.

This caught me by surprise; I didn't know Belfi had a connection to Ricci. My curiosity piqued, and I wanted to inquire further, but seeing the sadness and exhaustion in Rachel's eyes, I decided against probing. I didn't want to add to her burden, and I respected her need for space and time to process her grief, so instead, I offered a warm smile and a gentle pat on her shoulder.

"Take care of yourself and the children, Rachel. And remember, I'm just a phone call away if you need anything, even if it's just someone to talk to."

She nodded appreciatively, and I left.

As I drove home, my thoughts returned to Belfi's unexpected presence. I wondered how he knew Ricci and what had led him to visit Rachel on this sorrowful day.

My curiosity about Belfi's connection to Ricci and his sudden appearance at Rachel's house continued to nag at me. I couldn't shake the feeling that there was more to it than met the eye.

When I worked with Belfi, he seemed self-centered and only concerned with his interests. His call to Rachel didn't sit right with me, and I was determined to find out what he was up to.

I knew he was not there for Rachel or the children. Belfi was the kind of person who only cared about himself. I didn't know he had a son until Marla mentioned Jarred was his, even though I worked with Belfi for over a year.

While trying to acquire him as a client, he seemed egocentric, self-absorbed, and self-centered. Now, suddenly, he cares about Rachel. That seemed out of the ordinary, out of character for him, and as a friend of Rachel, I am determined to find out why Belfi is being so nice.

The door shut behind me with a soft click, sealing off the world outside. The confines of my apartment embraced me, a familiar sanctuary from the relentless pace of the day's events. The day's weight hung heavily upon my shoulders, a tangible presence that followed me through the threshold, demanding acknowledgment.

I shed the trappings of my professional self as I moved through the space, each step taking me further from the lawyer and closer to the simple comforts of solitude. The kitchen, with its promise of escape, beckoned. The bottle of wine stood on the countertop, the glass catching the faint light, a sentinel of solace in the quiet of my kitchen.

With relief, I uncorked the bottle, the sound echoing through the room's silence, and poured myself a generous glass.

The rich aroma of the wine filled the air, teasing my senses and promising a temporary escape from the realities that plagued my mind. Sipping the velvety liquid, I felt its warmth spreading through my body, easing the tension and inviting a moment of tranquility amid chaos.

Each sip served as a small respite, allowing me to savor the flavors and momentarily forget the burdens that weighed me down. I found comfort in the simple pleasure of that glass of wine, a brief pause to unwind and replenish my spirit.

As I sat in my apartment, the weight of my thoughts pressing against me again, I knew I had to escape the confines of my familiar surroundings. The walls seemed to close in on me, trapping me in a cycle of worry and uncertainty.

Determinedly, I hastily grabbed my coat from the hook. It was time to break free from the grip of my thoughts.

I have to get out of this place to replace this feeling with something else. Downing the remaining wine, I text Francine.

ME: WANNA GO OUT?

FRANNY: WHAT! ON A WORKDAY, WHO ARE YOU, AND WHAT HAVE YOU DONE WITH MY BEST FRIEND?

Choosing self-preservation, I opted to spend time with Francine while avoiding mentioning my day. The last thing I need is the pitfall of being pitied by confiding in my friend. (I'll tell her in the morning.)

ME: GET READY; I'M COMING OVER.

FRANNY: CAN COLLINS COME?

My steps came to a halt as I reread her last text.

Collins? I hadn't seen him in over three years; his eyes always revealed his affection for me. He has sent me texts recently, but I ignored them, deliberately avoiding any form of communication.

I found myself at a loss for words, unsure of what to say to him in response. Standing there, at the unexpected crossroads of our past and present, I was momentarily adrift in the sea of unspoken words and complicated histories. The years had slipped by since college, each of us orbiting the other, sometimes drawing near, sometimes spinning away into the vastness of our separate lives.

He had been ready to anchor us together, to set a course for a shared future, but I wasn't prepared to drop my sails. I wasn't ready to be moored. So, I cut the line, setting us adrift once more. And yet, through Francine, he remained a fixed point on the horizon of my world, never entirely disappearing from view.

Our encounters, sporadic as they were, had become a pattern etched into the fabric of our interactions. He would reappear, a ghost from my past, and we would slip into the familiar rhythm of what we once had. We would walk the streets of the city, wrapped in the comfortable cloak of nostalgia, dine in the warm glow of intimate eateries, and sometimes, in moments as fleeting as they were tender, our lips would meet in a stolen kiss, a whisper of what could have been.

But like a reflex, I would retreat, pulling back into the safety of my solitude. It was a dance we had perfected, each step, each turn, each retreat choreographed by a history we could neither fully embrace nor entirely escape. It was a cycle, a pattern of nearness and distance, a series of romantic moments that flared like shooting stars only to fade into the night.

ME: UM, SURE.

The realization hit me with the force of a gale, the expectation that I would shrink and diminish myself into a more palatable, more conservative version of myself because of him. For a fleeting moment, I entertained the thought, the idea of tempering my actions, moderating my expressions, becoming a shadowed version of the person I had fought so hard to become.

Fuck that.

I felt the need to let off steam, to release the built-up tension and frustration inside me; if he doesn't like it, he is welcome to fuck off.

We arrived at the nightclub around 8:30 pm, after having much-needed food to act as a sponge in my stomach as I drank myself to oblivion.

The music was loud, and the drinks were flowing. We made our way straight to the bar; I subtly caught the bartender's attention and gestured for him to come closer. I confidently ordered an apple martini while Franny and Collin ordered rounds of shots. I had never quite acquired a liking for the acrid taste of hard liquor.

I leaned back in my seat, watching my companions line up the shots before them. They were eager to partake in the ritual, tossing back the small glasses of liquor with practiced ease. Their faces contorted momentarily as they braved the intense taste and sensation.

Meanwhile, I sat there, calmly cradling my martini.

Another round by Fat Joe feat Chris Brown, one of my favorite songs, filled the air. Francine flashed me a smile, and we couldn't resist the urge to hit the dance floor together, belting out the lyrics at the top of our lungs, not caring who hears us.

As I swayed to the rhythm of the music, I felt someone's presence behind me, matching my movements with their own. Turning around, I locked eyes with Collin, who had now grabbed my waist and inched me closer to him.

Despite the nagging thought of stopping, the alcohol coursing through my veins urged me to keep dancing. I let go of my inhibitions, allowing the music to guide my movements as I surrendered to the euphoria of the moment. As our bodies swayed in synchrony, his body so close to me, I couldn't help but notice a newfound air of masculinity radiating from him. It was as if time had sculpted him into a more refined version of the person I once knew.

With every beat of the music, our proximity grew closer, his gaze locked onto mine, his eyes filled with a mixture of longing and desire.

As the world around us faded into the background, he leaned in, his breath warm against my skin, his lips inches away from mine. I instinctively turned my face away, avoiding his attempt to kiss me as my phone vibrated.

Thanking the gods for the distraction, I quickly reached for my phone.

GRUMPY: I THOUGHT YOU WERE GOING TO TEXT ME WHEN YOU GOT HOME!

ME: I'M NOT HOME.

GRUMPY: WHERE ARE YOU?

Ignoring the last text, I shoved the phone back into my pocket.
"Everything alright?"
Collin asked with an intense look.
"Yeah."
Trying my best to sound nonchalant.
We returned to where Francine was seated, talking to someone who would probably be her next hook-up. The music still pulsating in the air.
I could feel his eyes on me, searching for a response to his rejected advances. Forcing a smile, I joined Francine and her victim... 'date,' hoping to divert the attention away from the awkward moment.
My phone buzzed incessantly in my pocket, demanding my attention.
"Are you going to get that?"
Collin asked with what looked like annoyance in his eyes.
Irritated, I finally reached into my pocket and retrieved it.

GRUMPY: WHERE ARE YOU, BRITTNEY?

GRUMPY: ANSWER ME

GRUMPY: IF HE PUTS HIS HAND ON YOU AGAIN, I WILL BREAK HIS ARM.

I froze with the last text. Is he here? Frantically, I started scanning the room, my eyes darting from one face to another, searching for any sign of him.

GRUMPY: DO I HAVE YOUR ATTENTION NOW CUPCAKE?

I turned to Francine, suggesting we should leave, but she was engrossed in conversation and seemed reluctant to end the night so soon.

Collin was now at the bar ordering more drinks, so I headed to the bathroom to strategize my escape.

Glad the bathroom was empty, I hurriedly locked the door behind me and entered the small stall. I couldn't help but stare at the previous messages 'crazy' had sent, wondering how he knew where I was.

Thinking that I was probably losing my mind, I reached for the stall door, but the bathroom door opening stopped my attempts. (I locked it; didn't I lock it?) silently having a conversation with myself.

As footsteps drew closer, my heart skipped a beat, and my mind raced with anticipation. The stall door swung open, revealing a familiar figure standing before me.

His face was twisted with anger, his jaw clenched tightly, and his eyes bore into mine with an intensity that made my knees buckle, but why did that make him look even sexier? I need therapy.

He walked into the tight stall, grabbing my neck, his grip firm yet strangely gentle. He leaned closer to me, inches away from my ear. He said,

"Why are you here, Brittney?" His voice cut through the tension between us like a thick fog.

"I needed to let off some steam," I admitted, my voice a mix of defiance and raw honesty that I couldn't contain.

He stared at me, and I watched as his jaw tightened, a visible sign of the storm of emotions brewing within him. The air around us seemed to crackle, charged with an unspoken intensity.

"Let off steam? Meaning you were looking to get fucked?" The words fell between us, crude and jarring.

The vulgarity of his question hung in the air, a stark and ugly echo of my internal turmoil. It sounded disgusting, even though, in the darkest corners of my mind, it was precisely what I had contemplated. But hearing it voiced so crudely stripped the act of any of the rebellion or release I had imagined.

Okay, maybe it wasn't the ideal way to shed the skin of my past, to break away from the virginity that seemed to be just another shackle. But I was desperate to feel something, anything, other than the hurt that had become my companion.

Collin was not part of my plan, but how was I supposed to explain anything to this man? His reaction indicated that he interpreted my lack of response as an answer.

"We're leaving," he declared with a finality that brooked no argument, his hand clasping mine with an urgency that pulled me towards the door.

I resisted, planting my feet firmly. "I came with Francine and Collin, and I can't just leave them," I protested, my voice a mix of responsibility and reluctance.

At the mention of another man's name, I saw his jaw clench tighter, the line of it hardening like set stone.

"My brothers will make sure they get home safe," he assured me, his tone leaving no room for doubt, no space for questions.

A torrent of questions surged within me, each a wave cresting with curiosity and concern. They pressed against the back of my tongue, eager for release, yet I held them back, choosing silence over inquiry. There was a time for questions, for unraveling mysteries and seeking truths, but instinct whispered that this was not that moment.

He parked his phantom in the alley behind the club. Opening the passenger door for me, he gently guided me in; as I settled into the car, he reached with a firm yet gentle touch, fastening the seat belt securely across my chest.

As his presence filled the seat next to me, I felt a sense of safety, reassurance, and intimidation, a tether connecting us.

Not a word passed between us, and our unspoken thoughts hung heavy in the air; it reminded me of the evening we shared the pizza.

Bringing the car to a gentle stop, he turned off the engine and exited the vehicle; with graceful strides, he circled the car, arrived at my side, and gracefully opened the door.

He guided me towards my apartment door, patiently waiting as I fumbled with my keys to unlock the door. Once inside, he smoothly followed, stepping into my world confidently.

Wait a minute, "How did you know where I lived?" I asked, staring at him.

He casually took his coat off, ignoring my question and throwing it on my couch. He then rolled up his sleeves, revealing striking tattoos on his forearms. He strode to where I was standing. Grabbing my throat gently, his nose brushed against my neck, and I felt his warm breath as he inhaled deeply.

"You wanted to get fucked, Brittney?" His voice filled with venom.

Fuck, he won't let that go.

"Answer me."

"Yes... . No... ... I don't know."

His gaze held a complex blend of intense and conflicting emotions while gently rubbing his thumb over my lower lip.

His eyes never left mine. He unzipped my dress, letting it fall. Kneeling, he pulled my hips forward, inhaling.

"Mhhh."

He stood up, slowly lifting me off the floor. Instinctively, I wrapped my legs around his waist, and he led me into my bedroom; he then slowly placed me on the bed.

Without a word, his hands found their way to my back, pulling me closer and closing my mouth with his.

"You belong to me." He spoke.

Wait, what?

He ripped my panties off before I could utter a word, helping them find a new home in his pocket. He then grabbed my legs and pulled me closer to the edge of the bed. His hands moved to my thighs, parting them slowly, "You're so fucking wet." he said, looking up at me with hooded eyes. His tongue found my clit hungrily, licking my glistening juices dripping down my ass.

"I've dreamed of this." He spoke again, flattening his tongue against my clit, greedily licking from the top to the back, lifting my legs for a better vantage point. He tugged my clit with his tongue flicking over the sensitive nub turning my moans into screaming as I felt my organism getting closer.

"Leo."

Grabbing his head roughly, guiding him as I rode my organism out all over his face. He licked up every drop before climbing on top of me and kissing me.

"You are ours now, Cupcake."

"What do you mean?"

"Go to sleep," he said, smirking. "You'll soon find out."

Exhausted and not wanting to fight him, I allowed my sleep to take over; my last feeling was Leonardo covering me with my blanket and kissing my forehead.

CHAPTER 11
BRITTNEY

I decided to take a much-needed day off from work and embark on a long, contemplative drive to Connecticut to visit my mother.

Before heading out, I popped over Francine's apartment down the hall to ensure she got home safely. I knocked on her door, but there was no response. Slightly worried, I texted her. My phone immediately buzzed with her reply— she was on her way home. I couldn't help but chuckle as she added that her date had been a disaster.

We needed to plan a girls' night to talk about last night's occurrences.

Driving to Connecticut offered me a chance to escape and clear my mind. The road stretched ahead, allowing me to sort through my thoughts. Away from the demands of my daily life and ... ...them.

The upcoming departure with the men loomed over my mind like a storm cloud. We had shared intense moments together, but the complexities of our situation weighed heavily on my conscience.

I needed this time alone, away from their magnetic presence, to process my feelings and make sense of what the fuck is happening to my life.

Taking charge of my accommodation, I proactively booked a hotel in San Diego, a deliberate choice to maintain a sense of personal space. I ensured the hotel had a spa because I foresee myself needing relaxation every evening after dealing with the men and their father.

As I drove on the open road, the changing views outside matched the thoughts in my mind. The quiet and solitude gave me time to reflect on my emotions and desires.

With every mile I traveled, I felt lighter, as if I were letting go of the things weighing me down. The road became a metaphor for my journey, helping me unravel my thoughts and find clarity.

Two hours later, I arrived at my mom's place. Deep down, I wished she lived closer to me, but I understand now why she chose to stay away from the busy city life. Stamford seemed better for her, offering a more peaceful and relaxed environment. Typically, it would only take me an hour to reach her, but the never-ending traffic made the journey longer.

As soon as I pulled into the driveway, Max, my mom's dog, greeted me with a cacophony of barks. He was always so excited to see me, and I couldn't help but love him. I would have a dog if it weren't for my hectic schedule. Their companionship and unconditional love are exceptional.

About a year ago, my mother made a decision that brought a new sense of companionship into her life - she decided to get Max. I was excited for her, mainly since she lived alone. It seemed like the perfect choice, a four-legged friend to share her days with and fill her home with vitality and joy.

I vividly remember the day she introduced me to her new canine companion. A playful ball of fur with bright, inquisitive eyes greeted me, wagging its tail with an infectious enthusiasm.
The dog's presence seemed to light up the room, and I could see the immediate bond that had formed between my mother and her furry friend.

As I spent time with them during my visits, it became evident that this dog had become more than just a pet - he was family.

"Hi, boy," I said to the over-excited dog.

"Who's a good boy?" I exclaimed, laughing as Max enthusiastically jumped up, nearly knocking me off balance. His wagging tail and wet kisses filled me with joy. I bent to his level, returning his affection with gentle pats and scratches behind his ears. Max was a bundle of love and excitement, always ready to shower me with his canine affection.

"Baby, is that you?" I heard my mother call out.

"Yes, Mom."

"I'm in the kitchen."

Making my way to the kitchen, Max closely followed me, his paws clicking against the hardwood floor.

I could hear my mother bustling around, the clinking of dishes, and the aroma of home-cooked food filling the air. As I entered the kitchen, a warm smile spread across my face. My mother stood by the stove, her hands busy with pots and pans.

Max wagged his tail eagerly, anticipating some scraps from the delicious meal being prepared.

She wiped her hands on her apron, her eyes lighting up joyfully as she saw me. Dropping everything, she rushed towards me and enveloped me in the tightest hug. It was a hug filled with warmth and love. The kind of hug made all the worries and stresses melt away, leaving only a deep sense of comfort and belonging. At that moment, I knew I was home.

"Baby, what a pleasant surprise. Are you hungry?"

"Starving," I replied, a pang of hunger gnawing at my stomach: the long drive and the anticipation of seeing my mother had left me famished. The enticing aroma wafting from the kitchen only intensified my craving for a satisfying meal.

I playfully stole a few bites here and there, much to my mother's amusement. We shared laughter and exchanged lighthearted banter as we put the finishing touches on the meal. It was a joyful and playful moment, reminding me of our bond and the joy of spending time with loved ones in the kitchen.

An hour later, with my stomach happily satiated and my mind at ease, I leaned back in my chair, a contented smile gracing my face. The warmth of my mother's home and the love permeating every corner of the room had worked magic on me.

The worries and stresses that had weighed me down seemed to melt away, replaced by a sense of tranquility and inner peace. I cherished these moments, the simple pleasures of good food, laughter, and the comforting presence of family.

At that moment, I couldn't help but feel grateful for the respite from the chaos of the outside world and the rejuvenating power of home and loved ones.

"Mom, I need to talk to you about something," I said, my voice tinged with sadness at the thought of being so far away from her.

"I wanted to let you know that I'll be flying to California for a work trip in two days. It will be a week-long assignment, and I wanted to ensure you were ok with me leaving."

My mother paused momentarily, her eyes searching mine before a smile formed on her lips. "Oh, darling, that's wonderful!" she exclaimed. "I'm so proud of you and all the opportunities that come your way. Don't worry about me; I'll be just fine here. You go and make the most of this trip!"

I felt relief, grateful for my mother's understanding and support. With her blessing, I knew I could embark on this journey with a lighter heart.

We spent the rest of the time talking, laughing, and playing Scrabble, and to my delight, I emerged victorious as the reigning champion. The evening flew by in a blur of shared stories, playful banter, and the comforting warmth of family bonds. As the clock neared ten pm, I knew it was time to bid my mother farewell and make my way back home.

Hugging my mother tightly, I whispered words of love and gratitude into her ear. Her eyes twinkled with pride and affection as she wished me a safe journey. Stepping out into the cool night air, I carried with me the memories of a joyful reunion and the reassurance that our bond would always remain unbreakable no matter how far apart we may be.

Getting into my car, Max's tail wagging goodbye from the front porch, I started the engine. I drove away, the road ahead filled with anticipation for the adventures that awaited me in California.

CHAPTER 12

BRITTNEY

Age Nine

"I'm still and always will be the reigning champion!"

Marcello's triumphant shout echoed as he sank the winning shot. Our basketball matches had become a cherished tradition, a regular fixture every time my uncle came over – and that was nearly every day.

"I let you win!"

I managed to call out between breaths, my hands resting on my sides as I tried to catch my breath. My chest heaved, and I felt a mixture of exhaustion and exhilaration after our intense basketball match.

Marcello stood a few feet away, a playful grin on his face, clearly enjoying my feeble attempt to save face. He chuckled, wiping the sweat from his forehead with his hand.

"Oh, really? That's the best excuse you've got?" he teased, his tone lighthearted but victorious.

"I didn't want to make you feel bad, Marc," I said, laughter bubbling.

My uncle Marcello— or Marc, as I liked to call him to provoke a reaction— had always been a good sport about our playful banter. He insisted that he was too young to be called 'uncle,' so I took every opportunity to remind him of his age and see his mock protests.

Marc flashed a mock glare my way, his lips curling into a half-smile. "You enjoy tormenting me, don't you?" he retorted, shaking his head in mock exasperation.

I shrugged, the grin on my face unabashed.

"What are nieces for, if not to keep their 'not-uncles' on their toes?" I teased, using air quotes around 'not-uncles' for dramatic effect.

He chuckled, the lines around his eyes crinkling with amusement.

"I should've seen this coming when you were just a little troublemaker," he mused, recalling the countless times I'd managed to get under his skin, even as a child.

"And now I'm a big troublemaker," I quipped, bumping my shoulder against his playfully as we walked.

The sun began to dip below the horizon, casting a warm, golden glow over the surroundings. Marc feigned a sigh, his expression comically resigned.

"Yeah, yeah. Some things never change," he replied, his tone dripping with affection.

"Like those wrinkles," I teased, using my fingers to draw imaginary lines on his face. Marc halted in his tracks, his playful expression feigning innocence.

"What wrinkles?" he replied.

"Don't act like you don't see all of them. Satellites can pick them up," I continued with a mischievous grin, fully aware of his good-natured tolerance for my teasing.

Before I could react, Marc swooped in, lifting me off my feet and launching into a full-scale tickle assault.

Laughter bubbled out of me uncontrollably as I squirmed and wriggled in his firm grasp. With a quick twist, I managed to slip out of his hold and dashed toward the backyard, the fading daylight casting long shadows across the grass.

Marc was in hot pursuit, his laughter echoing through the air. Our playful chase took us around the yard, a dance of dodges and near-captures that had us both breathless. The wind tousled my hair as I sprinted, my heart pounding with exhilaration and sheer joy.

He closed the gap between us with surprising speed, and before I could react, I found myself tumbling onto the soft grass. His mischievous grin promised a payback I couldn't escape.

Laughter erupted from us as he launched into a full-fledged tickle assault, his fingers dancing over my sides and under my arms. The sensation was almost too much to bear, my laughter uncontrollable and my pleas for mercy mingling with his chuckles.

"Say you're sorry!" he demanded playfully, his fingers relentless in their tickling.

"Your wrinkles should be sorry!" I blurted out between fits of laughter, a retort that earned me another round of ticklish torment.

"I won't stop until you say you're sorry," he declared, determination in his eyes and mischief in his voice.

"Marcello, quit tormenting your niece," I heard my mother's voice float through the air from the open kitchen window. "And both of you get cleaned up. Dinner is ready."

Marc and I exchanged a playful glance, his fingers still hovering menacingly near my ribs.

"Well, it seems we have a ceasefire," he conceded with a chuckle. Slowly, he withdrew his hands, and I took the opportunity to sit up, brushing grass off my clothes.

"Your mother has saved you this time," he said, adopting a mock stern expression before his face broke into a grin. "But don't think you've won."

"Of course not," I replied with an exaggerated sigh.

As we made our way to the kitchen, I greeted my mother with a warm kiss on the cheek before moving to wash my hands.

Marc and I quickly jumped in to help her set the table, arranging plates, utensils, and glasses in a synchronized rhythm. The clinking of dishes and the soft hum of conversation filled the air.

A few minutes later, we all took our seats around the table, a spread of delicious food before us.

The room was filled with the comforting aroma of a home-cooked meal, and the atmosphere was light with shared stories and cherished moments.

As we dug into the meal, the conversation flowed effortlessly. Stories and anecdotes from the day were shared, accompanied by hearty laughter that seemed to echo through every corner of the house.

CHAPTER 13

LEONARDO

The moment I laid eyes on her, I felt a seismic shift in my world. Without a shred of exaggeration, she was the most breathtaking woman I had ever seen. Her presence was like a force of nature, undeniable.

Overwhelming.

Utterly captivating.

Her body was a masterpiece of proportion, a statuesque form that was elegant and commanding. She moved with a poise that seemed to accentuate her tall frame, her silhouette a study in curves and grace that could stir desire with the simplest of gestures. When she walked, it was as if the air around her was charged, and I found myself reacting in primal and involuntary ways.

The sway of her hips was a rhythm all its own, a gentle undulation that was at once innocent and intensely provocative. It was a dance of shadow and light, each movement a silent siren song resonating deeply within me.

Her skin held the luminous glow of health and vitality, a canvas of natural beauty that seemed to radiate its soft light. Her eyes, a mesmerizing blend of hazel and deep brown, shifted with the changing light, their shimmery depths holding stories and secrets one could spend a lifetime uncovering.

Her hair was a cascade of waves, each strand a testament to a rich and diverse heritage. It framed her face with elegance and a statement of identity, a proud declaration of her unique beauty.

Yet, it was not solely her physical attributes that defined her allure. Brittney carried herself with an air of confidence that was as attractive as any physical trait. She moved through the world with effortless grace and infectious self-assuredness. Her scent was as if she was enveloped in an aura that was at once intoxicating and comforting, a fragrance that seemed to imprint itself on your senses.

The perfection of her breasts, the curve of her back descending to that mesmerizing ass— it was a siren's call to something deep and instinctual within me. I had harbored a longing to explore the softness of her skin, to discover the taste of her lips, a yearning that was both exquisite and torturous.

As she departed the boardroom, leaving a wake of stirred emotions and lingering glances, I knew I wasn't alone in my desire. My usually composed brothers shared the same look of unspoken hunger, a sign of Brittney's effect on us all.

At that moment, I understood with clarity that was as jarring as it was profound— I was utterly and irrevocably screwed.

My brothers and I have always been close-knit, bound not only by blood but by the bounds of trust and shared experiences.

Our support for one another creates a sense of family that surpasses mere genetic ties. My father's intellect and astute business acumen have propelled him to accumulate wealth, his sharp mind serving as the driving force behind his financial success.

As the eldest in the family, the responsibility of taking over the family business falls on my shoulders, shaping my path and defining my future. Though it may not have been my initial plan, refusing my father's request or decision is not an option.

My brothers and I were forced to attend law school, and after graduation, our present was ownership of Charles LLP.

I recently stumbled upon information that confirmed my suspicion of my father being more than a 'businessman'; he was also a crook and a fucking liar; that's why we are all in this situation now; we were compelled to prioritize his needs and demands above everything else. Under his influence, we were coerced into flying to New York City against our will.

Despite the façade he presents to others, we see through his mask and recognize the true nature of his character. We are aware of his manipulative and deceitful ways.

We aim to find the best lawyer to aid him in his legal matters.

When he mentioned Brittney, I felt nothing until I tasted that sweet cunt; now, there is no way in hell I will let him near her.

So, my brothers and I decided to take her with us under false pretenses. This is the only way we will be able to protect her. I hope that once she learns the truth, she will forgive us.

Brittney was one of our brightest employees, and ever since she landed Belfi as a client, I have been keeping tabs on her, and so has my father.

Despite our usual practice of taking pictures of new hires, Sonny was right; the photographs did not capture her true beauty. I hate to think what my father will do when he lays eyes on her.

"What time is it?"

I asked Dominic.

Smirking, "Five minutes after the last time you asked."

"Ass Hole."

"Don't worry, she'll be here," Sonny said, smiling.

"I will fucking kill you both."

As the eldest sibling, I have always taken on the role of looking after my brothers. Throughout our lives, we have rarely been apart for more than a week. Our father forced us to attend the same prestigious college and law school, thus sharing a rental apartment.

Our close bond has kept us connected and allowed us to create cherished memories together.

Sonny has an unmatched skill and an uncanny ability to penetrate even the most secure system; Dom is a towering figure with bulging muscles and a formidable presence. He is the go-to person when we need someone to sing like a canary. He enjoyed inflicting pain, so much so that I really think he needs therapy.

And I'm the mastermind behind every operation.

As I looked at my watch again for the hundredth time, hoping she didn't stand us up but also wishing she would so I could go over to her apartment and punish her by making her juices flow all over my face again, that was sexy as hell.

From the corner of my eyes, I saw her sleek black SUV gliding towards us. I stepped out of my truck and leaned against it, anticipation building as I awaited her arrival.

She parked her car next to ours and gracefully stepped out. My dick jerked, captivated by her beauty and the promise of what was to come.

"Traffic." She spoke.

I grabbed her waist, pulled her closer to me, and kissed her passionately. She always smells and tastes incredible.

My brothers stood next to us, watching as I devoured her with my tongue. If we weren't running late, I would eat her right here.

"Get in the car," I said as I pulled away from her, my cock upset.

"Excuse me?"

Fuck, I love when she defies me.

Softly, "Get in the car cupcake... . Please." She smiled and got in the back seat of the truck.

As I closed her door, my brothers watched me with mischievous smirks, their eyes filled with amusement and knowing... fucking idiots.

"What!"

I hissed.

"Ohhh, nothin'," Sonny says, heading towards the driver's side door.

Ignoring them both, I took my seat next to Brittney.

CHAPTER 14

LEONARDO

Thirty minutes later, we were in the air.

I flew commercial once, and the experience was enough to convince me that I would never do it again. From the long lines to the cramped seats and lack of privacy, it was a far cry from the comfort and convenience I was accustomed to. From that day on, I made sure to stick to private flights, where I could enjoy luxurious and stress-free travel experiences.

I invested in an airline and bought a couple of private planes for the family. The Bombardier we were flying in was a little on the small side, but it only carried eight passengers and crew, so it was plenty spacious.

As soon as we were in the air, I pulled out my laptop and got to work answering the pile of emails that had accumulated in my inbox. With my finally uninterrupted time, I could focus and respond efficiently. Engrossed in my work, I lost track of time and didn't realize three hours had passed since our departure.

"Where is she?" I didn't need to mention her name; they knew exactly who I was referring to.

"She was tired, so I told her to nap in the back," Dom replied.

Being a frequent flyer, I had customized my private planes to include bedrooms. Understanding the importance of rest and comfort during long flights, I wanted to create a space where I could relax, sleep, and rejuvenate while in the air.

The bedrooms were equipped with cozy beds, soft lighting, and personalized amenities, providing a peaceful sanctuary amidst the clouds.

Opening the door to the bedroom, I see Brittney lying on her stomach, legs in the air, reading a book. Fuck, ... that ass. The sight made my cock throb. Casually strolling towards her, it took everything I had not to rip her jeans off and ass fuck that tight little hole.

I took a seat next to her.

"Dominic said it was ok."

She sat up, looking at me nervously.

Softly, I reassured her, "It is."

Her eyes met mine, captivating me, drawing me into their depths, Fuck it; I launched for her lips, taking her breath away. At that moment, time stood still, and the world around us faded away, leaving only the sensation of her soft lips against mine.

My manhood grew with every moan she made and every taste her lips provided. I needed her now, my dick ready to rip my inseam open. I sat her on my lap without breaking our kiss; she started grinding softly on my now rock-hard cock.

"Ahhh Fuck".

If she doesn't slow down, I will cream in my pants like a fucking teenager. Gripping her hips, I stationed her; she flashed me a devilishly alluring grin that stirred an intoxicating blend of desire and excitement within me.

I ripped her shirt off and undid her black lace bra, leaving her full, beautiful breasts exposed. Greedily reaching for both breasts, I put one nipple in my mouth and sucked hard, then the other; I knew I would leave marks, and the thought made me suck harder and squeeze tighter.

I stood up, holding her firmly, then gently placing her on the bed. I pulled off her pants and black lace panties, which I smelled before putting them in my pocket.

I was determined to take every piece of underwear she owned; imagining her walking around without panties because of me was a thought I would make a reality.

My face was between her legs instantly, and her smell had me losing my fucking mind. I could see just how wet she was when I pushed her legs further apart; her entrance was slightly open for me, and her wetness leaked out.

I have never made love; I fuck... ... . hard, but this, this will be different; I wanted to claim every inch of her sexy body and rid her of any man that touched, kissed, or fucked her before. After I'm done with her, she will only remember my name.

"You're always so wet for me, Cupcake."

She moaned as I kissed her swollen bud and tongued her from top to bottom, slipping one, two, and then three fingers into her slippery folds.

"You're so fucking tight."

I stood up, unbuttoned my shirt, and let it fall while watching her naked body on display for me. As I was undoing my pants, I noticed some blood on the comforter. Stopping my movements, looking between her and the sheets, not wanting to make her feel uncomfortable, I softly said, "Are you a virgin, Cupcake?"

She jolted up and sat with her legs pulled to her chest, her face turning plum, instantly regretting asking.

She only nodded.

God, no one claimed this goddess yet?

Even though I wanted to feel her wet virgin pussy on my cock, I couldn't have her first time like this.

Sitting down next to her, caressing her face,

"Not like this, ok?"

Hoping she'd understand, I grabbed my shirt from the back of the chair. As I stood up, a heavy sense of guilt washed over me, crashing against my conscience like a relentless tidal wave.

Avoiding her gaze became my instinct, a means of self-preservation against the onslaught of emotions I feared would mirror back at me from her eyes. With a heavy heart, I quietly returned to the front of the plane where my brothers were sleeping.

As I settled into my seat, the weight of my decision settled in, mingling with the engines' drone and the aircraft's rhythmic hum. Guilt, like an unwelcome companion, refused to leave my side. I closed my eyes, but the turmoil within me churned relentlessly; a storm of conflicted emotions mirrored the turbulence outside the plane's windows.

CHAPTER 15

LEONARDO

The plane landed 2 hours later, as the miles unfolded beneath the wheels, I couldn't escape the nagging question of what occupied her mind at that very moment. Her steadfast avoidance of my gaze and the palpable silence between us were like uncharted territories, urging exploration and understanding. It was a barrier, not just of distance but of unspoken words waiting to be unraveled.

In the heart of New York, where the city's pulse echoed through towering skyscrapers, Sonny unearthed a piece of information with his formidable computer skills. It was revealed that she had discreetly booked a hotel room for herself. Swiftly responding to this revelation, my brothers and I decided to intervene. We believed that our home, with its expansive rooms and welcoming ambiance, would provide her with comfort and serve as a sanctuary where she could find solace.

As I continued to drive, putting more distance between us and the bustling city, I glanced in the rear-view mirror to where Brittney sat in the back seat. The widening gap between us mirrored her evident desire to create space, yet her growing anxiety was palpable. Fidgety movements and the clenching of her hands betrayed the inner turmoil she was experiencing.

"Are we headed to my hotel?" she inquired, the uncertainty in her voice only adding to her allure. God, she's gorgeous when she's nervous, I couldn't help but think.

"You're staying with us," Sonny replied, his voice commanding assurance as he reached over to caress her thigh.

The history of shared experiences with my brothers lingered in my mind. I knew keeping Brittney exclusively for myself was futile.

"What! No, I have a reservation at the Four Seasons downtown."

"Not anymore," Dominic said with the most malevolent grin I had ever witnessed.

She sighed and shook her head, leaning back in her seat. She seemed to have grasped that going against us would be an uphill battle, the formidable force she was up against.

We arrived at our destination shortly after.

I quickly made my way from the driver's side, eager to assist her. I placed my arm around her waist, but she abruptly pulled away from my grasp, her body language tense and guarded.

"I'd rather Sonny shows me to my room."

Fuck, she is pissed.

Sonny grinned while taking her hand and leading her to the front door. I wanted to wring his neck, watching him stare at her ass while we walked up the stairs to her room.

We shared a decent-sized house. I slept on the third floor, which also housed my office, and Dom and Sonny shared the second floor.

We had an indoor pool that provided a secluded retreat, complete with elegant décor and a tranquil atmosphere, an outdoor pool that boasted luxurious lounge chairs and umbrellas, a state-of-the-art gymnasium filled with the latest equipment, a fully furnished basement with a media room, a cozy seating area, game room (Sonny's idea) and a private spa.

An army of diligent maids' butlers, security, and skilled cooks ready to attend to our every need. After long days of relentless work and commitment, we craved a sanctuary to unwind and rejuvenate. The help lived in quarters detached from the main house except for Jeffrey, our butler who served my family for over thirty years. He is one of the very few people not related to us whom we trusted.

Brittney's room, nestled on the third floor, was a source of genuine satisfaction for me. Sonny, ever efficient, had called ahead, ensuring the maid prepared her room in advance.

As she stepped into her new haven, I couldn't help but revel in the amazement twinkling in her eyes. It was a seemingly small gesture, yet her exuded joy and excitement resonated deeply within me. At that moment, I yearned to be responsible for bringing such happiness into her daily life.

Her bedroom was generous in size and adorned with a king-sized bed. A balcony, a walk-in closet, and an ensuite bathroom, which we would share, completed the luxurious space.

"This is amazing," she marveled.

"Only the best for you," Dom chimed in, his intrusion into her space evident.

Shaking my head with a fond smile as I exited the room, I advised, "Unpack and rest; breakfast is at 8. See you then." My brothers followed suit, leaving Brittney to acclimate to her new surroundings.

CHAPTER 16

BRITTNEY

My resolve was ironclad, a fortress built upon the indignity I had suffered. No matter how potent, his physical allure could not compensate for the humiliation that still burned fresh in my memory. So, what if I was a virgin? That gave him no right to leave me exposed, vulnerable, and ablaze with unfulfilled desire on his bed— a bed that had promised ecstasy but delivered only shame.

And now, with the audacity of one who knows not the depth of their transgression, he sought to smooth over the jagged edges of the night with niceties. No, I would not yield. The anger within me was a shield, a barrier against his charm and disarming looks.

I had maintained a steely silence throughout the ride, a silence that was both my armor and my protest. He was close enough to touch, yet I kept him at a distance, an emotional chasm I was determined to preserve. This silence would be my companion, my declaration of independence from the turmoil he had caused.

I vowed to continue this vigil of disregard for the rest of the week.

My room was nothing short of luxurious; the centerpiece was a magnificent king-size bed adorned with plush pillows and silky sheets that promised nights of blissful comfort.

A walk-in closet awaited, ready to house my tiny wardrobe with its neatly organized shelves and racks. And through the glass doors, a private balcony beckoned, offering a breathtaking view of the surrounding landscape.

Every detail had been meticulously attended to, creating an ambiance of indulgence and tranquility. As I stepped into this haven of luxury, a mixture of awe and gratitude washed over me, tinged with a hint of suspicion about the intentions behind such grand accommodation.

It was around three in the morning, and I was exhausted. I rang Francine, and even though I knew she might not answer, I promised to call her as soon as I landed... . Better late than never. After leaving a short voicemail, I entered the biggest ensuite I have ever stepped foot in.

It took me over ten minutes to figure out the shower; it had an array of controls and buttons adorning the panel. There were buttons for different water pressure, temperature settings, and even specialized massage settings. At one point, I had it with the knobs; I was ready to take a bird bath in the sink, but thank God, I figured it out (somewhat).

Walking out of the bathroom to my new bedroom for the next week, a pleasant surprise awaited me; a pair of cozy pajamas was laid out neatly as if someone had thoughtfully prepared them for me.

Assuming it was the maid, I made a mental note to thank her... ...them... in the morning.

As I settled into the bed, I couldn't help but marvel at the luxurious feel of the sheets. They were incredibly soft and smooth, like a gentle embrace from the clouds. I thought I must order two for myself when I return to New York.

The blaring sound of the alarm shattered the room's tranquility, jolting me awake with annoyance and frustration.

Cursing under my breath, I fumbled to find the alarm clock and silence its obnoxious noise. I groggily checked the clock.

7 am.

It was as if the universe had conspired to wake me up at a time when even the roosters were contemplating hitting the snooze button.

Waking early was typically not a struggle for me; my body was attuned to the rhythms of the day, beginning with the sunrise. But last night's rest had been elusive, a fleeting thing grasped only in the smallest hours of the morning. Just two hours ago, I had finally succumbed to the sweet lure of sleep, and now, resentment simmered within me at being robbed of the rest I so desperately needed.

I yearned to possess the power to lasso the sun, gently pulling it back into the horizon and coaxing the moon to go back to its rightful place in the darkened sky. The prospect of reclaiming those peaceful moments of slumber enticed me, tempting me to linger in the realm of dreams just a little longer.

With all the grace of a clumsy flamingo on roller skates, I toppled off the bed and landed on the floor in a spectacular display of morning gymnastics. I crawled to the bathroom, dragging myself inch by inch across the floor. Each movement felt like an Olympic feat, as if I were participating in the Floor-Crawling Championships.

Finally reaching the bathroom, I mustered the strength to stand up. Squinting at my blurred reflection in the mirror, I attempted to put on my best "I'm ready to conquer the day" face, which looked more like a confused penguin trying to impersonate a confident lion.

It was going to be an interesting day.

I dedicated some time to applying my makeup, skillfully concealing any signs of sleep deprivation, and utilizing Francine's technique for eye makeup. Following her approach, I aimed for a natural yet elegant look, ensuring that my appearance reflected both poise and a touch of sophistication. As I meticulously blended the hues and accentuated my eyes, I felt a subtle boost in confidence, ready to face whatever the day had in store with a polished and composed demeanor.

I meticulously chose a green business dress, its color exuding professionalism and sophistication. To complement the ensemble, I opted for a pair of sleek black Louboutin heels, adding a touch of elegance to the overall look. The refined dress and classic footwear combined aimed to convey a polished and confident appearance as I prepared for the day ahead. As I descended the stairs, the sounds of lively conversation grew louder, guiding me toward the welcoming embrace of the kitchen.

The aroma of freshly brewed coffee instantly lifted my spirits. I opened the door, revealing a sight that caught me off guard. Three impeccably dressed, handsome men sat at the table, indulging in a breakfast fit for royalty.

The table was adorned with an array of delectable dishes. The tantalizing aroma of freshly baked pastries and sizzling bacon filled the room, making my stomach rumble in anticipation.

It was as if I had stumbled upon a scene from a movie where everything was picture-perfect and effortlessly glamorous. (Why the hell don't I live like this?)

A sudden hush fell over the room as I stepped into the kitchen. The three men at the table redirected their focus toward me, their eyes locked onto mine. A palpable tension lingered as I became the center of their scrutiny. "Damn," I overheard Dom mutter, his eyes carefully assessing me from head to toe.

"Are you hungry?" Sonny asked, but the look in his eyes made it difficult to tell if he was referring to food or something else.

"The chef can make you whatever you want," Leo said as I ignored him.

I grabbed the cup of coffee that Sonny offered me.

"Thanks, Sonny," I said, emphasizing Sonny.

Leo sighed, and a faint laughter bubbled inside me.

As I drank my much-needed caffeine, I listened to the conversation between the men.

"Baby girl, you will stay here today and meet with our father tomorrow," Dom declared with a twinkle of curiosity in his eyes. The playful nicknames the men had bestowed upon me sparked an interest, but my immediate concern shifted to the unfolding situation that demanded my attention.

"What do you mean stay here? I am here for a job, and my job is not to lounge around in this house," I retorted, my hands gesturing emphatically at the vast expanse surrounding us.

"Our father will not be available today," Dom explained, studying my expression for any signs of understanding or dissent.

Infuriated by the lack of prior information, I fired back, "So why did I fly here yesterday?" The frustration lingered, leaving me in the dark about the abrupt change in plans.

Sonny, sensing my discontent, approached from behind, wrapping his arms around me in a comforting gesture and planting a reassuring kiss on my head.

"Don't be upset, princess. I promise I'll make it up to you later," he assured me, gently tilting my head to kiss my cheek near the side of my mouth. My heart raced as I glanced at Leo, attempting to gauge his reaction, yet he remained composed and seemingly unfazed.

Among the three brothers, Sonny emerged as the more hands-on and fun-loving personality. His vibrant and playful demeanor made him appear as the trio's jokester, and this light-hearted charm created a deeper connection between us. Sonny's easygoing nature and propensity for physical affection made him approachable, and I found myself drawn to the sense of warmth and camaraderie he exuded.

"I had the maids pick up some swimsuits for you. Change, swim, read a book, watch a movie, whatever you want, and we'll return soon. Ok, Cupcake?" Sonny suggested with a lighthearted tone.

An unsettling feeling crept over me as I sensed that something suspicious was happening. There was an air of secrecy, and I couldn't shake the intuition that there was more to this situation than met the eye.

"I'll make the best of it," I responded with a forced smile, determined to play it cool. Deep down, however, a burning resolve ignited within me to uncover the truth behind their behavior and decipher the enigma surrounding this unexpected turn of events.

CHAPTER 17
BRITTNEY

Age 13

I wasn't lost on the subtle shift in my uncle's demeanor and appearance. The playful spark that once lit up his eyes seemed dimmed, and his laughter was not as hearty as before. It was as if life had cast a shadow over him, altering his essence.

He had lost weight, a fact that couldn't escape my notice no matter how much they tried to downplay it. Whenever I broached the subject, my mother and he exchanged glances, their assurances masking a more profound truth.

But I knew. I could sense the unspoken words, the unsung worries that hung heavy in the air. Something wasn't right, and their attempts to shield me from it only fueled my determination to uncover their hidden reality.

As the days passed, my mother's presence at home became increasingly scarce, like a fleeting shadow slipping through our lives. The weight of her absence settled heavily on my heart, and I yearned for the warmth of her smile and the soothing sound of her voice.

Frustration and concern gnawed at me, the uncertainty of her actions clawing at the edges of my thoughts. I knew something had shifted, something beyond the ordinary busyness of life. The need to unravel the mystery grew stronger each day until it became an unshakeable determination.

One afternoon, I entered her room's private sanctum, seeking the answers that eluded me.

As I quietly stepped inside, the air in her room felt charged with trepidation and resolve. The soft rays of sunlight filtering through the curtains cast a gentle glow as if lending me courage for what lay ahead.

I rummaged through her drawer, each paper shuffled, feeling like an intrusion into her world. And then, among the mundane documents, my eyes snagged on a name that sent shockwaves- my uncle's name, etched on a hospital bill. My heart plummeted, and I clutched the paper, my fingers trembling.

As I read through the lines of medical jargon, the truth unfolded before me like a cruel revelation.

Pancreatic cancer – words that carried a weight beyond measure. The room seemed to spin around me as I grappled with the enormity of what I had discovered. A lump formed in my throat, choking back a flood of emotions that threatened to consume me.

The paper slipped from my fingers, falling onto the floor as I sank onto the edge of her bed. Thoughts whirled in my mind, memories of my uncle flashing before me – his laughter, warmth, and unwavering presence in our lives.

It was as if the ground had shifted beneath me, casting a shadow of uncertainty over the world I had known.

Grief mingled with a surge of anger, an unfairness that clawed at my chest. How could this be happening? Why had no one told me? The questions reverberated in my mind, echoing in the room's silence.

Seated around the polished dining room table, a scene that had become a fleeting rarity, the three of us were an island amidst the currents of our own lives.

My uncle's presence, a steady anchor of laughter and companionship, felt comforting and disconcerting as his eyes, which once held a mischievous twinkle, now reflected a somber depth.

My mother, the pillar of our small family, her smile weary but determined, struggled to bridge the growing gap that her relentless schedule had forged. Amidst the clinking of cutlery and the murmur of conversation, I found myself lost in my thoughts, tracing patterns on my plate with my fork.

The aroma of the lovingly prepared meal seemed to lose its appeal, overshadowed by the weight of unspoken concerns that had taken residence in my heart.

My gaze shifted to my uncle, who had been quieter than usual, his usually animated demeanor replaced by a thoughtful silence. It was as if a shadow had fallen across him, a shadow that I couldn't ignore any longer. The truth had been festering within me, a question I couldn't contain any further.

I looked up, my eyes meeting my mother's for a fleeting moment before returning to my plate. The words were on the tip of my tongue, a question that had gnawed at me for too long.

"Why didn't you tell me?" I finally uttered, my voice barely above a whisper, the question hanging heavy in the air.

The room seemed to hold its breath as my words lingered, a fragile tension wrapping around us. My uncle's gaze met mine, his expression a mixture of surprise and understanding, while my mother's eyes shimmered with regret and sadness.

As I set it down, my fork clinked against my plate, the sound of punctuation to the moment's weight. I could feel their eyes on me, their silent acknowledgment of the question finally voiced.

My mother's voice was gentle, laden with the weight of unspoken explanations.

"We didn't want to burden you," She began, her words carrying a mixture of apology and reassurance.

"With everything you have going on, we thought it best to shield you from this."

My uncle's hand found mine.

"We wanted to protect you," he added, his voice soft but unwavering. "You have your dreams and aspirations, and we didn't want this to cast a shadow over them."

I looked from one to the other, their love and concern evident in their eyes. It was a sentiment that both touched my heart and stirred a wellspring of emotions within me. The realization that they had chosen silence out of love and a desire to preserve my journey resonated deeply.

Tears welled in my eyes as I let their words settle within me, the weight of their unspoken sacrifices lifting the veil of my understanding. I reached for my mother's hand, feeling her touch's warmth and our bond's strength.

"I appreciate your concern," I finally said, my voice teetering with emotion. But I want to be there for both of you. We're family, and we face things together."

A tender smile passed between us, a shared understanding that transcended words. At that moment, around that dining room table, I felt the barriers erected by silence crumble, replaced by a renewed sense of unity and a shared determination to face the challenges ahead, hand in hand.

CHAPTER 18

BRITTNEY

Present

An hour later, I luxuriously reclined by the pristine outdoor pool, embraced by the sun's soothing rays and adorned in an elegant all-white two-piece swimsuit. The maids, with Matilda taking the lead, had exhibited an exceptional level of dedication to ensuring my comfort within the opulent confines of the house.

Matilda, in particular, stood out with her commitment to attending to my every need. Her efforts added a unique warmth to the air of mystery that enveloped the estate. To accentuate this hospitality, Matilda graciously presented me with a refreshing fruit platter accompanied by a glass of chilled champagne. Her attentiveness went above and beyond, ensuring that my glass remained consistently replenished, offering a continuous supply of bubbly to enhance the leisurely atmosphere.

As I allowed myself to drift into a momentary nap on the plush lounge chair, Matilda demonstrated her thoughtfulness by adjusting the umbrella's position, shielding me from the sun's direct rays. In this tranquil setting, a whimsical and playful thought crossed my mind – the idea of fitting Matilda into my suitcase and carrying her to New York with me when I departed.

Standing about 5 feet 3 inches and carrying some extra weight, Matilda defied stereotypes with her dedicated service. Her appearance, characterized by chunky glasses reminiscent of my nana's and the retro apron she wore, added a unique charm and familiarity to the grandeur of the surroundings. Matilda's presence became an unexpected and delightful highlight, turning a simple afternoon by the pool into a memorable experience within the lavish estate.

As I heard the front door slam shut and footsteps ascending the stairs, I quickly snatched the softest towel I could find, pondering if the men had a secret enchanted warehouse filled with tiny elves that conjured up all these luxuriously soft items.

Eager to join them, I hurriedly made my way up the stairs.

On the 2nd floor landing, headed towards the bedrooms, my attention was abruptly caught by the sound of heated arguing emanating from the third floor. The familiarity of the voices left no doubt that Leo was engaged in the dispute.

Curiosity piqued, and I made my way toward the source. As I reached Leo's door, I mustered the courage to knock lightly, my hand lingering in mid-air for a moment before making contact with the wood,

"Come in, cupcake." Opening the door, a shiver ran down my spine as I caught sight of the three men gathered in Leo's room, their eyes fixed on me.

"It didn't go well, did it?" I said as my gaze fixated on the shattered lamp strewn across the floor.

With an effortless nonchalance, Leo glided his hand over the nape of his neck, the simple act of loosening his tie transforming into a display of understated sensuality. His every move seemed choreographed to perfection, leaving me to wonder if I'd find him gracing the glossy pages of GQ magazine,

Caught in the act of staring, he responded with the sexiest grin, a silent acknowledgment of our shared tension. As he sauntered in my direction, his movements held a magnetic allure. In one fluid motion, he undid the towel, letting it cascade to the floor, and the abrupt exposure left my body tingling with goosebumps from the chill in the air.

His words, delivered with a confident yet playful tone, shattered the charged silence. "The bathing suit fits perfectly," he declared.

Throughout the years, I've cultivated a deep appreciation and love for my body, recognizing its inherent value despite not conforming to society's narrow ideals of being skinny. The journey towards self-love hasn't always been smooth, marked by moments when I succumbed to the pressures of unrealistic beauty standards, yearning for a shape that wasn't my own. In my teenage years, I faced teasing because of features like a not-so-flat belly or the presence of cellulite. However, as time unfolded, I embarked on a transformative journey towards self-acceptance. I learned to embrace the unique features of my body, seeing them not as flaws but as testaments to its strength and resilience. The mirror, once a source of comparison and self-criticism, now reflects a body that tells a profound story of self-acceptance and self-love. No longer tethered to society's unrealistic expectations, I've forged a path to appreciate and celebrate the beautiful narrative that my body conveys— a narrative of strength, authenticity, and personal triumph.

But amidst all the self-acceptance and love for my body, I had never experienced anything quite like the way these three gorgeous men were looking at me. Their hungry gazes transcended mere physical hunger.

Feeling a sudden surge of self-consciousness, I subconsciously placed my hands around my breasts, instinctively trying to cover the unexpected exposure of my very exposed cleavage.

As Leo's piercing gaze bore into me, his expression grew increasingly intense, his eyes filled with desire.

"What are you doing, Cupcake?"

"I... I was just... I'm nervous."

I managed to stammer, my voice barely audible.

The strength I had felt moments ago seemed to dissipate, leaving me feeling vulnerable and small under his piercing gaze. My hands nervously tightened around my breasts as if seeking comfort and protection from the overwhelming intensity of the situation.

He reached out and gently moved my trembling hands away from my breasts, his touch surprisingly tender despite the intensity in his eyes.

"No need to hide yourself." He murmured, his voice softer now.

"You have nothing to be ashamed of. You are a goddamn queen." His fingers lingered on my skin for a brief moment before slowly retracting.

Noticing my weariness, "I don't think she believes me." he said, his voice raised, intensely looking at me but clearly not talking to me.

"Maybe we should show her," Sonny said from beside me, his suggestive tone sending a shiver down my spine. Confusion and concern flashed in my eyes as I looked to Leo for clarification.

Glancing over at Sonny, I saw him grinning with hooded eyes, a provocative lick of his lips adding to the charged atmosphere. Dom stood behind me, his presence tangible, and I could feel the intensity of his desire against my back.

Fuck.

Leo closed in on me, his presence becoming more intense as he leaned closer, his warm breath tickling my ear.

"We'll take care of you."

His words were cryptic, leaving me with more questions than answers. In that split second, as his lips touched mine, time seemed to stand still. The confusion and questions that swirled in my mind were momentarily silenced by the warmth and intensity of his kiss.

There was so much passion in his kiss, opening my lips and using that fantastic tongue as if he was conveying something beyond words.

A soft moan escaped my mouth, blending with his groans. He then effortlessly lifted me in his arms and carried me towards his bed.

As the intensity of our kiss grew, an unexpected awareness settled around us like an invisible force. Sensing a presence, I reluctantly opened my eyes, only to find the two brothers standing there, their gazes fixed on me.

Leo, sensing their presence, broke the kiss and turned to them with a mischievous grin. Without saying a word, they closed the distance, joining us on the bed with a shared understanding.

I let out a surprised gasp as his hand connected with my ass, sending a jolt of mixed sensations through my body. The playful yet possessive gesture made my heart race even faster. With a gentle grip, he lowered me back down onto the bed.

"On your hands and knees... ... ... Now! Cupcake!" He said, breathing heavily, "Show us that wet sexy pussy."

Usually, I wouldn't allow him to speak to me in such a manner, but at that moment, a desire to explore the unknown led me to follow their lead willingly.

"Goddamn, you're perfect," Dom said, his voice now carrying a deeper, darker tone.

As I felt the cool air against my exposed skin, I couldn't help but roll my eyes playfully, knowing all too well that it was Leo who had just ripped off my swimsuit bottom. With a smirk, he locked eyes with me, his gaze filled with desire and a hint of amusement as if daring me to challenge his bold move.

"That juicy pussy tastes even better."

"Oh yeah?" Dom said.

As the weight of the bed shifted, I felt myself being gently lifted, my body settling onto Dom's lap as he laid down on his back, his strong arms securely holding me close. He then gently pulled me until I was aligned with his mouth, licking his lip ring; he bore his gaze at me before pulling my hips down on him and tasting me softly.

"Oh, Dom," whispering his name, I glanced down to where we connected. "Don't stop."

His nails dug into my flesh as his tongue took control. He looked absolutely amazing from this angle, his chiseled features illuminated by a soft glow, his eyes filled with desire as they met mine.

Lost in the intoxicating sensation, I grabbed a handful of his hair, tugging roughly as pleasure surged through me. His groans mingled with my moans, creating a symphony of ecstasy that echoed throughout the room. My eyes shifted to Sonny, who stood before me, his gaze fixed on our passionate encounter. The longing in his eyes only fueled the moment's intensity, creating a thrilling sense of anticipation. Completely exposed his masculine physique on full display, adorned with an array of captivating tattoos that adorned his skin, but all I was able to concentrate on was his hand stroking his dick, pre-cum escaping and landing on the carpet beneath his feet (he's so big). The anticipation built as I wondered what it would be like to experience him inside me, to feel his heat and intensity.

Parting my thighs wider, I arched my back, riding Dom's face hard, feeling that familiar sensation build up,

"Dominic... ... ohhh... ohhh... . Dom."

I screamed as the most rippling organism I have ever felt tore through me. Concerned about potentially suffocating him, I attempted to lift myself off him, but he firmly held onto my thighs, refusing to let go, licking every drop.

He then carefully guided me to sit next to him on the bed, licking his lips of the last bit of cum coating his mouth, then used the back of his hand to wipe the rest away.

"You're right," he said, lips glistening, never losing eye contact. "She does taste incredible." Making me blush.

Leo sat on the edge of the bed, his eyes fixed on me. With a firm pull, he lifted me onto him, my body gravitating toward his presence. As I settled on top of him, my fingers traced along the contours of his sculpted muscles; his intricate tattoos, previously concealed beneath layers of clothing, caught my attention.

"Ready, cupcake?"

My eager nod indicated my readiness and anticipation. With a self-assured smirk, he effortlessly lifted me gently in his strong arms and laid me down on my back. Pulling my top down, he exposed my breasts.

"Fuck." I heard the brothers say in unison.

His eyes gleamed with mischief as his gaze traveled down my body, pausing on the love marks he had left on me a few nights ago. A sly grin spread across his face, revealing his satisfaction at the lingering evidence of our passionate encounter.

I felt his hand gently cup my breasts. The warmth of his touch spread, igniting fire within me. His fingers explored the curve and contours; leaning in, he wrapped my nipple between his teeth, the sensation unbearable, "Leo," I managed to utter, "Please." I was wet with anticipation, and the wait was killing me; I wanted him now.

Grinning, "Greedy." he said.

With each gentle suck, he seemed to draw the pain away, replacing it with a deep, intoxicating pleasure that consumed my every thought. The world around us faded into oblivion as we became lost in the raw passion of the moment.

He then released his grip on me and slowly sat up. His breath was heavy, matching my rhythm as we both tried to catch our breath and gather our senses. My breasts were now suffused with pink. He carefully positioned himself between my legs, his hands bracing his weight on either side of me. Our bodies aligned perfectly, fitting together like two puzzle pieces. I could feel the heat radiating from his skin. As he slowly lowered himself onto me, inch by delicious inch, "Leo," I screamed, feeling the tension in the room heighten.

"Fuck, you're so tight," he groaned. "Breath," he added.

The sharp pang of initial discomfort gradually melted away, replaced by waves of pleasure that surged with each thrust.

"You're mine," he said, pressing himself deeper into me, "mine," he pushed even deeper. His lips captured mine in a searing, demanding kiss, igniting a fire within me that burned with raw desire. With each thrust, he delved deeper into the depths of my being, setting my senses ablaze.

Moans of pleasure escaped my parted lips, filling the air with a symphony of ecstasy. As our bodies moved in perfect harmony, the intensity of our connection intensified, driving us both to the brink of madness. I arched my back, offering myself fully to him, as he relentlessly pushed the boundaries of pleasure, his movements fueled by a primal need.

"Cum for me." He said between kisses.

The friction between us, the electrifying touch of skin against skin, sent shivers of delight coursing through my veins. I clutched at him, my nails digging into his back, my body trembling. I surrendered to the waves of pleasure that washed over me, my body shaking uncontrollably as the intensity of our connection reached its peak. Ecstasy coursed through every inch of my being as I released myself in a powerful climax, unable to contain the overwhelming sensation that consumed me.

"Leo!" I cried out, my heart pounding in my chest.

"Fuck," he says, laying his head by my neck, pumping into me, his length and force almost too much. Explicit expressions spilled from his lips, punctuating each thrust as he came in me in a fiery climax that shook us both to the core.

"Damn, baby." He said as the haze gradually dissipated.

I became aware of Dom's and Sonny's presence beside me. Dom's strong arms encircled me, lifting me effortlessly and settling me onto his lap as soon as Leo pulled out of me.

Dripping from Leo's and my cum- Dom seemed not to care. His touch, once again, ignited a fire within me, stoking the embers of passion that still lingered from our previous encounter.

He eagerly wasted no time as he aligned me on top of him and slowly guided me down on his massive dick.

"Ah Fuck" he said, eyes intently staring at me, "You feel amazing." Enveloping me in his arms, pulling me close until our bodies molded together seamlessly, stopping my movements, his head nestled against my shoulder, his warm breath caressing my skin. He then gently kissed my shoulder as if apologizing for what was to come.

He grabbed the back of my head, pulling my hair tight. Pain and pleasure engulfed me, but right when I opened my mouth, he took my lips, crushing onto them hard, kissing me with such passion I forgot it was Dom for a second. I always expected him to be rough, and I was looking forward to that, but this... . this was unexpected.

I bit his lip hard, causing him to bleed. He groaned in my mouth and started his movements again; this time, he was rough and hard, and I loved every bit of it. He laid down, grabbed my ass, pulling himself deeper in me; he then grabbed my neck, blocking my airway, while he fucked me mercilessly.

"This is what you like? huh, baby girl?" He growled, his grip tightening as his thrusts grew more forceful. The sheer intensity of my pleasure took me aback, surprised that I thoroughly enjoyed this wild and unbridled encounter. In my mind, I had always pictured myself as a tender and passionate lover, but Dom had shattered those expectations, revealing a side of me I never knew existed.

"Yes, ...ha... . harder." I managed to utter; he let go of my neck, needing both hands on my ass to pull me deeper into him.

He delivered a sharp and forceful slap to my ass, the impact sending a jolt of both pain and pleasure through my body. I could feel the sting lingering, knowing it would likely leave a mark.

He then guided me forward, leaning me over.

"Open your mouth."

Not knowing why but complying, he then unexpectedly spat in my mouth. The act took me by surprise, and I could taste the mix of his saliva and the lingering desire between us. He followed it with a rough, passionate kiss, our lips colliding with an intensity that matched the heat of the moment.

Sonny was behind me, rubbing my cheek where Dom left his mark. He and Dom exchanged glances, their eyes locked in a silent conversation that seemed to transcend words. It was as if they had an understanding. Then Dom slowed his pace. Sonny aligned himself as I gasped. "It won't fit," I spoke. A worried expression crept across my face.

"Trust us, Princess," Sonny said as he entered me slowly.

"Nooo," I firmly voiced my disagreement.

"You can handle it, baby girl," Dom said while grinning, chest heaving.

Sonny noticed my tension and paused; his eyes filled with concern. "Relax, baby," he whispered, his voice gentle and soothing. "I'll go slow and make sure you're comfortable." His touch was soft as he applied lubricant to his dick and my ass.

I took a deep breath, trying to relax and trust Sonny's words. With each slow, careful movement, he gradually eased himself inside me. The sensation was intense, a mix of pleasure and discomfort. Sonny's hands caressed my body, reassuring me that I was in safe hands.

As he continued to enter me, I focused on maintaining a sense of calm, letting my body adjust to the new sensations. Sonny's patience and attentiveness were evident, and it helped alleviate my initial tension. With each passing moment, the discomfort subsided, replaced by a growing pleasure that began to wash over me.

"Good girl," he said as he grabbed my neck, pulling me towards him, kissing my lips as Dom resumed his rhythmic movements inside me.

"Are you okay, princess?" he whispered against my lips.

All I could do was nod, unable to find words to express the overwhelming sensations that consumed me. With each nod, the intensity grew, and Dom continued to delve deeper inside me, pushing the boundaries of pleasure.

I couldn't believe how my sexual experience had escalated so quickly. From being a virgin to having two massive men inside me, working together to bring me to the peak of pleasure, it was an overwhelming sensation that I never thought I would experience. The intensity of their movements, the way they synchronized their actions, and their sheer size filled me, stretching my limits and pushing me beyond what I had imagined possible.

The way Leo stood before me, stroking himself, his eyes fixed on the erotic scene unfolding. It was a potent combination of pleasure and submission, knowing that I was being watched by him while being ravished by his brothers.

My body reacted instinctively, arching and writhing with passion, as my eyes involuntarily rolled back, overwhelmed by the intensity of the pleasure coursing through me, feeling the urge to... ... . No... .

"Stop," I managed to utter, my voice trembling with unease. Dom, sensing my hesitation, swiftly placed his hand on the back of my neck, his touch both gentle and reassuring. His eyes bore into mine, filled with genuine concern and a hint of confusion, as he struggled to comprehend what might be troubling me. I could feel his heavy breath against my skin,

"What's wrong, Baby girl? Is it too much for you?"

"I'm going to... to pee!"

I screamed, my voice echoing through the room. The moment's intensity had peaked, and I couldn't longer suppress my urgent need.

"Good," he responded.

Without missing a beat, both men synchronized their movements, plunging deeper into the depths of pleasure.

"Dom... . Sonny," I managed to yell; the sensation was overwhelming, and Sonny's thrusts grew more urgent as Dom's movements became faster and more forceful. I could feel the pressure building within me, a primal urge that demanded release. As they continued to plunge deep inside me, my body responded in kind, my inner walls tightening around them.

And then it happened. A wave of pleasure washed over me, starting from the depths of my core and radiating outward. I arched my back, a cry escaping my lips as I released in a powerful surge. My body convulsed with the force of my orgasm; Dom and Sonny's groans mingled with my moans as they both reached their climax.

"Goddamnit Princess," Sonny said from behind me, breathing heavily.

Leo stroked himself faster, his desire evident in his eyes. The sight of him pleasuring himself drove me crazy. I couldn't tear my gaze away from him as his hand moved with purpose, his movements becoming more urgent as he approached his climax.

"Fuck, Fuck, Fuck." He said, releasing an impressive amount of hot cum onto my breast with a satisfied groan.

We all collapsed onto the bed, our bodies covered in a sheen of sweat, utterly spent from our passionate encounter. Dom pulled me close to him, his head resting on my neck as he placed gentle kisses on my skin. The room grew quiet as Leo and Sonny exited, leaving us in peaceful solitude.

I closed my eyes, feeling contentment and connection with Dom, cherishing our intimate moment.

CHAPTER 19

BRITTNEY

Leo reentered the bedroom, his sculpted physique adorned only by a pair of snug-fitting boxers. With an outstretched hand, he beckoned me to join him. Ignoring Dom's disapproving glance, I willingly followed Leo's lead, following him into the en-suite bathroom, where he had thoughtfully prepared a warm, inviting bath just for me.

With gentle guidance, Leo clasped my hand, supporting my waist as I eased myself into the welcoming embrace of the bathtub. The soothing warmth of the water enveloped my body, creating a sense of comfort.

As I settled into the bath, Leo leaned against the side of the tub, taking the loofah in his hand. His touch was gentle, methodically washing my body with careful attention to every curve and contour. Despite the water taking on a pinkish hue, Leo seemed unfazed, wholly absorbed in the intimate task at hand.

I was finally able to observe him closely, trying to unravel the enigma that was Leo. It surprised me that he was the one attending to me in this intimate way, as I had always associated such tenderness with Sonny, not him.

"That tickles," I said, giggling while he washed my feet.

"You're my type of perfect cupcake." He whispered.

Just when I thought I was starting to understand him, he uttered something that caught me off guard— those moments of contradiction kept me on my toes with him.

The washing seemed to go on forever, punctuated by his occasional pauses to place gentle kisses on the different parts of my body he found himself near.

"Go get dressed. I'll see you downstairs," Leo said, his lips brushing against my forehead as he spoke. With those words, he signaled the end of our intimate bath time.

Stepping into the inviting atmosphere of my bedroom, I was pleasantly surprised to find a beautiful yellow sundress artfully laid out on the bed. Its open back, elegantly secured with a delicate string, and the form-fitting design that accentuated the curves in all the right places presented a stark departure from the clothes I had initially brought with me. The low neckline added a touch of allure to the ensemble, offering a perfect blend of style and comfort.

Gratitude filled me as I embraced the thoughtful gesture, appreciating the vibrant color and the light, flowing fabric of the dress. It seemed someone had carefully chosen this attire, anticipating the occasion and my taste. With a swift yet deliberate motion, I changed into the dress, savoring the luxurious feel of the material against my skin.

As I made my way downstairs, the aroma of food greeted me, leading me straight to the kitchen. Sonny and Dom were already seated on the island, enjoying their meal. Dom looked up and grinned when he saw me. "Hey beautiful, I made you a plate," he said warmly, placing the food he had prepared on the counter next to me.

Sonny, ever the affectionate one, approached me and gently kissed my forehead, a sweet gesture that made me feel cherished.

"This is too much."

"You need your strength," Dom whispered seductively in my ear, his words sending a shiver down my spine, warming my core.

The intimate moment was interrupted when Leo, dressed impeccably in one of his signature three-piece suits, entered the kitchen. His suit was a masterpiece of tailoring, a charcoal gray ensemble that exuded sophistication and refinement. The jacket hugged his broad shoulders while the vest added a touch of timeless elegance. The crisp white shirt beneath the suit jacket provided a striking contrast, and a silk tie in a deep shade of burgundy completed the ensemble with a subtle yet captivating touch.

His dark hair, meticulously styled, framed a face that seemed carved by an artist's hand. A strong jawline led to a hint of stubble, enhancing the rugged allure that made him equal parts refined and untamed. His piercing blue eyes held an intensity that hinted at a wealth of emotions beneath the composed exterior— windows to a complex and intriguing soul. The air seemed to shift as he sat next to me; the room instantly transformed into a backdrop befitting his distinguished appearance.

"When will I meet your father?"

The question hung in the air, freezing the room in an instant. Sonny and Dom exchanged glances, their eyes filled with curiosity, as they turned their attention towards Leo, waiting for his response.

"Soon."

Leo's response echoed in the air, leaving a hint of mystery and aloofness. He grabbed a plate of food and proceeded to eat, seemingly unbothered by the question's weight. As I watched him, frustration filled me. Trying to decipher Leo's intentions was impossible; understanding Mandarin Chinese would have been simpler.

"What do you mean? I'll be leaving soon, and I haven't even seen him." I pressed, my frustration mounting.

"I said soon!" Leo's reply was evasive. Abruptly pushing his plate away, he shot me a glance that spoke volumes— anger simmering in his eyes, his jaw locked. The atmosphere in the kitchen grew tense as he turned and swiftly left, leaving me perplexed and yearning for answers to the mysteries shrouding his actions.

I turned my gaze to Sonny and Dom, silently pleading for them to shed some light on the situation, hoping they could clarify Leo's cryptic behavior.

"Why don't you stay for a bit longer, princess?" Sonny suggested.

"I have a job, and my life is in New York."

"Technically, we are your bosses."

"I have a life," I said frustrated.

"Let's talk about this later," Dom said, looking at Sonny with warning.

Before I could answer, their phones vibrated almost simultaneously.

"Shit," Sonny said, looking at me, rubbing the back of his neck. "We'll be back as soon as we can." And just like that, they were gone.

CHAPTER 20

BRITTNEY

Age 15

With my uncle now under our roof, a decision born of necessity and a desire to be closer during this trying time, our home took on an air of bittersweet togetherness. The once spare bedroom became his sanctuary, where he navigated the tides of his illness with a quiet strength that humbled and inspired me.

Days turned into a montage of shared moments and simple pleasures. I juggled school and my newfound role as a caregiver, all the while cherishing the time I spent by his side.

We'd sit on the porch in the afternoons, the sunlight casting a warm glow as we shared stories, laughter, and the comfortable silence that often accompanies genuine companionship.

As weeks turned into months, the reality of his condition began to cast its shadow. The cancer, relentless and unforgiving, had woven its threads through his body, stealing away his vitality with each passing day. Yet, in the face of this inevitability, my uncle's spirit remained unbroken.

We faced the harsh truth together, navigating a complex labyrinth of doctor's visits, treatments, and the sobering conversations that peppered our days. My mother's tireless work continued her determination to provide the best care, evident in every exhausted but determined step.

Despite the weight of the situation, an underlying current of gratitude flowed through our lives. Gratitude for the time we had, for the chance to be present for one another in ways that extended beyond words. Gratitude for the shared laughter that rang through our home, a stark contrast to the heavy reality that often threatened to consume us.

As the seasons changed, so did my perspective. Our bond deepened, shaped not only by family ties but by the shared journey we found ourselves on.

While the specter of loss loomed on the horizon, it was in these moments that I learned the true power of connection: being there for someone when they needed it the most.

My mother's dedication to supporting my uncle during his illness was nothing short of extraordinary. Her days seemed to blur together, a relentless cycle of work and responsibility, all to ensure he received the care he needed.

From early mornings to late nights, she would leave our home with a determined look, the weight of the world on her shoulders. Her absence was felt keenly in the quiet moments, a reminder of the sacrifices she was making to alleviate his suffering.

I watched her from the sidelines, a mix of admiration and concern welling within me. Her strength was a force to be reckoned with, a testament to the depths of a mother's love and the lengths she was willing to go to ensure the well-being of her family.

At times, I wished I could shoulder some of her burden and ease the worry lines that etched onto her face. But I knew that her drive came from a place of profound love, a determination to provide comfort and support to my uncle in his time of need.

The approaching date of my birthday, just two months away, carried a weight of hope and desperation. In a somewhat irrational notion, I found myself clinging to the belief that if only my uncle could hold on until that particular day, I could utilize my birthday wish to miraculously banish his sickness.

Logically, I knew this was nonsensical, yet it became a lifeline, a way to channel my determination and willpower for his sake.

As time ticked away, I immersed myself in the preparations for my birthday celebration. Strangely, my uncle appeared to be positively engaged in helping me plan this significant event.

We meticulously curated each detail, sharing laughter and moments of joy. It was as if planning and looking forward to something greater had a tangible effect on his well-being. His participation filled me with cautious optimism, and I dared to believe my desperate hope might be working.

The daily planning sessions became a routine, a shared mission that both distracted us from the grim reality and offered a glimmer of possibility. I noticed subtle changes in my uncle – a newfound energy, a brighter smile, and a resilience that spoke of a fighting spirit.

Incredibly, there were moments of respite from the heavy cloud of illness that had hovered over us. We even managed to engage in activities that we used to enjoy together. Playing basketball, our favorite pastime, was now a testament to his progress. The sound of his laughter on the court was a stark contrast to the days when his health had cast a somber shadow over our lives.

As I returned home from school, weary from my academic pursuits, the prospect of shooting hoops with my uncle became a beacon of light. With each dribble, each pass, it felt as if we were defying the odds, pushing back against the inevitable.

And so, my upcoming birthday took on a new significance. It was no longer just a celebration of my existence; it symbolized our shared journey, a tangible manifestation of our hopes and dreams.

As the days continued to march forward, I clung to the belief that this special day could mark a turning point.

The long-awaited day of my birthday had finally arrived, ushered in by excitement and anticipation. My mother had thoughtfully taken the day off from her demanding schedule to ensure that this day would be unique.

Although I had entertained the idea of a lively gathering with my friends, my mother suggested a more intimate celebration, given the circumstances, seemed fitting. With a mixture of reluctance and understanding, I agreed to her proposition.

As the day unfolded, I couldn't contain my enthusiasm. Every moment seemed infused with an electric energy, a sense of joy that only birthdays could bring. Bursting with eagerness, I raced into my uncle's room, ready to partake in our cherished tradition of making a birthday wish together.

"Unc, wake up! It's time," I announced, my voice brimming with the exuberance that only birthdays could evoke.

However, my excitement was met with a stark contrast. He remained still, lost in the embrace of sleep as if the fervor of the day had yet to reach him. My enthusiasm wavered, replaced by a growing unease.

"Unc," I called again, the tone of my voice now tinged with concern.

Yet, there was no response, no acknowledgment of my presence. A wave of anxiety began to wash over me, eroding the initial jubilation. My attempts to rouse him felt futile, his unmoving form a stark reminder of the uncertainty that could engulf even the brightest moments.

I gently nudged his shoulder, a mixture of fear and urgency propelling me forward.

"Marc, come on, wake up," I implored, my voice a fragile plea in the face of mounting worry.

Finally, a flicker of awareness danced in his eyes, followed by a gentle smile that reassured my frantic heart.

"Hey there, birthday girl," he greeted, his voice a comforting melody that brushed away my apprehensions.

A sigh of relief escaped me, mingling with the tears in my eyes.

"You had me worried," I confessed, my words carrying the weight of the emotions that had surged through me.

Chuckling softly, he shifted, propping himself up against the pillows.

"Couldn't miss celebrating with you, could I?" he teased his attempt at humor, a soothing balm to my frayed nerves.

A relieved laugh bubbled from within me. As I met his gaze, I realized that this moment, this exchange, was a gift in itself. His presence, his unwavering spirit, was already fulfilling my birthday wish.

With an affectionate smile, I embraced him tightly.

"Having you here is the best gift. Happy birthday to me, indeed."

In the warmth of his presence, there was a sense of unbreakable unity in that embrace.

As the day unfolded, my mother and I worked together in the kitchen, preparing my cherished favorite dish with care and devotion. Balloons adorned the space, their vibrant colors dancing in the sunlight that streamed through the windows. Every corner of our home seemed to sparkle with anticipation, transformed by our efforts into a realm of celebration.

Yet, amidst the hustle and bustle, a shadow of concern lingered. My uncle, a figure of strength and warmth, remained confined to his bed, his absence a reminder of the fragility of life.

We understood that this day was not just mine but also his shared moment of connection and love.

Entering his room, excited for him to see what we have done, I softly called out to him,

"Time to wake up, Unc; everything is ready," I said softly.

His stillness was met with growing panic.

No, no,...

"Marc!" I cried out, my voice echoing the fear that had taken hold of my heart. Fearing the worst, I screamed for my mother, my pleas carrying the weight of my dread.

In a heartbeat, my mother was by my side, her concern mirrored in her eyes.

"What's wrong, baby?" she asked soothingly.

"He's not waking up," I managed to choke out, my voice trembling as tears welled in my eyes. The words themselves were a terrifying admission, a stark confrontation with the unthinkable.

With a sense of urgency, my mother approached his bedside, her movements cautious yet purposeful. She leaned over, her hand pressed to his neck as she searched for the faintest sign of life. The following seconds felt like an eternity, a suspended moment of anguish.

"Baby, call 911 now!" Her command shattered the stillness, snapping me into action.

Numbly, I stumbled out of the room, my mind racing as I fumbled for my mother's phone. My trembling fingers dialed the numbers, each digit a painful reminder of the urgency in the air.

As the dispatcher's voice echoed through the receiver, I conveyed the dire situation, my words a shaky testament to the turmoil gripping our home.

It felt like an eternity as I waited for the ambulance to arrive, the minutes stretching into an agonizing eternity.

When the paramedics finally arrived, their efforts were swift yet solemn. The room was filled with a tense urgency as they worked to revive him, their actions a flurry of expertise and determination. Yet, despite their best efforts, the room was soon shrouded in heavy silence, punctuated only by the stifled sobs that escaped my lips.

In that heart-wrenching moment, the truth became painfully clear. My uncle had slipped away, his battle with illness coming to an end. He hadn't made it to my birthday celebration, and the realization felt like a cruel twist of fate.

The room was filled with a palpable sense of loss, an insurmountable void. My favorite uncle, the pillar of strength and love that had anchored my life, was gone. The celebration that had begun with such promise had been extinguished, leaving behind a sea of sorrow and disbelief.

As tears streamed down my face, I clung to my mother.

My birthday had turned into a day of heartbreak, a stark reminder of life's fragility.

CHAPTER 21

BRITTNEY

Present

After talking to Franny and Mom, I spent some time reading. I had never had this much free time and didn't know what to do with it. The men left yesterday evening, and I felt a bit restless.

Sonny texted me last night, saying they won't return until today. I was upset but also worried, and being confined within the house's walls, regardless of its size and luxury, had limitations.

I sat in the cozy reading nook, surrounded by shelves adorned with books of various genres. The afternoon sunlight streamed through the window, glowing warmly on the inviting space. My fingers traced the spines of the novels, contemplating which one would provide the perfect escape.

The silence in the room echoed the emptiness I felt within. The men's absence left me grappling with a mix of emotions— a sense of liberation yet a yearning for their presence. My phone buzzed, disrupting the tranquility, as Franny's text illuminated the screen. It was a comforting exchange, a brief respite from the solitude.

As I opened the chosen book, the familiar scent of aged paper filled the air. The characters and worlds within the pages became my companions, offering an escape from the lingering uncertainties. The luxury of time, once an elusive concept, now stretched before me, and I allowed myself to immerse in the written realms, momentarily forgetting the confines of my surroundings.

The anticipation of the men's return mingled with a subtle restlessness, prompting me to glance at the clock. The vastness of the luxurious house felt both comforting and isolating, leaving me to navigate the uncharted waters of solitude.

The idea of spending my newfound free time exploring California tugged at my adventurous spirit. The expansive, luxurious house had offered a temporary sanctuary, but the allure of the unfamiliar surroundings beckoned me.

I contemplated going to the gym for a workout, however, the desire to seize the opportunity and explore the beauty of California outweighed the familiarity of a gym session. The prospect of discovering new sights and experiences fueled my determination to step beyond the confines of the opulent residence.

With a sense of excitement and anticipation, I headed toward the front door. The prospect of embarking on a solo adventure, immersing myself in the vibrant culture of California, and breathing in the coastal air invigorated my spirits. I envisioned calling an Uber, ready to embrace the spontaneity of exploration.

As I opened the door, a man came running towards me, causing me to startle and jump back slightly to avoid a collision. Surprised by the sudden encounter, I looked at him with slight confusion.

"I'm sorry, ma'am, I cannot let you leave."

"What do you mean?"

"Mr. Charles specifically told me not to let you leave the house."

"What, are you going to hold me against my will? The last time I checked, that's called kidnapping."

"I'm sorry, Ms. Wright."

How the fuck does he know my last name. Who is this fucker.

Reluctantly, I stepped back as the man approached, allowing him to open the front door for me.

"Orders are orders," he said, patiently waiting for me to walk back into the house, his expression unreadable.

As soon as the door was closed, I sprinted up the stairs, my heart pounding in my chest, reaching Leo's room in five seconds.

I meticulously combed through Leo's room with curiosity, determined to unravel the mystery surrounding him. I carefully inspected every corner, peered under the bed, and rummaged through drawers, hoping to stumble upon a hidden compartment or a secret stash of documents.

I felt a sense of urgency as I scoured the room, knowing that time was ticking away. My hands moved swiftly, shuffling through papers, turning over trinkets, and even examining the backs of picture frames. I couldn't shake the feeling that there was something important I was missing, something that held the key to understanding the enigmatic circumstances I found myself in.

Minutes turned into an hour, and frustration began to creep in. The lack of significant discovery weighed heavily on me, intensifying my desire to uncover the truth. It was as if Leo's room held a secret that taunted me, just out of reach.

As the sound of approaching footsteps echoed through the hallway, panic surged within me. Without hesitation, I abandoned my search and sprinted toward the en-suite bathroom, seeking refuge within its confines. My heart pounded in my chest as I shut the bathroom door behind me, breathing heavily as anxiety washed over me.

Inside the safety of my bedroom, I leaned against the locked door, my mind racing with questions and possibilities.

A newfound determination outweighed the disappointment of coming up empty-handed in my search. I knew I had to find answers, to uncover the truth behind the secrets that seemed to surround me.

A few seconds later, my bedroom door swung open, and my heart skipped a beat as Leo entered.

"Hey, cupcake," he said, smiling.

"What do you want, Leo?" I mustered all my composure and tried to sound calm, yet there was a hint of annoyance as I spoke to him.

"I just had an interesting conversation with Brandon," Leo said, catching my attention.

I looked at him, puzzled.

"Who?" I asked, genuinely curious.

"Security," my annoyance resurfaced as I recalled my less-than-pleasant encounter with that particular individual. I sighed and sat on my bed, crossing my arms and waiting for Leo to continue.

"It's not safe for you to go out by yourself," he stated, concern lacing his words. I let out a frustrated chuckle.

"Well, it seems like I might as well start learning Mandarin Chinese," I remarked sarcastically, hinting at the difficulty of understanding Leo's intentions and actions.

Leo's face contorted in confusion as he tried to understand my mention of learning Mandarin. His brows furrowed, and he tilted his head slightly, clearly perplexed by my comment.

Brushing away Leo's confused look, I continued with my question, "Why?"

"Trust me."

"I don't know you well enough to trust you."

"You trusted me enough to taste that sweet pussy and fuck you." He had the nerve to say while licking his lips.

"Fuck you"

"You promise?"

He walked towards me with a determined stride, stopping right before me. With a gentle touch, he held my chin, tilting it up to meet his gaze. His lips drew closer, and with desire in his eyes, he leaned down and kissed me passionately...

"Promise you'll fuck me," he said between kisses.

My heart raced as I watched his every move, his eyes never leaving mine as he removed his belt, slowly undoing the button and zipper of his trousers. My breath caught in my throat as he revealed himself, confident and unashamed. But then again, he had nothing to be ashamed about.

I felt a surge of desire, my body responding to his presence in an instinctual way. I swallowed hard, trying to contain the overwhelming sensations coursing through me, not wanting to let my desire show too openly.

He leaned closer to me, his voice low and husky.

"Open your mouth," he whispered, his breath sending shivers down my spine. I hesitated momentarily, unsure of what I was about to do, but my desire overpowered any doubts.

As his manhood brushed against my tongue, a deep, guttural groan escaped his mouth. The sound was laced with pleasure, a raw expression of the sensations coursing through his body. "Damn, baby".

His hand found its way to my hair, gripping it firmly as he guided himself deeper into my mouth. His gaze remained locked with mine, intensifying our connection.

"Shiiitttt," he breathed, moving in and out of my mouth with deliberate slowness. His sheer size made it challenging for me to take him in completely, causing my movements to be slightly uncoordinated and messy.

But every time I struggled, he only seemed to revel in it, relishing our intimate connection's raw, unfiltered sensations. My mouth, wet and warm, continued to envelop him as he savored each moment, prolonging the pleasure that pulsed between us.

"Just like that baby."

He said while forcing my mouth to take more of him, fucking my mouth with more force; as I gagged and felt my vision blur, he pulled back slightly, granting me a brief respite to catch my breath.

"Swallow. Every. Drop."

He commanded, with his head tilted back, he grabbed my hair even tighter, forcing himself further down my throat. I tasted a mixture of saltiness and warmth exploding down my throat. "Jesus," he groaned. Gagging at the taste and surprised by the amount of cum- but I did what he asked, swallowing all of him.

"Good girl," he praised, now looking into my eyes, releasing his hold on me while catching his breath and rubbing my chin.

"Your turn, gorgeous," he said while pushing me to the middle of the bed. He lifted my dress and ripped my panties off. Inhaling them, he then pocketed them. I couldn't help but roll my eyes.

"Spread your legs."

I complied, eagerly waiting for what was next.

"Yes, just like that, baby," he said while inserting his finger in me.

"So fucking wet," he said as he got on his knees, lifted my ass, placing my legs over his shoulder,

"So goddamn sexy," he said again right before he tasted me. I moaned as he circled his tongue around my core.

"Please," I managed to say in between breaths.

Leo inserted a finger in me, then two, then three.

This man is driving me wild. He curled his fingers, and Oh. My. God, the sensation had me seeing stars. My breath quickened as he picked up his pace.

"Leo!"

I screamed while my movement and his fingers found a rhythm. Looking down at Leo and the connection between his mouth and my core drove me wild. When our eyes connected, seeing this handsome man's raw desire for me pushed me to my breaking point. My organism rippled through me like a tidal wave.

"Fuck baby," he said while I squirted in his mouth and face. He tried his best to sop it all up, but by the wetness of his face, I could tell he was unsuccessful.

Leo, unable to contain his impatience, eagerly tore off his shirt. Seeing his impressive physique, I opened my legs wider, welcoming him with equal enthusiasm.

He thrust painfully in me like a man possessed, but by the third stroke, the pain turned into pleasure, and I was grabbing his ass, pushing him deeper.

"Goddamn baby, you are so fucking tight," he said. I bit the side of his neck, which drove him even more insane. Groaning, he grabbed my ass, lifting me slightly, "I need to be deeper in you" this man is insatiable.

Every thrust.

Every kiss.

Every touch brought me closer to him.

I felt my organism build up, and before long, I was coating his dick with my wetness yet again.

"You're mine cupcake," he murmured as he groaned and released his load in me.

He stayed in me for quite some time. It seems like he refused to detach from me, and I was not going to say a word about that.

After our breathing returned to normal, he moved the sweat-soaked hair from my face, tucking it gently behind my ear. His fingers traced a delicate path along my cheek, leaving a trail of warmth in their wake. In the quiet aftermath of our shared passion, the room seemed to hold its breath as if honoring the intimacy unfolding.

His eyes, still smoldering with desire, met mine, creating a connection that transcended the physical realm. The vulnerability at that moment was tender and raw as if our souls had borne themselves to each other.

"Beautiful," he whispered, his voice a velvety caress that resonated in the hushed space. The weight of his gaze lingered on my face, a silent acknowledgment of the shared intensity that had transpired.

I lay there, caught between the aftermath of pleasure and the anticipation of what might come next. The air crackled with a unique energy, a blend of satisfaction and the lingering hunger for more.

With a gentle touch, he cupped my face, his thumb tracing the outline of my lips. Each gesture felt deliberate, as if he was savoring the remnants of our shared experience. The world outside seemed to fade away, leaving only the echo of our connection.

In that suspended moment, I became acutely aware of the sweat-drenched sheets beneath us, the scent of our shared passion lingering in the air. The vulnerability of being exposed, not just physically but emotionally, added a layer of intimacy that transcended the ordinary.

As he leaned to place a soft kiss on my forehead, I closed my eyes, absorbing the tenderness of the gesture. The room, once filled with the fervor of desire, now cradled us in a serene embrace.

Our entwined bodies, still humming with the aftermath of pleasure, found solace in the stillness of the night.

The morning sunlight streamed into the room, gently awakening me from my slumber. I intended to sleep longer, but it seemed the day had different plans for me.

As I opened my eyes, I noticed Leo lying next to me, peacefully asleep. A mixture of emotions washed over me as I took in his relaxed form, resisting the temptation to give in to my desires.

Leo's arm was tucked under his head, and the other rested on his torso. The rise and fall of his chest indicated a deep sleep.

It felt surreal, as if I were trapped in a dream. Perhaps I would soon wake up in my familiar New York City apartment, away from this intense and complicated situation.

Carefully, I tried to extricate myself from the bed, mindful of the soreness in my body that reminded me of the passionate night we had shared.

As I quietly moved, "Where are you going, cupcake?" he said, lying in the same position. "Uh-uh, not so fast," Leo murmured, his voice husky as he pulled me back towards him, his grip firm on my waist. His lips found their way to my neck, planting soft kisses. The heat of his body against mine only intensified my desire, and I couldn't deny the effect he had on me.

I sighed softly, torn between surrendering to the moment and maintaining my resolve to uncover the secrets between us.

It wasn't fair how he knew exactly what he was doing to me, playing with my emotions and desires.

But yesterday, I decided to play along, to go with the flow until I could unearth the truth that Leo and his brothers were hiding from me.

With reluctance, I gently pushed against his chest, breaking the enchanting hold he had on me. "I need to take a shower," I reiterated, my voice laced with a hint of frustration.

Meeting his intense gaze, I silently communicated my desire to maintain some semblance of control and understanding in our complicated situation.

"You mean we need to shower," emphasizing 'we.' He said as he lifted me and carried me to the bathroom.

The warm water cascaded over our bodies as Leo turned on the shower. Stepping inside, I felt his strong presence behind me, his hands guiding me under the gentle spray.

His touch was possessive as he reached for the shampoo, his fingers delicately massaging my scalp. With each stroke, he planted soft kisses on my neck. The sensations intensified as his hands moved down, skillfully lathering the body wash onto my skin, his touch tracing every curve and contour.

Time seemed to stand still as Leo took his time, paying attention to every inch of my body. His hands glided over my breasts, the lather creating a sensual glide that heightened my senses. I couldn't help but gasp as his fingers trailed down to my ass.

Lost in the moment, I surrendered to his care and desire.

Once satisfied, he turned his attention to himself, thoroughly washing his body with precision. As the water cascaded over his sculpted physique, I couldn't help but admire how his muscles glistened, his confidence and masculinity exuding from every pore.

With the show complete, Leo turned off the water, creating a stillness mirrored our newfound tranquility. Wrapping a towel around his waist, he reached for another, gently drying me off with a tenderness that spoke volumes of his desire to care for me.

"Leo,"

I said, looking into his eyes as he dried my body.

"Yes,"

he replied, his gaze locked with mine.

"I want to see the town,"

I stated, my determination clear in my voice.

Leo seemed to sense that I had already won this fight, even before it had begun. He let out a sigh, realizing that he couldn't deny me what I desired.

"We can go to dinner tonight. Would you like that?"

He offered, his voice tinged with resignation.

A smile tugged at the corners of my lips as I tried to hide my excitement. "I would love that," I replied, unable to contain my enthusiasm.

"I'll make the arrangements. In the meantime, go get dressed and get some breakfast," Leo instructed, his tone slightly commanding.

I nodded, playing my part in this intricate game of deceit and intrigue. As I walked away, I couldn't help but feel a sense of satisfaction.

If they weren't willing to share any information, then I would have to resort to pretending, lying, and deceiving, just like them, to uncover the truth.

The stage was set, and I was ready to play my role.

CHAPTER 22

BRITTNEY

My spirits soared like a jolly Saint Nick spreading holiday cheer throughout the day. I made a deliberate effort to express affection towards the men before they departed, taking at least a minute to tongue them down.

"I'll pick you up at 8. Be ready." Leo said.

With determination fueling my every move, I embarked on my plan to deceive and escape.

As the minutes ticked by after the men's departure, I seized the opportunity to visit the gym. For nearly three hours, I dedicated myself to lifting weights and pushing my body to its limits on the treadmill.

This physical training would, in my mind, grant me the strength and agility necessary to fend off any potential interference from the formidable brothers.

Oh, how foolish I was to believe that a mere three hours in the gym could thwart their power. If Popeye could eat spinach and become strong in a few seconds, then I could work out once in over six months and fend off three powerful men .... right? I shook my head at my naivety, realizing the magnitude of the challenge ahead.

After indulging in another refreshing shower, I meticulously applied my makeup, trying to enhance my features, silently wishing Francine was here to help. As I carefully blended the shades and accentuated my eyes, a familiar buzz reverberated through the room, signaling a notification on my phone.

GRUMPY: SORRY, I CAN'T MAKE IT TONIGHT. SONNY AND DOM WILL BE YOUR DATES

I couldn't help but feel disappointed as I realized Leo wouldn't be there, but I quickly pushed those thoughts aside.

Ever the attentive assistant, Matilda had prepared a stunning brown silk dress adorned with delicate lace, tracing intricate patterns along the bodice. The dress featured elegant spaghetti straps that gracefully embraced the shoulders, leading to an alluring open back that added a touch of sophistication. The silky fabric cascaded down in gentle folds, accentuating the wearer's figure subtly yet alluringly.

To complement the ensemble, she had chosen a pair of black strapped shoes, their design seamlessly blending with the dress's elegance. The shoes added a finishing touch, enhancing the overall aesthetic of the outfit. Additionally, Matilda thoughtfully selected a set of jewelry to complete the look – a pair of dangling silver earrings that caught the light with every movement and a delicate bracelet that adorned the wrist, adding a subtle sparkle to the ensemble.

As I slipped into the dress, the smooth and luxurious fabric caressed my skin, evoking a sense of pure indulgence. I made a mental note to 'remember' this dress when it was time for me to depart.

Descending the stairs with purpose, I found Sonny and Dom eagerly waiting for me by the entrance. Both men looked absolutely impeccable, exuding an air of refined elegance.

Sonny wore a sleek all-black suit that exuded both sophistication and charm. The tailored jacket featured a slim, modern cut, enhancing his muscular frame. The lapels were adorned with a subtle sheen, catching the light just right. The jacket seamlessly hugged his shoulders and tapered down to the waist, creating a refined silhouette.

Beneath the jacket, Sonny sported a crisply pressed black shirt, its fabric contrasting subtly with the suit. The shirt's collar stood with a perfect balance of sharpness, adding a touch of elegance to the ensemble. The suit trousers followed the same tailored precision, tapering down the legs and pooling gracefully over polished black dress shoes.

A vibrant yellow tie, a bold choice that injected a pop of color into the ensemble, completed the look. The perfectly knotted tie drew attention to his face, highlighting the charismatic features that made Sonny irresistible. The ensemble exuded confidence and style, reflecting Sonny's personality with every carefully chosen detail.

Dom's black suit epitomized refined elegance, tailored to perfection with a modern flair. The jacket, adorned with meticulous stitching, accentuated his broad shoulders, while the sleeves embraced his arms with a snug fit, subtly hinting at the strength beneath.

Beneath the impeccably crafted jacket, Dom wore a shirt that mirrored the shade of my dress. The fabric clung to him with precision, emphasizing his muscular physique. The shirt's hue, matching seamlessly with my attire, created an unspoken connection, lending a sense of intimacy to the occasion.

The suit trousers continued the theme of sartorial excellence, skimming his legs in a tailored fit before cascading elegantly over polished black dress shoes. The ensemble not only exuded authority but also, with subtle coordination, established a visual harmony, subtly acknowledging the underlying connection between us.

As they turned their heads upon hearing my footsteps, I couldn't help but revel in the smug satisfaction that crossed my lips. Their immediate reactions, a slight shift in their posture, and the way their gazes intensified silently confirmed their desire for me.

Closing the distance between us, I was enraptured by their passionate kisses. First, Dom lifted me off my feet while kissing me, "You look stunning, baby," he said, breaking our kiss.

Sonny snatched me from his arms and kissed me, "you do," he said while helping himself to a handful of my ass- momentarily lost myself in the whirlwind of sensations.

Collecting my thoughts, a mischievous smile graced my lips as we made our way outside.

Waiting for us was a sleek limousine symbolizing opulence and luxury. Stepping into the vehicle, I knew that this evening held the promise of new revelations and unexpected encounters.

With a gracious gesture, Dom opened the limousine door and extended his hand towards me. I gladly accepted his offer, allowing the warmth of his touch to ignite a flicker of anticipation within me.

As we settled into the plush seats, Sonny effortlessly retrieved a bottle of champagne and poured me a glass with a practiced ease that spoke of familiarity.

Curiosity getting the better of me, I couldn't help but inquire about Leo's absence, my eyes carefully studying the expressions on their faces for any subtle hints or shifts in demeanor.

"Why wasn't Leo able to join us?"

I asked, the words slipping from my lips with a gentle curiosity lacing my tone.

Dom's response was tinged with irritation, his voice betraying a hint of frustration.

"He had some business to attend to."

His words laden with tension. Sensing their sensitivity around the topic, I quickly decided to let it rest, not wanting to raise any suspicions or delve deeper into the matter.

Sonny redirected the conversation with a sly smirk adorning his lips.

"It should take us about 15 minutes to reach our destination, right, Dom?" he interjected, his gaze locking with mine momentarily, eliciting a playful spark in his eyes that hinted at hidden desires.

"Yeah, just about," Dominic replied.

Finding myself in a familiar territory, encountering them whose intentions were clear; their desire for me written all over their faces and eyes and as if my body had a mind of its own- against my will, it succumbed to their advances, unable to say no.

The two men flanked me on either side, their presence engulfing me. Sonny reached out, swiftly taking hold of my drink and gently setting it aside.

"Cum for us, baby girl," he said as his lips met mine with an undeniable hunger.

In an assertive move, Dom's hand clasped my thigh, guiding my leg onto his lap, his fingers tracing a path of tantalizing sensation. He froze when his thumb grazed my core.

"Naughty girl!" he said, smirking.

His gaze intensified as he locked eyes with me, a realization dawning upon him. At that moment, he recognized my bold choice, the decision to forgo any undergarments. A mixture of surprise and desire flickered in his eyes. Making me giggle.

He inserted a finger in me, took it out, and put it next to my mouth. I eagerly licked his finger while he intently looked at me, groaning.

"Fuck" he said getting on all fours smelling my core. "You smell fucking amazing," he said before diving in. Sonny pulled my face in his direction and kissed me mercilessly.

"You have to come now for us," Sonny's voice was a command that brooked no argument, his hands guiding me with a firm gentleness that left me no choice but to surrender.

And I did. I came undone at their coaxing, a release of tension that had been building, coiling tighter and tighter until it burst forth in a rush of overwhelming sensation. It was a moment of pure abandon, a cresting wave that broke over me, leaving me breathless and shuddering.

Aware of the limited time we had, their focus shifted. Both composed themselves, readjusting their attire and ensuring their appearance was presentable, helping me do the same.

As the limo door swung open, Sonny's remark about our close call drew a mischievous smile from his lips.

His hand found mine, guiding me with an air of confident purpose towards the restaurant's entrance. Envious onlookers followed our every move, their eyes fixated on my captivating dates.

The surge of jealousy and rage within me was undeniable, fueled by the possessiveness that stirred deep within me.

Seated at our table, I noticed the lingering glances from other women in the establishment; their admiration mingled with a tinge of envy. The waitress appeared promptly, her undivided attention seemingly reserved for Sonny and Dom as they effortlessly placed their orders without glancing at the menu or her.

I felt annoyed at her overt display of interest, desperately wishing for a sharper weapon than the butter knife resting innocently beside my plate.

Minutes later, our food and drinks arrived, delivered by the same waitress who seemed too eager to prolong her interactions with my irresistible companions.

"Would you like anything else?" she asked, her eyes shamelessly ogling my boyfriends, provoking a simmering rage within me.

With a clenched jaw, I locked my gaze on her, the intensity of my glare communicating a clear message. Sonny and Dom exchanged knowing smirks, relishing the dynamic at play.

"NO... ... no," I responded curtly, my words laced with a barely contained hostility. The audacity of her following statement further fueled my frustration.

"Let me know if you need anything else," she ventured, oblivious to the seething fury behind my eyes.

"I will," I replied through gritted teeth, the desire to possess a sharper weapon intensifying with every passing second.

Despite the waitress's irritating presence, the food's impeccable quality salvaged the evening. We dined, indulged in delightful conversation, and savored every moment.

As the evening progressed, my plan to escape the captivating allure of these men began to take shape.

Step 1 subtly weaving its way into the fabric of our interaction.

"I need to use the ladies' room,"

I declared, hastily rising from the table and approaching the restroom sign.

Step 1 had been successfully executed, and now it was time to move on to Step 2.

As I hurried along, I discreetly called for an Uber, grateful that the restaurant's location in San Diego meant that taxis operated throughout the night, much like in New York.

True to my words, I did need to use the restroom, so I made a brief stop to relieve myself while my ride drew nearer.

While washing my hands, a notification chimed on my phone, signaling that the Uber was only a minute away.

Perfect timing.

Step 3 of my plan involved slipping out of the restaurant unnoticed.

Fortunately, the bathroom was on the opposite side of our table, allowing me to make a casual exit without raising any suspicion.

Stepping outside, I took a moment to double-check the license plate and confirm the driver's intended passenger to ensure I was getting into the correct Uber. One can never be too cautious.

As I settled into the backseat, contemplating the next move, I realized that I hadn't planned beyond this point. I never thought I'd get to this point.

Step 4 was a vague concept, overshadowed by the urgency of escape.

But I was resourceful and would have to rely on my instincts and improvisation. Rather than heading straight to the airport, I took a calculated risk.

"Do you happen to know Jimmy Charles? The founder of Charles LLP?" I inquired, pulling up a picture of him on my phone, hoping that visual aid would assist the driver.

The Uber driver glanced at the photo on my phone and nodded, a flicker of recognition crossing his face. "Oh yeah, that's Jimmy Charles— big shot around these parts. What do you need with him?" he asked, his curiosity piqued.

Leaning back in my seat, I offered a friendly smile. "Just some business matters. I appreciate your help," I replied, not delving into the details. "Please take me to him," I requested, placing my trust in the unexpected turn of events.

CHAPTER 23

BRITTNEY

After a grueling 45-minute journey, I finally arrived at what appeared to be Jimmy's residence. My phone was flooded with missed calls and messages from Sonny, Dominic, and Leo.

I knew they would be furious, but my determination to uncover the truth outweighed my guilt or fear. It was well past 11 p.m., and I only hoped Jimmy was still awake. Otherwise, my efforts would be in vain.

"I'm here to see Jimmy. Please let him know it's Brittney— " I began to say to the security guard stationed at the front gate.

"Hold on," he interrupted, his voice curt.

After a brief pause, he signaled for my driver to proceed as the gate slowly lifted. The oblivious driver maneuvered the vehicle towards the front of the house, nearly colliding with a statue along the way. The opulence and sheer wealth on display left me... . Us.. astounded. It was hard to fathom the magnitude of possessions amassed by a single individual.

As I stepped out of the vehicle, I briefly considered asking the driver to wait, but I resisted the impulse.

Taking deliberate steps, I walked up the grand staircase towards the imposing front door. Just as I approached, the door swung open with force, held by a stern-looking guard. I hesitated momentarily, turning my head to watch my only means of escape disappear beyond the compound's confines. Doubts gnawed at me, hoping I was making the right decision, but it was too late to turn back.

I summoned all my strength and continued my determined march toward the house.

Once inside, the guard guided me down a hallway, leading me to what I could only assume was Jimmy's office.

The air was tense with anticipation, and my heart pounded. This was my chance to seek the truth and confront the mysteries surrounding me.

He led me to what looked like an office. "Have a seat," he said as he hurriedly walked back in the direction he had come from.

I sat as instructed, feeling a mix of anticipation and unease. The guard left, leaving me alone in the room, and the weight of uncertainty settled upon me.

The minutes stretched into what felt like an eternity until finally, Jimmy entered the room, dressed in luxurious pajamas and a silk robe. But it was the neckpiece that stole the show— an ostentatious statement piece that practically screamed, "Look at me, I've made it!"

I couldn't help but glance at the wall clock, realizing how late it was. Perhaps my impulsive decision to come here was ill-advised.

Jimmy was a handsome older man, exuding a certain charisma and confidence. Standing over six feet tall, he possessed gray hair and piercing blue eyes. The resemblance between him and his sons was undeniable.

His well-kept beard added a touch of maturity and sophistication. As our eyes met, I sensed a hint of something in his gaze. Was it... ... lust? I quickly dismissed the thought, attempting to conceal my discomfort.

"I apologize for intruding at such a late hour," I began, my voice betraying a hint of nervousness. It was nearly midnight, and I questioned the wisdom of my actions.

"To what do I owe the pleasure?" Jimmy responded, his eyes lingering on me, particularly my cleavage.

I shifted uncomfortably, feeling the weight of his gaze.

"I was brought here to assist you with a case," I replied, attempting to maintain composure despite my growing uncertainty.

"Really?" he responded, his tongue lightly grazing his lips as he walked towards his massive mahogany desk and took a seat.

"Is that what my boys told you?" The question hung in the air, laden with unspoken implications.

Did they deceive me? If so, what was the real reason for my presence here?

"You look nothing like your father," he continued, his words laced with a sharpness that caught me off guard. My father? Confusion clouded my thoughts as I struggled to process his remark.

"My father?" I repeated, seeking clarification.

"You are more beautiful than your picture," he said, his gaze unwavering. His statement left me both puzzled and intrigued. What did he mean? And how did he know my father?

"Do you know my father?" I asked, momentarily setting aside the previous comment.

Smirking, he opened his desk drawer and pulled out an envelope. He placed the envelope on the desk, opened another drawer, and placed a gun on top of it.

If I wasn't shaking before, I was shaking now.

"I now see why my boys kept you from me. You must have a juicy cunt."

Surprised by that statement, I stood up, ready to leave the room and run back to New York.

"SIT DOWN," he yelled, startling me to my core.

Obliging his command, I sat down.

He lifted the gun and pointed it my way. Breathing heavily and sweating profusely even though the central air was on full blast, I gathered all my strength, "How do you know my father?" At this point, I couldn't care about a case; I doubt there even was one. If he is going to shoot me, he can at least tell me about the man who ran out on me and my mother all those years ago.

We heard a 'BOOM' when he was about to speak.

The abrupt and resonant noise reverberated through the air, halting our conversation. Jimmy and I exchanged puzzled glances before our attention shifted toward the source of the disturbance - the office door. With an echoing creak, the door swung open, revealing a furious Leo framed against the dimly lit room.

Leo's anger was palpable, radiating from every pore. His eyes blazed with fiery indignation, and his clenched fists trembled with pent-up emotion. It was as if a storm of wrath had been unleashed in that confined space, creating an unmistakable aura of rage that filled the room.

Sonny and Dom, flanking Leo on either side, shared his intensity. Their presence heightened the charged atmosphere, creating an almost tangible tension. Leo's gaze, charged with fury, briefly met mine, and an unexpected warmth surged through me - a peculiar response to the chaotic scene unfolding.

Leo moved purposefully towards Jimmy, propelled by his anger, positioning himself as a shield between Jimmy and me. It was a silent yet powerful declaration of protection amid the escalating chaos. Simultaneously, Sonny moved swiftly to my side, his grip on my arm tightening with a possessive edge, a clear manifestation of his protective instinct.

However, the most striking transformation was happening with Dom. His usual composed demeanor shattered, replaced by an unrestrained fury emanating from every fiber of his being. The fire in his eyes burned unprecedentedly, revealing a side of Dom that had remained hidden until now. It was a chilling sight, as if he stood on the precipice, ready to unleash a storm of rage capable of shaking the very foundations of their world.

"Ah, boys," Jimmy said so casually.

"What are you doing— Jimmy," Leo said, his eyes fixed on the gun. A hint of defiance laced his voice as he addressed his father by his first name.

"You were supposed to bring her to me!"

"Change of plans."

"Because of her, ...some stupid bitch?...... You defy me? Your own flesh and blood?"

As Jimmy's anger reached its crescendo, his voice grew louder and more intense. Each word erupted from his mouth with a force that propelled specks of spittle into the air.

Sonny's grasp around my arm tightened, a dual expression of reassurance and caution compelling me to recognize his presence amid the chaos that enveloped us. Yielding to the silent command, I shifted my attention to Sonny, only to be met with a disquieting spectacle.

His eyes, typically radiating warmth and affection, now bore an intense and unbridled rage. Flames of fury flickered in his gaze as he directed his penetrating stare toward his father. The simmering anger within him appeared to loom over his entire presence, casting a profound shadow that threatened to engulf the room. It was a transformative moment like Sonny had tapped into a reservoir of emotions previously concealed beneath his composed exterior. "Let. Her. Go."

Tilting his head to the side, his eyes shifted from his sons. He then started laughing— like I laughed when I saw Kevin Hart live.

Leo threw something in his direction; from where I was sitting, all I could make out was they were pictures. Jimmy abruptly stopped laughing when he saw the photos, jaw twitching; he reached for one picture, scanned it, and threw it back on his desk. He stood up, grabbed the envelope he had placed on his desk earlier, and walked towards Leo, thrusting the envelope with great force in his chest.

"Take this and get the fuck out."

Looking around the room

"ALL OF YOU"

Happy to oblige, I promptly rose from my seat, hastening my steps toward the door. Leo, with a patient demeanor, allowed everyone else to exit the room before turning to follow suit.

CHAPTER 24

SONNY

Impatience brewed within me as we sat at the dinner table. Every passing minute felt like an eternity, my mind consumed with the desire to be in the privacy of our sanctuary.

The tempting thought of having her all to myself, away from prying eyes, fueled an urgency that made the food before us lose its appeal. With each forced bite, I silently longed for the moment when we could escape the confines of the restaurant and watch her ride my dick until she cums all over it.

A flicker of jealousy danced in her eyes as she observed the waitress lavishing us with attention. Little did she know that her doubts were unfounded, for our gaze remained fixed solely upon her. If only she could perceive the truth, she would realize that no external distractions could diminish the intensity of our devotion. However, a mischievous smile played upon my lips as I observed her growing jealousy.

Though I yearned to reassure her and ease her doubts, a part of me couldn't help but relish the knowledge that I held such sway over her heart. The tinge of excitement that arose from watching her jealousy only heightened the anticipation.

Every action she took seemed to exude an irresistible attraction, whether it was her seductive allure, infectious happiness, fiery anger, or even moments of jealousy. No matter her emotion, she carried herself with captivating grace and confidence like a goddess descended from the heavens.

In the tapestry of my romantic encounters, I have traversed a varied landscape, embracing the company of women of different shapes and sizes. Each possessed unique captivation and left an indelible mark on my memories.

There was something about Brittney that attracted me strongly. It felt like an invisible force pulling me closer to her.

I realized that deceiving her by bringing her to the west coast under false pretenses would eventually bite us in the ass, and I fucking told Leo to tell her the truth, but that jerk-off never listens.

Leo, being the eldest among us, had always been our protector. He shielded Dom and me from the relentless abuse inflicted by our fathers, shouldering the brunt of the assaults and beatings that Jimmy unleashed upon us. With courage and a deep sense of responsibility, Leo endured the pain and suffering to keep us safe. When the time came, when he was old enough, he made the bold decision to take us away, liberating us from the suffocating walls of that house.

In his selflessness, Leo became our guiding light, leading us toward a life where we could escape the darkness that once haunted us. Leo's intelligence shone brilliantly, and we never lacked anything under his guidance. Despite the pain and suffering we endured, our mother seemed oblivious, turning a blind eye to Jimmy's cruelty.

It fueled a deep-seated resentment, a feeling of betrayal that lingered in my heart. Determined not to repeat past mistakes, I vowed to protect my future children with unwavering devotion, ready to shield them from harm.

We were trapped in Jimmy's grasp again just a few years ago. We were forced into his service and given a grim directive: to deliver Brittney to him. Yet, our encounter with her had ignited an unexpected flame within us.

We fell irrevocably in love with her, and our instincts screamed for us to protect her at all costs. It became clear that the only way to ensure her safety was to bring her back with us, even if it meant defying the ruthless orders that bound us.

In a dangerous game of survival, we became her guardians, ready to face the consequences of our actions and shield her from the darkness that threatened to consume us all.

CHAPTER 25

SONNY

The restaurant's atmosphere shifted from casual banter to palpable tension as Dom and I exchanged concerned glances. Brittney had excused herself to the restroom nearly fifteen minutes ago, and her prolonged absence made us increasingly uneasy.

"I hope she's not drowning the waitress in the toilet," I quipped to Dom, trying to lighten the mood, though my watch betrayed my growing impatience. His expression mirrored my concern, and without a word, we both rose from our seats, heading towards the bathroom.

With one hand covering my eyes, I opened the door slightly with my other, "Brittney?" peeking through my fingers, "Princess?"

Dom, more direct and more anxious, shoved the door wide open, muttering a sharp "bitch" and hitting my shoulder as he barged in. We scanned the empty restroom, the stalls standing silent and unoccupied. Thankfully, there was no one else in there.

Frustration clawed at me as I uttered a low, guttural "Fuck," my hand instinctively reaching for the tracker app on my phone. The decision to discreetly plant a tracker on Brittney's car during our time in New York, initially a precautionary measure, now emerged as a fateful move.

The app's interface illuminated my face in an ethereal glow as I urgently navigated its features. A knot tightened in my stomach, the tracker revealing Brittney's whereabouts.

This seemingly excessive precaution had transformed into a pivotal safeguard. Leo's unexpected appearance at that club a few months ago became a twist of fate, averting a potential catastrophe that threatened to alter the very fabric of our existence.

Rage surged within me, contemplating what could have transpired had Leo not intervened. The mental images of Brittney entangled with that fucker Collins fueled my anger. In the recesses of my mind, dark scenarios played out, each one a manifestation of my protective instincts pushed to their limit.

Upon our return to California, I discreetly affixed a tracker to Brittney's phone. What initially seemed a cautious measure emerged as a source of profound relief. Dom and Leo wholeheartedly endorsed my decision to discreetly place the tracker on Brittney's phone without her knowledge.

A few seconds later, the quiet tension shattered with an abruptness that matched the unexpected intensity of my voice. "HOLY SHIT," I exclaimed, the words escaping my lips with a fervor that resonated through the air, far louder than I had intended.

"What," Dom said, glancing at my phone.

"We have to go. Now!" The urgency in my voice propelled me out of the bathroom, my heart pounding.

I fumbled for my phone as I dialed Leo's number. "Leo," I said, my voice laced with urgency, "Get to Jimmy's house NOW."

The gravity of the situation hung in the air, fueling my need for immediate action. Time was of the essence, and I knew that Leo's presence could make all the difference in the tumultuous events about to unfold.

My brothers and I worked well together, and we had a remarkable synergy. We had our individual talents, which complimented each other perfectly, resulting in impressive outcomes. I wouldn't trade them for anything.

We tore through the streets at a reckless 100 in a 55, breaking every speed limit. In what felt like an adrenaline-fueled blur, we reached Jimmy's house in record time. The screeching halt of our car coincided with Leo pulling up simultaneously.

Perfect.

The sight of our car triggered an almost instantaneous reaction from the guard; the gate swung open smoothly, betraying none of the usual hesitations. It was as though the urgency of our arrival had communicated itself to him, prompting an uncharacteristically swift response.

The front door of Jimmy's house loomed ahead, and I wasted no time, using my foot to swing it open forcefully. The adrenaline coursing through my veins propelled me forward, each step driven by the pressing need for haste.

However, just as we approached the threshold, an unwelcome obstacle materialized in the form of the obstinate guard attempting to block our path. He arrogantly underestimated the urgency that fueled our mission. His futile attempt to impede our progress only heightened the tension in the air, the stakes escalating with each passing moment.

I couldn't help but grin, and with calculated movement, I expertly disarmed him, leaving him bewildered and unsure of how to react. Using his weapon, I knocked him on the side of his head with so much force I was uncertain if I killed him... . That wasn't my concern.

Following Leo down the hallway, we noticed Jimmy's office door was closed; I kicked the door open using the full strength of my leg, making it slam against the wall. I hope I broke that shit.

The scene that unfolded before us was stomach-churning; that motherfucker had his gun pointed menacingly at MY princess. The surge of rage threatened to overwhelm me, and it took every ounce of self-restraint not to lunge at him.

Summoning a reservoir of control, I resisted the primal instinct to confront him head-on. Instead, Leo and Dom moved swiftly, strategically placing themselves between the barrel of the gun and its intended target. Every fiber of my being screamed for retribution, yet I hesitated, acutely aware that our priority was to get Brittney to safety.

With gritted teeth and clenched fists, I jolted towards her. In a matter of heart-wrenching moments, we sought refuge in the sanctuary of Leo's truck, putting miles between us and the imminent danger lurking at Jimmy's house, abandoning the limo at Jimmy's house. That was my parting gift to him.

The drive back was shrouded in an oppressive silence, an unspoken agreement between us to refrain from piercing the thick veil of tension that clung to the air. Brittney, usually a lively presence, remained unusually quiet, her thoughts veiled behind a stoic expression. I mirrored her silence in solidarity, aware of the delicate equilibrium that had settled over the car— a stillness pregnant with unspoken emotions.

Seeking a connection, however tenuous, I tentatively placed my hand on her thigh. The abruptness of her recoil sent a jolt through the confined space, and a silent 'shit' reverberated in my mind.

The car came to a halt, and without a second thought, Brittney sprang out, leaving the door to swing shut almost reluctantly. She walked towards the house with determined strides, leaving us chasing after her. Inside, the air was charged with unspoken questions, the unsaid words echoing in the hollow space between us. Brittney ascended the staircase with a purpose that left us rooted at the foot, caught in a silent debate. Should I go after her?

"Goddamn it." Leo's voice broke the lingering silence, his words slicing through the heavy air, "I need a drink." Without waiting for a response, he headed towards the bar. The sound of liquid pouring echoed in the room as he filled his glass with a generous amount of scotch, the amber liquid cascading to the brim. In one swift motion, he brought the glass to his lips, and the scotch disappeared down his throat in an instant.

The ritual continued as Leo poured himself another round, and without a word, we followed suit.

CHAPTER 26

BRITTNEY

My emotions were in turmoil, a jumbled mess of anger, sadness, and confusion that left me feeling utterly overwhelmed.

The previous night had granted me a reprieve, the men wisely opting to leave me to the cacophony of my thoughts. But now, the clamor within demanded resolution, and I hungered for answers.

My reflection in the mirror revealed eyes swollen from the silent tears shed in the shadows of sleep. With meticulous care, I concealed the evidence beneath layers of makeup, constructing a façade to shield the world from the storm within. I snagged an oversized sweater and shorts, pulling them on quickly. They became a sort of shield, trying to hide the mess of emotions inside me. The mirror reflected a night of no sleep, but my eyes showed a determination to figure things out.

I walked with purpose through the halls, each step echoing the questions in my head. Before long, I stood in front of Leo's room, feeling the tension in the air, a sign that a confrontation was on the horizon.

I pounded his door with all my might, the sound echoing through the empty hallway. It swung open, and a confused Sonny stood on the opposite side.

"The door was unlocked, princess; you could have just come in."

"I wouldn't want to intrude on your highly classified information," I said, walking into the room.

Leo and Dom occupied the couch, prompting me to navigate towards them. I settled directly across, positioning myself in the center of an unspoken tableau. Hands tucked into his suit pockets, Sonny assumed a vigilant stance behind his brothers.

Surveying the trio, I closed my eyes briefly, a moment of internal fortification. Gathering my energy, I summoned the strength to confront the looming uncertainties.

"I want to know the truth about what's happening," I asserted, locking eyes with Leo. It was a collective understanding; he held the reins as the boss.

"Why did you go to Jimmy's house?"

Leo's counter-question hung in the air, a subtle but unmistakable attempt to shift the narrative. A sense of disbelief washed over me; was he trying to turn the tables on me?

Summoning my resolve, I pressed on. "How does Jimmy know my father?" The question lingered, a heavy silence settling in the room.

A low, ominous groan escaped Leo's lips, a sound that seemed to convey the weight of a burden. He hesitated as if caught in the balance between revealing and concealing. Leaning forward, he pushed the envelope across the table, the same one that had occupied pride of place on Jimmy's office desk just a few hours earlier.

I leaned back in my chair, my gaze fixated on the envelope as if it held the key to unraveling the mysteries surrounding us. A pregnant pause enveloped the room, tension crackling in the air. Just as my fingertips grazed the paper, Dom interjected with a cautionary tone, "There's no going back after you open it, Baby girl."

Their stare was intense and unyielding, causing my eyes to dart nervously in search of some sign of relief. I had an inner debate, trying to decide on the best course of action.

Narrowing my eyes defiantly, I asserted, "I am not a child." My hand reached out, seizing the envelope, and with a determined yank, I tore it open. The contents revealed within caused my eyes to widen, and my jaw dropped in sheer disbelief. The weight of the revelation compelled the contents to slip from my trembling hands, scattering on the floor like shards of shattered secrets.

Frantically, I rose from my seat, with an urgent need to distance myself from the disturbing images that now demanded a place in my consciousness. The room seemed to close in on me as the reality of the situation sank in.

In a blink, all three of them were at my side, their attempts to console me falling short as my emotions continued to run rampant. The air became tense, an overwhelming sense of disquiet permeating the space. Desperate for a breath that eluded me, I pulled away from their attempts at reassurance, a singular focus guiding me towards Leo's open balcony.

"Who is that?" With my back facing them, I hope that's not who I thought it was. After what felt like a lifetime, "Your father." Not knowing who said that, my mind went blank, even though I did not know the man; it was like a punch to the gut, the shock of the news leaving me reeling and disoriented. Some small part of me was hoping I would see Adam again, and he would make me understand why he walked out on me and my mother.

"Who is that?" I questioned, my back turned to them, a silent prayer echoing in my mind, hoping against hope that it wasn't who I feared.

After what felt like an eternity, the words I dreaded sliced through the air, "Your father." The revelation hung in the room, the weight of the truth settling over me like a suffocating shroud.

The speaker of those words remained a mystery, but it hardly mattered. The shock of the news left me reeling, my mind a blank canvas, unable to process the enormity of the revelation. Even though I had no prior knowledge of the man in question, it felt like a punch to the gut, the unexpected revelation leaving me disoriented and grappling with the sudden disruption of my reality.

A small, almost imperceptible part of me harbored a flicker of hope— that seeing Adam again would somehow provide answers, a rationale for why he had walked out on me and my mother. That hope was shattered after seeing the pictures of his decapitated head.

"Cupcake"

"Don't you fucking call me that," I yelled;- In one swift motion pivoting on my heels, I turned to confront them. Eyes burning, I scanned them, pausing momentarily to gather my thoughts and formulate a plan on how to proceed.

"How?" Was the only logical word that came out of my mouth; hot tears streamed down my face, leaving a trail of moisture in their wake. I felt sadness and helplessness as I stared at them, not breaking eye contact.

"HOW?" This time, I was practically screaming.

"Fuck" Sonny said, swiftly crossing the room, his arms wrapping around me in the tightest embrace I had ever experienced. Despite my attempts to break free, he held on steadfastly. Surrendering to the moment, I cried in his arms, the tears flowing freely as if releasing the floodgates of pent-up emotions.

Desperate to regain my composure, I pulled away and questioned with a barely audible voice, "What happened to him?" Sonny, still holding my shoulders, gently pulled me back, studying my now probably swollen, red eyes.

"We've got you, princess," he reassured, pulling me back into another tender embrace and gently kissing my head. An internal struggle urged me to break free, but the fear of unraveling kept me locked in his arms, teetering on the edge of an emotional precipice.

Enveloped in the warmth of another body behind me, gently pulling me closer, a soft voice whispered, "I'm sorry you had to find out this way, baby girl." Recognizing Dominic by the affectionate nickname, I welcomed the support and leaned the back of my head against his chest.

Opening my eyes, I swept the room until my gaze settled on Leo. He stood at a distance, hands tucked into his pockets, an air of uncertainty clouding his expression. It seemed he was grappling with the delicate task of navigating the moment's intricacies.

My eyes remained locked on Leo as I spoke, the weight of my words carrying through the room. "Tell me what happened."
"Jimmy."
His one-word revelation tore through me like a knife – Jimmy. His father killed my father. A chilling question gripped my mind – was I now a target, too?
"Why?" I questioned, my voice laden with a mixture of grief and disbelief.
Sighing heavily, Leo walked toward me, gently grabbing my arm and leading me away from his brothers. He guided me to the couch, settling down before pulling me onto his lap. Despite his efforts to wipe away the tears staining my cheeks, they persisted, making it impossible for him to eradicate the evidence of my emotional turmoil. Seeming to resign himself to this futility, he began to speak.
"Adam worked with Jimmy for several years," he explained, with Dom and Sonny flanking the couch. "Jimmy discovered that Adam was two-timing him. Aware that your father possessed recordings that could incriminate him and his partners, Jimmy wasn't willing to risk exposure. He decided to eliminate the threat."
As his words drowned me in a sea of disbelief and sorrow, I attempted to rise, but Leo held me tightly, rendering my efforts futile.
"What does he want with me?" I asked, my voice shaky.

Despite his apparent reluctance, Leo continued, "Adam was in New York a week before his death. Jimmy is convinced he went there to hide the evidence. Since you're the only family Adam had, he believes your father entrusted you with it."

"I don't know anything," I protested, shaking my head.

"We know," Leo assured me. In response to my questioning look, he added, "The day I stepped into your office, you didn't recognize me. If you had known about the evidence, you would have recognized me— or my brothers— immediately."

A heavy silence settled in the room as their words lingered, creating a tapestry of understanding woven with fear and uncertainty. Dom, breaking the silence, spoke with a calm assurance, "We're here to protect you, baby; we won't let anything happen to you."

Confusion clouded my thoughts, a dense fog that seemed impenetrable until he offered a lifeline of logic. Their family resemblance to Jimmy was unmistakable, and had I been privy to my father's secrets, I would have seen the connection instantly. Jimmy looked like all three of them combined, just older.

Leo's touch was a silent calmness to the gravity of the situation, his fingers brushing away the hair from my face with a tenderness that belied the turmoil swirling around us. "I... we needed to protect you," he confessed, his voice a soft murmur that resonated with a protective fervor.

His lips met mine in a gentle kiss, a bittersweet mingling of his resolve and my tears. "I'm sorry, cupcake; I should have told you sooner," he whispered against my mouth, his breath carrying the weight of regret.

Betrayal had brought me here, yet amid deception, a strange sense of trust in Leo anchored me. It was a trust born not of naivety but of the instinctive understanding that, despite everything, he intended to shield me from harm.

"Now what?" I asked, the adrenaline-fueled fear subsiding into a cold, focused calm.

Beside me, Dom's voice rumbled with a dark growl, carrying a lethal determination that sent a shiver down my spine. "We are going to kill that motherfucker."

Turning to face him, the pain that had once threatened to break me transformed into a steely resolve. As I stroked his ruggedly beautiful face, finally noticing the rough beard hinting at days without shaving, I softly said, "I want to help." The anger in my voice rang like a clear bell, marking a profound change within me.

Once a naive city girl whose only mistake was speeding on the highway, something had opened within me. A newfound strength and determination, an unyielding refusal to let anyone make me feel weak.

Minor.

Scared.

I had evolved, and now, as I stood facing the brewing storm, I vowed to be there when Jimmy's demise occurred. I promise to be the last one he sees.

CHAPTER 27

BRITTNEY

Age 15

The morning of Uncle Marcello's funeral dawned with a sky cloaked in mourning shades, a somber gray that seemed to press against the church windows with a silent, respectful weight. Inside, the air was still, heavy with the scent of lilies and the murmur of the gathered, all cloaked in the garb of grief.

I stood beside Mom, our hands clasped— a lifeline amidst the sea of condolences that flowed around us. The words from well-wishers were a constant hum, a drone of sorrowful clichés that people felt compelled to offer in the face of death. "I'm so sorry for your loss," they murmured, one after another, their eyes brimming with a shared pain.

But I remained silent.

It wasn't that their words didn't reach me or that the comfort they offered wasn't appreciated. It was just that my grief had rendered me mute, my voice buried beneath the weight of an unamenable loss.

Uncle Marcello had been a constant, a steady presence now gone, leaving behind a silence that seemed too profound to disturb with mere words.

Mom's hand tightened around mine, her presence a silent pillar of strength. Her face was a mask of serene sorrow, tears marking quiet paths down her cheeks.

As the service unfolded, the priest's voice a soothing cadence, a figure at the periphery of my vision caught my attention— a mysterious man standing alone, his presence an anomaly in the tapestry of familiar faces. He was a stark figure, his attire impeccable, but it was not his appearance that drew me— it was the sense of familiarity I couldn't place.

He stood at a distance, his gaze fixed on the proceedings with an intensity that seemed out of place. I had seen him before; I was sure of it. But where? The question nagged at me, a puzzle that demanded attention amidst the rituals of farewell.

The eulogies painted Uncle Marcello's life in vibrant strokes, but my focus was split, stolen away by the enigmatic stranger who seemed as much a part of the ceremony as the flowers and the tears.

As the final words were spoken and the congregation began to stir, ready to accompany Uncle Marcello on his last earthly journey, I decided. I extricated my hand from Mom's grasp and stepped toward the man, driven by a need to place him, to understand why he was here in this moment of finality.

But as I approached, he seemed to sense my intent. His eyes met mine, a flash of recognition— or was it a warning? — passing through his gaze before he turned away. I quickened my pace, a murmur of excuse me on my lips, but it was too late.

He slipped through the crowd with a grace that belied his size, his steps silent on the carpeted floor. By the time I reached the place where he had stood, he was gone, the church doors closing softly behind him.

I paused at the threshold, peering out into the drizzle that had begun to fall, the mysterious man a shadow that melted into the mist. Who was he? Why had his presence felt so significant? And why did he leave so abruptly upon my approach?

CHAPTER 28

DOMINIC

I cannot wait to tear that fucker limb to limb. I have never considered Jimmy my father, he has always been a sperm donor, and the thought of impaling my trench knife in his eye socket made my cock jerk.

The escalating pain and anger within me, intensified by the heart-wrenching sight of Brittney's tears, ignited a fierce yearning to burn the entire world down if it meant providing her with some measure of relief. In all my years, the depth of such intense emotions directed towards a woman was unfamiliar territory. Yet, with her, it was markedly distinct.

A profound connection existed, a bond transcending ordinary emotions' boundaries. The desire to shield her from the consuming turmoil she faced stirred within me like a primal instinct. This wasn't just about protecting her; it was an all-encompassing need to be her refuge in the storm, to stand as a bulwark against the forces threatening to drown her.

As the flames of anger and protectiveness flickered within, I realized that her presence had changed the world. The ordinary had morphed into something extraordinary, and the idea of burning down the world seemed like a radical, desperate gesture to carve out a space where she could find peace.

A whirlwind of feelings surged, and I couldn't deny the undeniable truth: I was in love. It seemed implausible given the short span of just a couple of months, but time held no sway over matters of the heart.

Every moment spent with her intensified the connection, deepening the roots of affection within me.

It was a sensation both exhilarating and terrifying, for love had the power to transform and redefine everything I thought I knew.

With each passing day, my heart whispered her name, confirming that this newfound love was an extraordinary force, one that would shape the course of my life forever.

There was a difference in my feelings for her. It wasn't a mere physical attraction or a desire for a fleeting encounter.

Instead, I longed to experience a deeper connection with her—intertwining our souls and becoming entwined in a sense of unity. This went beyond the realm of lust; it was a yearning for an emotional and spiritual bond.

The intensity of my emotions revealed itself in moments of jealousy and possessiveness. Seeing any man casting an admiring glance in her direction ignited a fierce anger within me. It was in those moments that I realized she was more than just a passing fling. She had become a fundamental part of my life, and the thought of another person encroaching upon what we had, filled me with an indescribable rage.

In her, I found not just a physical connection but a more profound connection of the heart and soul. She had become someone I wanted to protect, cherish, and share my life with— someone I wanted to build a future with. It was a realization that this was no ordinary affair but rather a love that had the power to transform our lives.

Brittney's presence significantly impacted Leo, too, making him act differently from how he usually behaves around others. He rarely showed affection to anyone, but with her, it was different. I noticed this when he kissed Brittney before boarding the plane in New York. It was evident that he had fallen hard for her, making me realize that I wasn't far behind.

Seeing Leo, who typically kept his emotions in check, openly displaying his affection for Brittney made me understand the depth of his feelings. It also made me aware of my own growing attraction towards her. It became clear that we were all headed down a path of love and emotional entanglement. The undeniable connection we shared with Brittney was something we couldn't resist, and it was bound to change our lives forever.

Amongst us, Sonny was the one who wore his emotions on his sleeve, unabashedly expressing them from the very moment we shared her.

I couldn't wait to kill Jimmy and his partner, whoever that asshole was; we have been frantically trying to place a face on his second in command ever since we came back home but haven't been able to. I give it to Jimmy; he cannot resist sharing sensitive information, especially with Leo.

As Brittney got up to leave the room, I followed close behind her, not ready to let her out of my sight.

I wanted to take all her hurt and pain away by any means necessary. Opening her bedroom door, I grabbed her waist, lifted her off her feet, and kissed her gently, not wanting to cause any more pain, be it pleasurable or not.

Whenever we made love, I consciously tried to commit every inch of her body to memory. I paid close attention to the places that elicited the most pleasure when we kissed, nibbled, or caressed her.

It was a sensual exploration, a quest to uncover the secrets that would bring her the greatest delight. Each encounter with her was an opportunity to learn to understand her desires on a profound level.

In the depths of my imagination, I pictured her adorned with a captivating tattoo. The idea ignited a spark of excitement as I imagined how it would accentuate her beauty and add an element of intrigue to her already alluring presence.

However, the thought of broaching her would have to wait until our mission was completed. There were priorities to attend to, and once the dust settled, I would eagerly bring up the idea, hoping it would be met with the same enthusiasm and desire for self-expression that I possessed.

As I carried her in my arms, a gentleness washed over me, unlike anything I had ever experienced. At that moment, I couldn't help but question my transformation. 'Who had I become?' The realization of my tenderness and deep-rooted care and affection for her amazed and startled me.

Her eyes, filled with lust, affected me. They softened my heart, melting away any defenses I had. I saw vulnerability and longing in their depths, which touched me deeply. The intense connection we shared made me feel protective and tender towards her. Her gaze had the power to awaken a gentleness within me that I didn't know existed.

She also awoke something else in me. Just the way she looked at me had a remarkable power to make me cum in my pants.

As she licked her bottom lip and bit it with hunger, a strong desire stirred within me. I struggled to maintain self-control, aware that her actions had the potential to push me beyond my limits. If she persisted in this enticing behavior, I couldn't guarantee that I would be able to resist the overwhelming temptation she presented.

My heart skipped a beat when I first saw her at the restaurant. In that instant, an intense desire surged through me, urging me to bend her sweet ass over and fuck her hard.

However, as I recognized her true identity, conflicting emotions enveloped me. Anger coursed through my veins, fueled by the realization that she was the intended target.

Yet, intertwined with that anger was an unexpected excitement. I soon discovered that my brothers had no intention of following through with the plan.

Suddenly, what seemed like a mundane job transformed into an exhilarating and unpredictable experience. What started as a monotonous assignment had evolved into a thrilling journey where the lines between duty and desire blurred. With her at the center of it all.

After hearing her screaming my name while I fucked her, she occupied my thoughts constantly, and I needed to hear her again.

Be inside her.

Every fucking second of the day.

The day she bit me and sucked my blood woke up the devil in me. That was the sexiest thing I have experienced, and I needed more. She is unaware of my penchant for pleasure mixed with pain, but it won't remain a secret for long.

As she took my tongue into her mouth, sucking on it with a provocative intensity, a deep and unrestrained groan escaped from deep within me. The intertwining of pleasure and desire left me intoxicated, lost in a haze of heightened sensations.

Needing to be inside her NOW.

With an urgency that consumed me, I lifted her while keeping our lips locked, swiftly removing her shorts in record time. I couldn't restrain myself any longer; patience was a luxury I couldn't afford in that moment of overpowering desire.

I undid my pants just to have enough room to pull myself out and thrust fully into her.

"Fuck, baby," I said as soon as her warmth wrapped around my throbbing cock. She arched her back, placing her feet on the bed, giving me more room to push inside her.

"Fuck"

My pace gradually decreased, not wanting to cum just yet, tracing kisses down her neck.

With a determined effort, I finally succeeded in removing her sweater, feeling a mix of relief and frustration. As I discarded it aside, a fleeting thought crossed my mind— to burn all her sweaters as a lighthearted retaliation for the struggle they had put me through.

I pulled her lace bra down, revealing her exquisite nipples to my hungry gaze. Succumbing to the irresistible temptation, I took my time, licking each one tenderly before yielding to the primal urge to bite her. As her moans filled the air, she gripped my hair tightly, her grasp sending waves of pleasure mingled with a delicious pain coursing through me. The torment of her grip only fueled my desire, driving me to greater heights of passion and insanity.

The time my girl squirted on my dick was the hottest thing. I craved for her to do it again, for that feeling was unlike any other. If it were possible, I would choose to exist within this woman.

I withdrew myself partially from her, then smoothly slid back inside, repeating this motion again and again.

The rhythm of our bodies became a dance of pleasure, building with each movement, until I sensed her surrendering beneath me.

A sense of satisfaction washed over me as I whispered, "Good girl," acknowledging her response to our shared intimacy.

"More," She panted as her grip tightened on my back, her fingers digging into my flesh, breaking the surface and leaving a mark.

Sensing her intensity, my pace quickened, driven by a primal need to satisfy her. I focused on balancing my force, mindful not to tear her apart.

"Cum... . on me, baby."

Watching her become undone by my doing, I could not control myself.

She came screaming my name... ... fuck, she is perfect.The woman before me wore the most intoxicating expressions when she reached the pinnacle of pleasure. I felt the wetness coating me, forcing me to blow my load in her.

I eased myself beside her, the warmth of her presence drawing me in. With a gentle pull, she nestled into the curve of my embrace. As she rested her head on my chest, her hand found a comfortable spot near my heart, seeking the rhythmic reassurance of its steady beats. The soft rise and fall of her breath against me created a tranquil cadence in the peaceful stillness of the room.

Inhaling deeply, I savored the sweet scent that enveloped her, a delicate fragrance that whispered familiarity and intimacy. With tender affection, I gently kissed the strands of her hair, the softness of the gesture carrying a promise of comfort and protection.

As the night unfolded around us, its serenity a gentle backdrop, we succumbed to the soothing embrace of our shared moment— the ambient sounds of the night, a symphony of tranquility, wrapped around us like a cocoon. In the peaceful union of our beings, we gradually drifted into the realm of dreams, our entwined selves finding respite in the serene embrace of each other's presence.

CHAPTER 29

BRITTNEY

Taking a nap and waking up next to Dom felt like a haven of tranquility, a brief respite from the tumult of emotions that defined my days. The desire to prolong those moments, to wake up beside him every day, echoed within me like a persistent melody, a comforting thought amid the chaos. However, as he quietly followed me to my room, it became apparent that this pursuit was more than a yearning for peace; it was a desperate need to escape the suffocating grip of grief that threatened to consume me.

Reflecting on our earlier conversation, the pain and hurt clawed their way back into my thoughts, a relentless torment that refused to be buried. Putting myself in Adam's shoes and attempting to imagine the depths of his anguish proved to be a mentally draining endeavor. The weight of the emotions pressed down on me like an unrelenting force, leaving me in a dark space, as if trapped in a room with the walls closing in on me.

In a desperate bid to regain control, I jumped off the bed abruptly, the urgency to expel the contents of my stomach overwhelming me. Hurrying to the restroom, I sank to the heated bathroom floor, the warmth offering a fleeting comfort against the internal storm. Placing my hand over my mouth, I fought to stifle the sobs that threatened to escape, not wanting Dom to hear the depths of my vulnerability.

A whisper cut through the air from the other side of the door, Dom's voice filled with concern. "Are you okay, baby?"

Taking a deep breath, I attempted to compose myself before responding. With a feeble voice, I managed to utter a hesitant "Yes," though conviction eluded my words. The tension in the room heightened when Dom tried to open the door, only to realize it was locked. "Baby, open the door," he urged, his concern palpable.

After a few more shaky breaths, I rose from the floor, but the spinning sensation in my head made my attempt useless. Flopping back down, I closed my eyes, hoping the darkness would calm the vertigo. The door was forced open, and all three men walked in, their presence adding layers to the charged atmosphere. They lifted me off the floor, carried me to my bed, and laid me down gently, their actions a silent reassurance of support.

As I mustered the strength to open my eyes, I saw Dom standing before me, clad only in his boxers. His defined muscles hinted at his dedication to working out, a physical testament to his strength. He sat on the bed, pulling me close, and I lay my head on his chest, closing my eyes to the comforting sound of his rapid heartbeat. In that moment, the realization that these men cared about me resonated deeply, a balm for the wounds that grief had inflicted.

"I'm calling the doctor," Leo asserted, a practical voice amid emotions.

"No, I'm fine," I insisted, though the fragility of my voice betrayed the facade of strength.

"No, you're not."

Lazily opening one eye, I looked at him and said, "Let me rest, and if I don't feel better after, then by all means."

"Fine," Leo replied, seemingly bothered but not wanting to upset me further. I smiled, closing my eyes and settling back on Dom's comfortable chest. Sleep once again claimed me, pulling me back into its comforting embrace, a temporary escape from the storm that raged within.

CHAPTER 30

BRITTNEY

As I stirred awake, a sense of slight improvement washed over me compared to earlier. Glancing at the clock, I discovered it was already past 4 am. The realization hit me that I had slept through the entire day and night, leaving me somewhat incredulous.

Reaching across the bed for Dom, my hand only finding the cold sheet, I sighed.

I reached for my phone, hoping that Francine would answer. The sound of her cheerful greeting brought a flood of emotions, reminding me of how much I had missed her.

At that moment, I couldn't bear to burden her with the weight of my troubles, so we engaged in lively conversation about various topics, immersing ourselves in the warmth of friendship and shared memories. The mere act of speaking to her alleviated some of the heaviness in my heart, offering a temporary respite from the worries that plagued me.

However, as our conversation flowed, the subject of her impending move crept into our discussion, casting a shadow of unease over the previously lighthearted atmosphere.

Francine had planned to depart a week ago but chose to delay her departure. She patiently waited for me to return to New York so that we could bid each other a proper goodbye.

However, uncertain about my plans and not wanting to disrupt her own, I urged her to depart as scheduled.

I reassured her that I would find a way to make it to Italy soon to see her. Although she expressed discontent with the idea, I was adamant about not having her alter her plans again for my sake.

And now, with just three days remaining until her departure, the reality of our impending separation weighed heavily on my heart.

"Oh shit,"

She said from the other end of the line.

"What," I sat up abruptly, the sudden movement causing the room to spin around me.

"I'm going to be late."

As I glanced at the time, my eyes widened in astonishment to see that we had been engrossed in our conversation for a staggering three hours.

"I'll call you later," I said, reluctant to end our conversation but aware that we both had responsibilities to attend to.

"I miss you,"

I said, trying to keep my composure, feeling the burning sensation in the back of my eyes.

"I miss you too."

I got out of bed and was in the bathroom for over an hour. I felt a strong pull to see my men, yet at the same time, I felt a deep resistance to the idea.

I eventually decided to head outside and soak up some sun, which would benefit my well-being.

Tiptoeing down the stairs, I made it to the backyard, and the sun's warmth on my skin was a welcomed sensation after spending so much time indoors.

I reclined on the pool chair, relishing the warmth of the sun's rays cascading over my body.

Matilda approached, delicately placing a tray of aromatic coffee and delectable pastries on the nearest table.

At that moment, I couldn't help but feel an overwhelming surge of gratitude towards her; I had never met someone so attentive to my needs. She would make a fantastic secretary; as a matter of fact, she could teach Jarred a thing or two, I thought to myself.

I grabbed the coffee and enjoyed the feeling of the warm liquid coating my throat. Under different circumstances, this place would be heaven.

"Glad to see you up."

Startled by the unexpected voice, my body jerked in surprise, nearly causing me to spill the scalding hot coffee.

"Didn't mean to startle you."

As I turned my head towards the source of the voice, my breath hitched in my throat, and I couldn't help but let out a soft gasp.

The sight before me was nothing short of mesmerizing. Sonny stood there, dressed in comfortable gray sweatpants, a black T-shirt, and a backward cap, his casual attire somehow making him even more irresistible.

Dom, in his blue jeans and crisp white shirt, exuded a rugged charm that was impossible to ignore.

And then there was Leo, the epitome of sophistication, clad in a perfectly tailored suit that accentuated his magnetic presence.

They approached me with a deliberate, almost hypnotic pace, and I had to bite my lip to suppress the tumultuous thoughts swirling in my mind.

Sonny gently lifted my legs and settled himself next to me on the reclining chair, placing my legs on his lap. His touch on my toes sent waves of relaxation coursing through my body, relieving the tension that had built up from the week. His skilled hands moved with gentle firmness, expertly kneading and massaging my aching feet. The sensation was heavenly, and I couldn't help but sigh contented.

Meanwhile, Leo's eyes lingered on the scene before him, a subtle hint of disappointment crossing his face. I could sense his desire to be beside me, sharing that intimate connection. Yet, he respected Sonny's claim to the spot, settling for a seat beside Dom, his gaze fixated on our intertwined legs.

As Sonny continued his ministrations, his fingers tracing delicate patterns on my skin, I couldn't help but notice the intensity in Leo's eyes. It was as if he longed to join in, to offer his touch and feel the warmth of my skin against his fingertips.

I leaned back, enjoying the sensation. It was a small indulgence amidst the chaos that surrounded us.

"Is there anything these men can't do?" I wondered aloud, my voice barely a whisper.

I heard Sonny let out a soft chuckle, a grin spreading across his face as he massaged my feet.

"How do you feel?" Sonny asked.

"Better,"

"We've come up with a plan to lure out Jimmy's partner," Leo revealed, breaking the news.

What did he say?

"What?"

"Focus, princess."

"How?"

I moved to sit up. Sonny's eyes briefly showed a hint of disappointment, but he quickly closed the distance between us, his hand finding its place on my thigh. His touch sent a shiver down my spine, and I couldn't help but relish in the comfort and closeness that came with it.

Leo's gaze was on Sonny's hand, then met my eyes before speaking again.

"He is in New York, and since they both think you have the evidence, we will lure them out with your look-a-like."

Leo's words hung in the air, the gravity of the situation sinking in. Jimmy's partner was in New York, and they believed that using a look-alike of mine would be the key to luring them out. However, I couldn't help but voice my doubts. Their plan seemed flawed, and I couldn't simply sit back and let someone else take my place.

"Do you have someone who looks like me?"

I asked, my voice tinged with skepticism. Their answer wasn't what I expected. Sonny's response indicated they hadn't found a suitable candidate yet but were working on it.

"That won't work,"

I stated firmly, my eyes narrowing as I looked at Leo and Dom.

"If anyone is going to be the bait, it should be me."

Leo interjected, his tone firm.

"No, you won't."

"Hell no," Sonny barked from next to me.

It was clear that they didn't want to put me in harm's way, but I couldn't stand idly by while others risked their lives for me.

"I understand your concern, Leo,"

I replied, my voice softer.

"But if there's a chance to end this and protect all of us, I want to be part of it. I won't let someone else take my place and face the danger that belongs to me."

Silence hung in the air momentarily as the three men exchanged glances, a mix of worry and consideration evident on their faces.

Finally, Leo spoke, his voice filled with concern.

"We'll need to plan carefully and ensure your safety," he said, gently touching hand.

"But if you're determined to be part of this, we'll do everything we can to protect you."

"Are you serious?" Sonny said, anger in his voice. Why are you even considering this?"

"She wants to help. We'll let her help, but we will ensure she's completely protected," Leo said to his brother.

Why are they talking like I'm not even here? "I'm not a child," I interjected. "I can take care of myself, and I'm doing this." The last statement directed towards Sonny.

The silence that followed was nerve-wracking.

Throughout the conversation, Dom remained silent, his face contorted with anger and frustration. His brows furrowed, and his jaw clenched tightly as he listened to our plans. It was evident that he disagreed with the decision to involve me.

But once I decided to take matters into my own hands, a surge of determination washed over me.

I believed that by confronting the situation head-on, I could finally find closure and put the painful past behind me. However, my decision seemed to catch the men off guard, and their reactions reflected apprehension.

"When are we leaving?" I asked, my gaze fixed on a distant point, avoiding direct eye contact with any of them.

Leo cleared his throat, breaking the silence as he consulted his watch. "We should leave within the next 48 hours," he replied, his tone measured and serious. "I'll make the necessary preparations and ensure our plan is foolproof."

Dom nodded in agreement, his expression solemn, finally speaking. "We'll need to gather more information and strategize before we proceed. This isn't something we can rush into blindly."

Sonny leaned forward, his voice filled with concern. "We'll do everything we can to ensure your safety, and we won't take any unnecessary risks. We need to approach this with caution and precision."

With an exasperated huff, Leo abruptly stood up, turned on his heel, and walked away, leaving me frustrated. He had a knack for being a complete jerk at times, yet there was an undeniable allure about him that I couldn't ignore.

As I watched his retreating figure, my mind wandered to all the times he had challenged me.

Teased me.

Igniting a fire within me.

It was a love-hate relationship that kept me on my toes, and I craved his infuriating presence and intoxicating charm.

CHAPTER 31

BRITTNEY

After our earlier discussion, I felt the urge to converse with Sonny. I could sense his frustration when I expressed my desire to assist with the plan, and I wanted to understand his perspective better.

Seeking him out, I finally discovered him in the gym, his chiseled form illuminated by the room's soft glow.

Sporting nothing but shorts and sneakers, his well-defined muscles were on display, reminding me of his rugged appeal. My heart fluttered as I approached, my emotions a mix of curiosity and a longing to bridge the gap between us.

"Mind if I join you?"

I asked, a tentative smile gracing my lips. My eyes wandered over his form, drawn to the strength he exuded.

He paused, his gaze meeting mine, and for a moment, it felt like the air between us held a silent conversation of its own.

"Sure,"

He replied.

As he focused on his workout, I took the opportunity to collect my thoughts while walking on the treadmill. The rhythmic sound of my footsteps matched the rhythm of my contemplation. I knew I had to choose my words carefully, expressing my feelings without causing any misunderstandings.

After a while, I gathered the courage to broach the topic.

"Sonny,"

I began, my voice steady yet cautious,

"I want you to know that I'm serious about helping. It's not about seeking attention or proving anything. I believe that we're stronger together."

He continued his exercise, his features masking any immediate reaction. I could tell he was mulling over my words, a war of emotions beneath his calm exterior.

"I get it, Brittney," he finally responded, his voice low and measured. "But this isn't like our usual operations. It's dangerous, and I can't have you risking yourself."

I nodded, acknowledging his concern.

"I understand that it's risky, Sonny. But we're in this together, aren't we? I want to help protect what we have, what you, Leo, and Dom have built."

He paused again, his eyes locking onto mine, a mixture of conflict and something softer residing within them.

"I just don't want to see you hurt," he admitted, his voice a whisper.

My heart swelled at his honesty. It was clear that beneath his tough exterior, he cared deeply for me, a fact I had always sensed but had rarely seen so plainly.

"I know Sonny,"

I said, my vulnerability laid bare.

"But I can handle myself. I want to prove that I'm not just some liability."

"I know you aren't."

He gracefully dismounted the exercise machine and closed the distance between us, his gaze unyielding. Without breaking eye contact, he walked around me, and suddenly, his strong arms gently lifted me off the treadmill, making my heart race.

In a husky voice, he whispered,

"I need to taste you, baby."

His words hung in the air like a promise, his intent clear and electrifying. With that simple statement, a veil of desire fell between us, igniting a primal yearning that had been building beneath the surface.

As he held me in his arms, emotions swirled within me.

Anticipation.

Vulnerability.

Raw emotions

My breath hitched as he leaned closer, his lips hovering just above mine, his warm breath sending waves of electricity across my skin.

Time seemed to stand still in that charged moment, the world around us fading into insignificance. It was just him and me, suspended in an intimate space where words were unnecessary, where every heartbeat conveyed the depth of our longing.

And then, as if driven by an irresistible force, our lips finally met in a fierce, passionate kiss.

His lips were soft yet demanding.

He gently carried me to the weight machine and settled down, his muscular frame supporting me on his lap. Our lips met again in a passionate kiss.

Amid our fervent kisses, he whispered,

"I love you, princess," his words a tender confession that sent my heart into a frenzy. Those three words, spoken sincerely, held a weight I couldn't ignore, and my emotions surged in response.

My heart swelled with the depth of his feelings, and I could hardly believe that the man I had fallen for was right here with me, holding me close.

As our kisses deepened, I lost myself in the moment's intensity.

Between breathless moments, I managed to utter, "I love you too." The words tumbled from my lips, carried by the whirlwind of sensations that his presence always invoked within me.

He continued to explore me with a blend of tenderness and fervor that left me breathless. His touch was a delicate storm, his movements a perfect fusion of gentleness and urgency.

He reached for my jogging pants and tore them by the crotch, leaving me exposed and vulnerable. He then lifted us both, pulling his shorts down and exposing himself.

Reaching for him, I could feel the weight and hardness of his dick in my grasp. His desire was evident; I looked up at him, our eyes locking in a heated exchange that spoke volumes without the need for words.

With a soft smile, I tightened my grip, relishing how he responded to my touch.

"Fuck, baby." He spoke.

My power over him was intoxicating, a heady mix of control and vulnerability that heightened our tension.

I could feel his pulse beneath my fingertips, a rhythmic beat that echoed the rhythm of my own heart. As I stroked him, his eyelids fluttered, his features a portrait of pleasure that I was creating. Each movement was deliberate, each touch designed to elicit the responses I craved from him.

He leaned into my touch, his eyes smoldering with a hunger that mirrored my own. I could see the raw desire etched across his features, a hunger that demanded to be sated.

"Are you teasing me, princess?" His voice was deep and dark.

My hand now dripping with his precum, I brought my glistening hand to my lips, my tongue flicking out to taste him, to experience the unique flavor of his desire. It was a way of letting him know that I craved him as much as he craved me. The slight saltiness mixed with a subtle sweetness sent a rush of arousal through me, making me ache for more.

"Christ," he whispered.

His chest rose and fell in rapid succession; his lips parted as he watched me, unable to tear his eyes away from the intimate display.

As I finally withdrew my fingers from my mouth, a low, guttural sound escaped his lips.

"You're going to be the death of me," he said, smiling at me.

His strong and possessive hands reached the back of my head. His touch was a silent command, urging me closer and pulling me into the gravitational pull of his lips. There was an urgency in how he kissed me, a hunger that matched mine.

Rising on my tiptoes, I aligned myself with him. The moment of contact was electric, a jolt of pleasure that threatened to send my senses spiraling out of control. But I held on, determined to savor every second of this tantalizing dance.

As I sank onto him, inch by delicious inch, a gasp of pleasure escaped my lips. His dick filled me, stretching and filling me in a way that left me breathless. I could feel the heat of him, the throbbing pulse of desire that matched my own.

But the reaction in his eyes truly stole my breath away. The way his gaze darkened, the intensity of his focus, it was as if I held his entire world.

"Fuck, you feel so good." He said.

The raw desire that flickered in his eyes was intoxicating, a confirmation that I had succeeded in pushing him to the edge.

I began moving, a slow and deliberate rhythm matching our heart pounding. Each thrust sent waves of pleasure radiating through me, each meeting of our bodies a symphony of sensations that had me teetering on the edge of ecstasy. His fingers dug into my hips, guiding me, urging me on as we moved together.

"Hold on, baby," he rasped, his grip on me tightening as if to anchor himself.

"You feel so good, I don't want to cum just yet."

His words, heavy with desire, only fueled my determination. I was on the precipice, teetering on the edge of a climax that promised to be explosive.

"Baby," he groaned, his eyes clenched shut, a beautiful display of his struggle for control.

But I was relentless, my body driven by a hunger that demanded satisfaction. I shifted my angle slightly, chasing that elusive sensation that would send me over the edge.

A soft gasp escaped his lips as my movements intensified, and I knew I was driving him to the brink. I was on a mission to shatter his restraint, to push us both into the sweet abyss of release.

His hands roamed my body, igniting every nerve as he held me against him, our connection growing more profound with every touch.

Unable to resist any longer, I leaned in and brushed my lips along the curve of his neck. The shiver that ran through him was palpable, his breath hitching as he fought for control.

"Shit baby, what are you doing to me" he managed to say between breaths.

My tongue traced a path over his heated skin, and his grip on me faltered for a moment.

Encouraged by his reaction, I quickened my pace, the need for release becoming almost unbearable. Our bodies moved in perfect synchronization, a symphony of desire that resonated through every fiber of our beings.

As I continued to move, my lips found his neck once more, and this time, I couldn't resist the urge to bite down gently, a surge of primal instinct coursing through me. His response was immediate, a low growl escaping his throat as his restraint finally shattered.

"Baby," he moaned, his fingers digging into my hips as he met my movements with a fervor that matched my own. We were two bodies entwined, lost in the intoxicating dance of pleasure, hurtling towards a shared climax that was now inevitable.

With a final, fierce collision, our bodies reached their breaking point, pleasure exploding like a firework deep within me. I cried out, my voice merging with his in a harmonious chorus of ecstasy as the world around us faded into a haze of sensation.

As our breathing slowed, as the echoes of pleasure subsided, I collapsed against him, our bodies still trembling in the aftermath. His arms enveloped me.

"Fuckkk baby"

"I didn't even get a chance to taste you."

CHAPTER 32

BRITTNEY

It's hard to believe how quickly time is passing. We are leaving tomorrow, and despite my excitement and anticipation, I can't help but feel a sense of trepidation and unease as my mind conjures up all sorts of worst-case scenarios that threaten to undermine my confidence and joy.

The men ran me through the plan over and over again. The plan was for me to meet Francine for brunch at Cafe T. We chose this particular spot because of the outdoor dining option, and my men will have a better vantage point.

Security personnel will be present among the diners, discreetly blending in with the crowd, yet ever watchful of their surroundings and any potential threats that may arise, thereby providing us with an added layer of protection and peace of mind.

I still haven't told Franny, and it's killing me inside. My men insisted I should tell her after we killed Jimmy's partner, not wanting her to become a liability. I disagreed with that but did not feel like arguing with them. They have been low-key upset ever since I told them I wanted to help.

Leo strolled into my room without knocking,

"Hey," I said, noticing him. Surprised, he was casually dressed in a black t-shirt and black jeans. He still looked incredible.

"How are you feeling?" he asked.

Nervous! "Fine."

"You don't have to do... ."

"I'm going," I told Leo, unfazed by their attempts to convince me otherwise.

I had heard it all before, their concerns and pleas falling on deaf ears. This time, I was determined to take matters into my own hands. I was tired of waiting, tired of living in uncertainty. It was time to face the challenges head-on and find the closure I sought.

With a hint of defiance, I added, "You've tried to change my mind so many times, but it won't work."

I was ready to prove myself and confront whatever lay ahead; nothing they said could deter me.

"Fine," Leo said, walking towards the couch and plopping down, his arms stretched out and resting on the cushions. A mischievous grin formed on his face as if he knew the effect he had on me.

It frustrated me to no end. His actions were deliberate, designed to provoke a response. I couldn't help but feel a mix of irritation and attraction.

He had a way of getting under my skin like no one else. It was infuriating yet strangely enticing. I took a deep breath, trying to compose myself. I wouldn't let him see how much he affected me.

"Come here, cupcake," he said with hooded eyes.

As I stood up and started walking towards Leo, he swiftly raised his hand, signaling me to stop. His gesture halted me mid-step, causing me to pause and gaze at him with frustration. I could see the playful glint in his eyes, a challenge hidden behind his confident demeanor. It was clear that he had something up his sleeve.

"Take your clothes off and crawl to me."

Without hesitating, I obediently followed his command. I slowly removed my clothes. With each garment that fell to the floor, the air around us seemed to grow heavier with desire. Once wholly undressed, I positioned myself on all fours and began crawling towards him, my heart pounding in my chest.

Seeing the bulge in his pants grow, my anticipation intensified, and I could feel the wetness between my thighs.

He spread his legs, inviting me closer, and I could sense the raw desire emanating from him. The throbbing ache within me matched the pulsating need in his gaze as I drew nearer.

His smile sent shivers down my spine as he grabbed a handful of my hair, gently guiding my head to the side. My neck was bare- vulnerable to his touch. His warm tongue trailed along the curve of my neck, leaving a tingling sensation in its wake. His breath against my skin heightened my senses, causing my body to respond with desire. His whispered words of praise, calling me a "good girl," sent a rush of heat through my veins.

He settled back onto the couch, his eyes fixed on me with a magnetic intensity. Slowly, his hand descended to his belt, deftly unfastening it as anticipation crackled in the air.

With a swift motion, he pulled the belt free, followed by his jeans and boxers, revealing his hardened desire with a single tug.

He lifted his t-shirt off in a tantalizing display, revealing his sculpted torso and perfectly defined muscles. As he sat back down, his eyes remained fixed on me. A wicked smile played on his lips as he sensually ran his tongue along the curve of his bottom lip.

Practically dripping now, I eagerly awaited any form of physical contact from this irresistible being.

"Sit," he said, motioning to his lap.

The command sent a jolt of excitement through my body, making my heart race. Without hesitation, I straddled his lap, feeling the heat radiating from his body as our skin made contact. His hands found their place on my waist, gripping me firmly.

The weight of his presence beneath me was electrifying. With a wicked grin, he whispered, "Now, put that gorgeous pussy on me."

I always liked hearing his filthy mouth when he fucks me, and he knows that.

As I descended onto his eager cock, our bodies merged in a perfect rhythm. He held onto my hips firmly, guiding my movements and intensifying the pleasure with each thrust. The sensation was electrifying, an exquisite blend of ecstasy and raw desire.

Our moans harmonized, filling the room with a symphony of passion as we surrendered ourselves to the intoxicating pleasure.

"Don't stop, baby," he said, groaning between his teeth. "You are so fucking wet."

He leaned forward, his lips capturing mine in a searing kiss. Our mouths melded together with a hunger and urgency that mirrored the intensity of our lovemaking.

He continued to thrust inside me with a primal rhythm; with each thrust, I felt a wave of ecstasy wash over me, building and intensifying with every movement.

"Goddamn," he said in between kisses.

He groaned in my mouth again, grabbing my ass.

"You feel so fucking good," groaning again. "Fuck," pounding in me harder.

The room was filled with the sound of our passionate moans as he released his warmth deep inside me. He nestled his head in the crook of my neck, his warm breath tickling my skin as he tried to catch his breath.

But his desire was insatiable, and he began moving inside me once more, his arousal growing once again to its impressive size.

He whispered in my ear, urging me to turn my head and look behind us. Curiosity getting the best of me, I glanced over my shoulder and caught sight of the mirror reflecting our passionate encounter.

He lifted me as we watched his hot white cum, the journey from my entrance, dripping on his erection, making its way down his balls, and ending on the carper. The view fueled fire within me. It was an erotic sight, an intimate display of our connection laid bare for us to witness.
"This is what you do to me, baby."
"This is what that tight wet pussy does to me."
Eagerly straddling him, riding him with fervor, his release mingled with the wetness between us, creating a symphony of erotic sounds. The rhythmic splashes and moans filled the air, intensifying the sensation that overwhelmed my senses. My head spun with a mixture of pleasure, desire, and the sheer intensity of the moment.
"Cum" he whispered in his deep, husky voice.
He shifted his position on the couch, lowering himself slightly, allowing my breasts to sway enticingly in front of his face. With hunger in his eyes, he reached out and took hold of one, his hand encompassing it possessively. The anticipation of his touch sent shivers of pleasure through me, and I bit my lip in anticipation.
His warm tongue traced circles around my nipple, and I let out a soft gasp, my body responding to his sensual caress. His eyes locked with mine as he continued to lick and suckle, reveling in the sight of my pleasure.
As his tongue continued to tease and please, a surge of pleasure built within me, reaching its crescendo.
And in that moment, he bit down on my sensitive nipple, sending a jolt of ecstasy through my body. The mix of pain and pleasure intensified the sensations, pushing me over the edge.
I couldn't hold back any longer, and I released with a powerful and prolonged orgasm that left me breathless and trembling in his arms. The intensity of the experience was overwhelming, and I clung to him, lost in a haze of blissful surrender.
"Goddamn, baby," he whispered hoarsely as his movements grew more desperate. I could feel his body tense beneath me, and his rhythm became erratic.

With a final thrust, he reached his climax again, his release surging through him in waves of pleasure. His breath was heavy against my skin as he held me close, savoring the moment of shared ecstasy. We lay there, tangled in each other's arms, the heat of our passion lingering in the air.

Trying to catch our breaths, "I can't wait for you to have my baby," he said, kissing me.

CHAPTER 33

BRITTNEY

After almost two months on the West Coast, I finally returned home. I have lived in New York for over ten years, and at this moment, I feel like a stranger.

The flight back was quiet— too quiet. I was nervous and went over the plan in my head while the men stared at their phones or tablets.

Despite their attempt to appear composed, there was an undeniable sense of nervousness among us. The high stakes of the mission weighed heavily on our minds, and the familiar streets of New York felt unfamiliar as uncertainty loomed.

"Ma'am"

"Huh,"

I muttered as the waiter stood next to me. Glancing at the menu, I quickly scanned the options and decided to go with the first thing I saw.

"I'll have the Chicken Caesar salad, please," I said, placing my order.

"Very good,"

The waiter replied, taking my menu and heading back inside.

The plan was in full effect. Before we left, I called Francine and asked her to meet me for lunch. She was ecstatic to hear that I would return to New York before her flight to Italy.

So here we were, sitting at a cozy café, with the anticipation hanging heavy in the air.

I could feel the watchful eyes of my men, observing our every move, waiting for the right moment to execute our plan. But I was so consumed by nervousness that I couldn't fully engage with Francine, who sat across from me, looking at me with concern as if I had sprouted three heads.

"What's up with you?"

Francine asked. I took a deep breath, gathering my thoughts and finding the right words to respond. How could I possibly explain the tangled web of danger, secrets, and forbidden desires that had consumed my life?

"Oh, nothing much,"

I replied, my voice trembling slightly. Sighing, I continued.

"It's complicated."

I hesitated for a moment, contemplating whether I should divulge any details. But ultimately, I decided it was best to shield Francine from the dark realities that plagued my existence.

"It's just work stuff, you know," I continued, forcing a smile. "Some challenging projects and high-pressure situations. Nothing that I can't handle."

I hoped that my vague response would be enough to satisfy her curiosity without arousing further suspicion.

Franny leaned forward, her eyes searching mine for a glimpse of the truth.

"Are you sure you're okay?" she asked softly, her concern evident in her voice. "You seem... different."

I reached across the table and took Franny's hand, trying to convey reassurance.

"I promise everything will be fine," I said, my voice filled with determination. "I have a lot on my plate right now, but I'll figure it out. You know me, always finding a way."

Franny nodded.

"Well, just remember that I'm here for you," she said, gently squeezing my hand. You don't have to face everything alone."

Her words touched my heart, reminding me of our incredible friendship. It pained me to keep her in the dark, but it was a necessary sacrifice to protect her from the dangerous world I had become entangled in.

"I appreciate that, Franny," I replied, my voice filled with gratitude. "And I'm grateful to have you in my life. You bring so much light and joy amidst all the chaos."

As we continued our lunch, I made a silent vow to myself. I would do whatever it took to keep Franny safe, even if it meant walking through the darkness alone. The secrets, the dangers, and the intimate encounters with my mysterious companions would remain hidden, locked away in the depths of my soul.

"GET DOWN!" someone yelled.

Without hesitation, I obeyed the command and quickly dropped to the floor. I glanced over at Francine, sitting across from me, and saw the fear in her eyes as she followed suit, taking cover under the table.

Time seemed to slow down as chaos erupted around us. The sounds of shattering glass, frantic voices, and furniture crashing filled the air. My heart raced in my chest, adrenaline coursing through my veins as I tried to make sense of the situation.

Crouched beneath the table, I focused on staying as still as possible, listening intently to the commotion. The fear and uncertainty hung in the air like a heavy fog.

Suddenly, I felt a hand on my elbow, gently pulling me upward. I cautiously peered out from under the table and saw one of my men, his face etched with concern. Without a word, he motioned for me to follow him.

As I rose to my feet, my heart pounding in my chest, I couldn't help but ask the burning question on my mind.

"Did we get him?" I said, my voice filled with fear.

Leo, standing beside me, met my gaze with a solemn expression. His eyes flickered as he spoke. "Yes," he said, his voice steady but tinged with caution. "But we need to be careful. Stay close to me."

Before I could process his words fully, my attention was drawn to the commotion unfolding in the distance. Two of our bodyguards were rushing towards an alley across the street from the restaurant, their guns drawn and ready for action.

My instincts took over without thinking twice, and I pushed my way past Leo, determined to see the situation for myself.

As I reached the alley, fear coursed through my veins at the scene before me.

The bodyguards stood next to a lifeless figure, their guns still raised, indicating that their target had been neutralized. The realization hit me that this person was the one who had posed a threat to my life.

In my pursuit of answers, I took a step closer, desperate to glimpse the face that had caused so much turmoil. But Leo, ever watchful and protective, swiftly intervened, gripping my elbow firmly as he pulled me back against him.

"Stay back," he cautioned. "It's not safe. Let my men handle it."
"I have to,"
I said in a low voice, my gaze fixed on him.

Leo, his eyes filled with worry, tightened his grip on my elbow as he responded, "Cupcake..."

Not allowing his words to deter me, I rose on my tiptoes, my heart pounding in my chest, and gently reached for his face, pressing my lips against his in a tender kiss. He responded with equal fervor, his hand finding the back of my neck, deepening the kiss.

It was a moment of connection and reassurance before I reluctantly pulled away, knowing that there was a task at hand.

Turning away from Leo, with each step I took, my eyes remained fixed on the lifeless figure lying before me. The sight that greeted me was chilling.

"Oh... my... god,"

I barely managed to utter, my hand instinctively rising to cover my mouth in shock and horror. The scene was gruesome, the pale skin of the deceased and the oversized suit they wore serving as a haunting reminder of their identity. Blood pooled around the back of their head, their eyes frozen in a wide-open stare. It was a sight that shook me to my core.

"Did you know?" I asked, turning to face Leo.

"No,"

His response was simple and concise, but it held a world of meaning. At that moment, I found comfort in the fact that Leo was unaware of the danger that had loomed over me. Knowing he hadn't deliberately kept me in the dark was a small comfort.

Memories flooded my mind, images of the countless hours I had spent working alongside Jarred. We collaborated on numerous projects, often staying late into the night.

But if Jarred had wanted me dead, why hadn't he acted within the confines of our workplace? Why had he chosen this particular moment, this public setting?

Questions swirled in my mind, threatening to consume me. How did Jarred know Jimmy? Was there a connection I had missed? It was a tangled web of uncertainty, and I knew I couldn't be consumed by these questions now.

"We have to go, Cupcake,"

Leo's urgent voice pulled me out of my thoughts, and he nearly lifted me off my feet as we hurried through the alley.

As we made our way towards the sleek black truck parked in front of the restaurant, my eyes couldn't help but stray towards the growing crowd. Curiosity burned within me, mingling with a hint of apprehension. What had drawn these onlookers, this sea of faces, to the crime scene? ... . Wait ... .

"Where is Francine?"

The words escaped my lips in a frantic plea as I ran across the street, narrowly avoiding a collision with a car. Ignoring the chaos around me, I pushed past anyone in my way, focusing solely on finding Francine.

"Francine!"

I called out, my voice filled with desperation and fear. My voice seemed distant, drowned out by the racing thoughts in my mind.

I scanned the area, my heart pounding, searching for any sign of her amidst the grim scene.

My breath caught in my throat as I stumbled upon the devastating sight before me. Sonny and Dom, their faces etched with anguish, were desperately attempting to revive Francine, their hands performing the rhythmic compressions of CPR. Blood stained the ground, a stark contrast against the pale pallor of her lifeless body.

Her eyes stared vacantly ahead, devoid of the vibrant spirit that once resided within them.

"No, no, no, Francine... please... wake up."

I choked out, my voice trembling. I knelt beside her, gently cradling her head in my lap, my trembling hands delicately brushing her hair away from her face. Time seemed to stand still as I whispered her name, my voice filled with a raw longing for her to respond, to come back to me.

Her pale complexion chilled me to the core, a stark reminder of the fragility of life. The world around me seemed to blur as tears welled up in my eyes, my grief threatening to consume me.

Dom or Sonny spoke, their words a distant echo amid my anguish, but their meaning was lost in the haze of my sorrow. All that mattered in that moment was the loss of my dear friend, the emptiness that now loomed in her absence.

I clung to the faint hope that she would awaken, that this nightmare would be a fleeting, terrifying dream. But as the moments stretched on, reality sank in, and the weight of her absence settled heavily upon my shoulders.

The tears flowed freely now, my sobs mixing with the cacophony of the surrounding chaos as I mourned the loss of someone who had become family to me.

A hand was on my shoulder, caressing me.

"I'm so sorry, baby girl."

CHAPTER 34

BRITTNEY

Waking up next to Sonny used to bring me peace, but now it only intensifies the pain in my heart. It's been a month since Francine's tragic death. I find myself wishing every day that I could disappear, that the world would swallow me whole and take away this unbearable grief, but life doesn't work that way, and I'm left to navigate this endless sea of sorrow on my own— the memories of her laughter.

Her warmth.

And her friendship haunts me, and I can't escape the emptiness without her.

The men wouldn't let me out of their sight. After Francine's funeral, I wasn't ready to leave New York, and Leo took it upon himself to buy a loft apartment where I could stay with them. The days were filled with kindness from the men, but my mind was fixated on the haunting memories of Francine. The image of her lifeless body on the ground, her eyes open but devoid of life, played on repeat in my mind. The pain of losing my best friend was unbearable, and it felt like a heavy weight that I carried with me wherever I went.

 The guilt of Francine's death weighed heavily on me. I blamed myself for getting involved and exposing her to danger.

The funeral was a bittersweet moment, filled with beauty and sadness. Francine looked stunning, but the finality of never seeing her again crushed me. I had to step out several times to collect myself, and Leo, Dom, and Sonny were by my side, offering unwavering support throughout the ordeal.

But after months together... ..always together, I felt suffocated by their constant presence; I knew I needed space to heal. While well-intentioned, the weight of their support felt overwhelming, and I craved solitude. I have to escape from them, even if it's just for a little while.

Gently slipping away from his arm wrapped around my waist, I went to the bathroom.

Ever since the "incident," they wouldn't let me sleep alone. Like I'm some fragile patient in an asylum, they took turns watching over me. I wouldn't say I liked being treated like a child, and the resentment grew towards them and even myself. The weight of their presence suffocated me, and I longed to break free from this suffocating cocoon.

 In the bathroom, I couldn't hold back the urge to throw up... again. It had happened almost every night for the past few weeks, but I didn't want to alarm the men. I mentioned I was going to see my mother today, which was true, but I also planned to visit the doctor while I was there. It's time to get checked out and figure out what's going on with my body.

The fear of what I might discover scared me, but I couldn't ignore the signs any longer. Deep down, I longed for the pain to go away. Sometimes, I felt like I couldn't go on, like I'd rather crawl up and die. But then I thought of my mother and the love we shared. She needed me, and I needed her. We were each other's anchor in this storm of grief and loss. I couldn't leave her, and she couldn't leave me.

Together, we would find the strength to keep going, to face the darkness, and find a glimmer of light amidst the shadows. And perhaps, with time, we could heal the wounds that seemed so unbearable now.

Lifting myself off the floor, I turned on the shower. The hot water cascaded over my body, soothing my tense muscles, but I couldn't wash away the pain inside. Tears mingled with the shower's spray as I let my emotions flow freely. It had become routine – crying in the shower almost daily, hidden from their watchful eyes.

I knew my grief was understandable; losing my best friend had shattered me. But there was something more, something deeper gnawing at me. My emotions felt raw, like a raging storm I couldn't control. Lately, I found myself snapping at the men, even when they were only trying to help. I couldn't stop the outbursts, the uncontrollable anger and frustration.

I felt lost, adrift in a sea of emotions, unable to find my way back to calm waters. It scared me how much control this storm had over me. I needed stability and some semblance of control, but I didn't know how.

The bedroom was dimly lit, with soft sunlight filtering through the curtains. I could feel their watchful eyes as I stepped out of the bathroom. Leo, Dom, and Sonny were all there, concern etched on their faces.

"How are you feeling today, Baby girl?" Dom asked gently, reaching out to touch my arm.

I shrugged off his touch, not wanting their pity.

"I'm fine," I replied tersely, avoiding their gaze.

Leo stepped forward, his intense gaze searching my face. "You don't seem fine, baby. We're worried about you."

I turned away, unable to meet his eyes. "I said I'm fine. I just needed some time alone."

Sonny sighed, his voice full of frustration. "You can't keep shutting us out, Cupcake. We're here for you."

I wanted to scream at them to leave me alone, to let my pain swallow me. But some of me knew I needed them and couldn't face this storm alone.

"I know," I finally admitted, my voice cracking with emotion." I just... I don't know how to handle all of this."

Leo stepped closer, wrapping his arms around me in a gentle embrace. "You don't have to handle it alone," he whispered. "We're here for you, always."

I felt tears welling up in my eyes, but I fought them back. I didn't want to break down before them, to show them how broken I was.

"I'm scared," I admitted, my voice barely a whisper. "I feel like I'm falling apart and don't know how to stop it."

Dom placed a hand on my shoulder, his touch reassuring. "We won't let you fall," he said firmly. "We'll catch you," embracing me.

I know what'll help!" Sonny declared with enthusiasm. "Food! It always makes me feel better. Are you hungry, princess?"

I nodded, my voice still muffled from Dom's hug. "Yes," I said, "but food won't fix this mess."

Sonny grinned. "Maybe not, but you still need to eat. What do you feel like eating? Anything you want, you'll get."

"I want chocolate-covered bacon," I blurted out, and suddenly, all three of them froze in disbelief. I could feel Dom's chest shaking from laughter as he held me.

"Chocolate-covered bacon?" Sonny repeated, his eyes widening.

Leo raised an eyebrow. "You sure that's what you want, Cupcake?"

I shrugged. "Why not? It's the perfect blend of sweet and savory."

Dom finally managed to speak, his laughter still bubbling up.

"Only you could come up with that combination."

I grinned. "Well, you did say anything."

Sonny shook his head, still trying to process my request. "Alright then, chocolate-covered bacon it is. I'll place the order."

Leo's taste and style never failed to amaze me. The loft we shared was nothing short of a masterpiece. The open-plan layout made the space feel even more expansive, and the kitchen was a chef's dream with top-of-the-line appliances and a sleek design.
Four spacious bedrooms, each with an ensuite bathroom, provided comfort and privacy. The living room was adorned with elegant furniture, and large windows allowed natural light to flood the entire space, offering a stunning view of Central Park.
But Leo's thoughtfulness didn't stop there. When he found out I love plants, he bought me a temperature-regulated greenhouse... a greenhouse! He placed it outside on the wrap-around balcony. I've always loved plants, and now I have my little oasis high above the bustling city.
It felt like a dream, and I couldn't believe I lived in such a magnificent place. Leo's gestures always overwhelmed me, and I couldn't help but feel incredibly grateful for everything he did for me.
The loft was undeniably stunning, but amidst its beauty, there were moments when my emotions threatened to overwhelm me. There were times when sickness and grief clouded my mind, making it challenging to appreciate the luxury and comfort around me fully.
When I pushed aside my sorrowful thoughts on the good days, I could see the loft for what it was – a sanctuary, a haven where Leo's love and care embraced me, even during the darkest times. But on those frequent occasions, my mind would drift back to Francine, and the pain of losing her would wash over me like a tidal wave.

In those moments, the loft's grandeur would fade into the background, and I would feel a deep ache in my heart. I longed for the times when I could fully enjoy the space, bask in its elegance, and embrace the life Leo had so generously crafted for us.

Despite my moments of guilt for pushing them away, most of the time, I couldn't bring myself to feel sorry. There were days when my emotions ran wild, and I lashed out, shutting them out as if I wanted to build walls around myself. Yet, they remained steadfast, refusing to abandon me. I couldn't help but wonder why they were still here and hadn't given up on me yet.

I went to the kitchen and joined the men, settling beside Sonny on the island. The plate of chocolate-covered bacon was right in front of me, but the smell of bacon was starting to make my stomach churn. I had to summon all my strength to keep myself from throwing up right then and there.

Sonny noticed my discomfort and put a concerned hand on my back. "Are you okay, Princess?" he asked, his worry etched on his face.

I tried to give him a reassuring smile, but it felt forced. "Yeah, just not feeling too great," I replied, my voice barely above a whisper.

Dom, who was sitting on the other side of the island, leaned over and peered at me with concern. "You want some water?" he offered, reaching for a glass.

I shook my head, my stomach churning even more. "No, thanks," I said, my hand instinctively moving to my belly.

Leo, standing by the stove, turned to look at me. "Maybe you should lie down for a bit," he suggested, his eyes filled with concern.

"No, I am seeing my mom today. I'll be fine," I said as I got up from the island, trying to hide the discomfort in my voice.

"You sure, Princess? We can go with you," Sonny offered.

I shook my head, not wanting to burden them further. "No, it's okay. I need to do this alone," I replied, trying to sound more confident than I felt.

Leo, ever the understanding one, nodded in agreement. "Alright, just take it easy. We'll be here when you get back," he said, giving me a reassuring smile.

I managed to smile a little, feeling grateful for their support. "Thanks, guys," I said softly.

As I walked towards the door, I felt their eyes on me, their concern palpable. I knew they were worried about me, but I needed this time alone to sort through my emotions and find some semblance of peace.

CHAPTER 35

BRITTNEY

Driving has always been a source of comfort for me. There's a certain freedom in hitting the open road, the wind rushing through the windows, and the world passing by. On my way to my mom's place, I decided to call the doctor's office. To my relief, they managed to fit me in for an appointment. I was eager to get some answers and hopefully find a way to feel better.

Arriving at the doctor's office, I couldn't help but feel nervous. I wanted to understand why I'd been feeling this way lately and maybe, just maybe, find a solution. The receptionist was kind, and after checking me in, I sat in the waiting room.

"Brittney, is that you?" I heard, looking up from the magazine I was reading. It was Dr. Simpson, our family doctor for years. Even after moving to NY after college, I still made the trip back here for my annual appointments because she's the best.

"Dr. Simpson, how are you?" I said, rising to my feet and giving her a warm hug.

"It's been what, five years now?" she remarked.

"Yeah, just about."

"Come, I have a few minutes. Let's go to my office."

Fuck, I don't feel like small talk, but I can't say no to her. I was silently praying she didn't ask any personal questions.

"Sit, sit," Dr. Simpson said, gesturing towards the chair in front of her desk as we walked into her office.

I sat, trying my best to hide my discomfort with the unsettling decorations in her office. The pictures on the wall and the pregnant sculpture on her desk constantly reminded me of things I'd instead not think about.

"Coffee? Tea? Water?" She offered.

"No thanks, I'm fine," I replied, not wanting anything to prolong the visit.

"So tell me, what have you been up to?" she asked while pouring some coffee.

"Nothing much," I replied, keeping my answers vague. I didn't want to burden her with my struggles. Dr. Simpson was my family practitioner, not a therapist, and I preferred to keep it that way.

She leaned back in her chair, sipping her coffee. "You know, Brandon started his practice a few months ago in Norwalk," she said, attempting to make casual conversation.

Here we go again, I thought to myself. Dr. Simpson had been trying to set me up with her son Brandon for years, and she never missed an opportunity to mention him.

"Look," she said, turning a picture around so I could view it. Of course, it was her and Brandon; they looked like they were on vacation.

"That's nice," I replied with a forced smile, not wanting to engage in the topic.

"He's such a catch, you know," she continued, oblivious to my lack of interest.

I nodded politely, not wanting to offend her. But inside, I was growing increasingly annoyed with the constant matchmaking attempts.

A knock at the door saved my sanity when the receptionist peeked her head in, "Sorry to interrupt, but Dr. Simpson, your next patient is here." she said... .Thank fuck.

"Great," she responded smiling, "Oh, and please show Ms. Wright to exam room 5." She then shifted her gaze to me, "I'll be in to see you in a few minutes."

I quickly nodded, relieved to have a way out of the awkward conversation. "Sure, that sounds good," I replied, trying my best to hide my true feelings.

The receptionist led me to the exam room, and I took a deep breath as I entered the small, sterile space. The familiar scent of disinfectant filled the air, triggering memories of past visits to the doctor's office.

As I sat on the examination table, I tried to push aside the thoughts of my recent loss and focus on the reason for my visit. I needed to address my health concerns, and seeing Dr. Simpson was the right decision.

A few minutes later, Dr. Simpson entered the room with a warm smile. "Sorry about the interruption earlier," she said apologetically. "Now, tell me, what can I help you with today?"

I took a moment to gather my thoughts before speaking. "Well, lately, I've been feeling more emotional than usual," I admitted. "And I've been experiencing some physical symptoms as well, like nausea and dizziness."

Dr. Simpson listened attentively as I described my symptoms. She asked follow-up questions and conducted a thorough examination. It felt good to have someone genuinely concerned about my well-being.

"I'll order some tests to see the cause," she said, typing a million miles a minute on her computer. "I'll be back in a few," she said as she left the room.

Sitting in the exam room, my anxiety mounted with each passing moment. The nurse had drawn what felt like gallons of blood, and I couldn't help but feel lightheaded and queasy. The urine samples didn't make the experience any better. I tried to distract myself by focusing on the bland, white walls, but my mind drifted back to all the "what ifs."

Finally, the nurse finished and assured me the doctor would review the results soon. I thanked her and was left alone again, waiting for the verdict. My mind was a whirlwind of worries and uncertainties. I couldn't shake the feeling that something was wrong, that my body had been affected by the emotional toll of recent events.

Time ticked by slowly, and I tried to stay composed, but the fear of bad news weighed heavily on me. I took deep breaths, trying to calm my racing heart. I kept reminding myself that I had to be strong for myself and my mother.

After what felt like an eternity, Dr. Simpson finally returned with the test results. I held my breath, waiting for her to speak.

"We will not have the blood results back until tomorrow, so when they arrive, I will call you. I doubt there will be no reason to drive back here for them."

"Great, thanks." Because I don't know what lie I would tell the guys if I needed to return to Connecticut tomorrow.

"But in the meantime, we have your urine test results."

The way she said that made me uneasy as if something was terribly wrong.

"You're pregnant, Brittney."

My heart skipped a beat, and the world seemed to stand still momentarily. Pregnant? The word echoed in my mind, and I couldn't believe what I heard. The shock was overwhelming, and I struggled to process the information.

Pregnant? How was that even possible? With everything that had happened, the last thing I expected was this. Panic set in, and a million thoughts raced through my mind.

I stammered, trying to find the right words to respond, but my voice failed me. Dr. Simpson looked at me with concern and understanding, giving me a moment to absorb the news.

"It's okay, Brittney. Take your time. This can be a lot to process," she said gently, offering me a reassuring smile.

Finally finding my voice, I managed to speak, "But... I can't be pregnant. With everything going on, how is this even possible?" Maybe getting fucked almost daily by three men without a condom helped. I tried my best to have them come anywhere but inside me during my ovulation days, but I guess my calculations were way off. I even tried not to have sex with them during those days, but one look at Dominic coming out of the shower with just a towel covering him, dripping wet, tossed that idea out the window fast.

Dr. Simpson nodded understandingly. "I know it's a lot to take in, but sometimes unexpected things happen. Stress and emotions can sometimes impact our bodies in ways we don't anticipate."

I felt tears welling up in my eyes as the reality of the situation sank in. How could I handle being pregnant when I could barely handle my own emotions? How could I be responsible for another life when I was struggling to keep myself together?

Dr. Simpson continued, "It's essential to remember that you're not alone, Brittney. I'm here to support you; resources are available to help you. It's okay to feel overwhelmed, but we'll work through it together. There are also other options if you are not ready to be a mother."

Taking a deep breath, I wiped away the tears and nodded. "Thank you, Dr. Simpson. I... I need some time to think."

"Of course, take all the time you need. And remember, if you have any questions or need someone to talk to, I'm here for you."

As I rose from the examination table, I couldn't shake the feeling of nervousness and uncertainty that washed over me. I needed to get out of there, away from the doctor's office, away from the news that turned my life upside down.

Dr. Simpson looked at me with a gentle smile.

"We'll contact you as soon as we have the blood test results. Take care of yourself."

"Thank you," I replied, my voice shaky.

CHAPTER 36

BRITTNEY

The drive to my mom's house was a fog of mixed emotions and thoughts swirling inside my head. Dr. Simpson's words echoed relentlessly, "You're pregnant, Brittney." The news hit me like a tidal wave, drowning me in a sea of uncertainty. How could this be happening? How will the guys react when I tell them? Which one of them is the father? Will they be happy or overwhelmed? Should I even tell them at all?

I grappled with the weight of the news, torn between the desire to share everything with the men who had become my family and the fear of burdening them with another challenge. As I parked the car in my mother's driveway, my hands trembled, and my heart pounded.

I took a deep breath and tried to clear my mind before stepping out of the car. Seeing my mother would provide some comfort, but I knew I couldn't avoid the inevitable conversation with the men for long. The truth would come out, and I needed to find the strength to face it, no matter how difficult it may be.

Startled by the knock on the window, I turned to see my mother's concerned face peering in. "Brittney, are you okay, honey?" I blinked a few times, realizing I was sitting in her driveway.

Taking a deep breath, I tried to muster a smile. "Yeah, Mom, just lost in my thoughts."

I opened the car door and stepped out of the car, and she gave me a big hug. At that moment, I felt like a little girl again, seeking solace and comfort in my mother's warm embrace. Her hug enveloped me with reassurance, love, and protection. It was exactly what I needed: a reminder that she would always be there no matter what life threw at me.

Reluctantly, she started to pull away, but I wasn't ready to let go. I tightened my grip, clinging to the safety and familiarity of her arms around me. To my relief, she understood my unspoken plea and reconnected her arms around me. We held each other tightly, not caring about the passing time or the world outside, finding comfort in being together.
When I finally decided to loosen my hold, she let go too, but her warm smile remained.

"Oh baby," my mother said softly, her eyes filled with concern and love. Her comforting words were all she needed to say, and I couldn't hold back the flood of tears any longer. All the pain, confusion, and anger poured out in heavy sobs.

"It'll be okay," she reassured me, gently wiping my tears. But would it be alright? I wondered if that was just something people said under challenging situations. What else could she say to make me feel better?

"Come on, let's go inside," she said, wrapping her arms around me tightly. With her comforting touch, we made our way into the house.

Inside, she guided me to the living room, where we settled on the couch. She wrapped a soft blanket around my shoulders, just like she used to when I was a child. It was a small gesture, but it brought a sense of comfort that I desperately needed.

Max had always been the chipper and intelligent companion I knew, but today, even he seemed affected by my emotions. It was as if he could sense my pain and was hurting too. I often marveled at his intelligence, and I couldn't help but think that he was the Einstein of German Shepherds.

As I sat on the couch, lost in my thoughts, Max came over and sat next to my feet, gazing up at me with his concerned eyes. It was like he was trying to understand my pain and offer comfort in his canine way. I smiled at him, "I'm okay, buddy, I promise," I said softly, rubbing his ears gently. I knew it was more for my reassurance than his, but having him by my side brought me joy.

"I'll make us some tea," Mom said.

As she disappeared into the kitchen, I couldn't help but chuckle. Tea was her remedy for everything. Headache? Tea. Stomach ache? Tea. Can't sleep? Tea. Can't concentrate? Tea. Want to lose weight? Tea. Want to gain weight? Tea. It seemed like she had a magical tea potion for every ailment or situation imaginable.

I playfully thought to myself, "I wonder if she has tea for being sad and depressed on the verge of suicide?" Of course, it was a dark and absurd thought, and I quickly shook it off. But at that moment, I realized just how much my mother's love for tea had become a running joke.

As my mother left to make tea, I was drawn to Max's comforting presence. I plopped myself down on the carpet next to him, and he immediately responded by resting his head on my lap. It was as if he could sense my distress and offered his silent support.

Stroking his fur, I looked into his deep, understanding eyes and felt a connection that was hard to put into words. He had been with me through so much, and now, in my moment of turmoil, he was here again, a constant source of comfort and companionship.

I couldn't shake the strange feeling that Max knew what was happening inside me. It was as if he could sense something growing in my belly, even before I was fully aware. I brushed the thought aside for the moment, not ready to confront the possibility of what it could mean.

"This is a secret between us," I whispered to Max, looking into his deep, understanding eyes. I decided to keep the news of my pregnancy a secret until I fully understood what was going on or at least got a feel for the men to know if they wanted a baby or not. Leo mentioned that he had wanted one before, but that was in the heat of the moment; he wasn't thinking straight, and people did change.

Max responded with a gentle nudge of his nose against my hand as if reassuring me that he was there for me, no matter what secrets I carried.

My mom returned to the room a few minutes later, carrying a tray with tea and snacks. I was about to head to the dining table, as we always did, but she stopped me with a surprising invitation, "Sit down. We'll have tea in the living room."

I couldn't believe my ears. We never ate or drank anything in the living room. My mom was quite strict about using the dining table for all our meals, with no exceptions. Something must be up for her to change the rules like this.

"Mom, are you okay?" I asked, feeling both shocked and curious.

She chuckled and reassured me, "Yes, I'm perfectly fine. Just thought we could use a change today. Sit down and enjoy the tea."

Still unsure about her sudden change, I sat back on the couch. As she poured the tea, the room was filled with the delightful aroma of oranges. As I took a sip, I could already feel a sense of relaxation washing over me. She was correct; tea and quality time together made a significant difference.

"You know you can talk to me about anything," she gently reminded me.

"I know," I replied, grateful for her understanding and support.

"Good," she said with a warm smile, getting up from her seat and joining me on the floor.

Sitting next to her, I felt safe. There was no need for words; her presence alone was enough. She picked up the remote and asked,
"So, what movie are we watching?"
She knew that I didn't like to be pushed and that sometimes all I needed was her comforting presence.

"Home Alone," I replied. I loved holiday movies, and Home Alone was one of my favorites. Even though it was only October, there was nothing wrong with indulging in a bit of holiday cheer.

"Home Alone it is," she said, starting the movie, and we both settled in to enjoy the rest of the afternoon together.

Over the next few hours, we laughed and joked about how stupid Harry and Marv were, falling for all of Kevin's clever tricks. Once you watch "Home Alone 1," you must watch 2 as well; it's practically a holiday law. But during the second movie, exhaustion caught up with me, and I drifted off to sleep.

As the movie played in the background, I entered a realm of dreams filled with memories of Francine, laughter, and shared secrets. However, my peaceful slumber was short-lived. Max's gentle nudging and whimpering roused me from my dreams.

"Shit, what time is it?" I whispered to myself. Gently sliding my phone from my pocket, I checked the time. It was much later than I had anticipated. Several missed calls and messages from the guys.

I slowly got up and headed to the kitchen to call Leo. My heart was heavy, burdened by my emotions and the knowledge of the secret I was carrying.

"Where are you? Are you okay?" Leo's voice sounded concerned as soon as he picked up the phone.

"I'm fine. I fell asleep watching a movie with Mom," I replied.

"I can come get you," he offered, his concern evident in every word.

"No," I quickly interjected, "it's late, and I think I'm going to stay here tonight."

There was a pause on the other end of the line, and I thought he might have hung up. "Cupcake, are you sure you're okay?" Leo asked, his tone softer, filled with genuine care and worry.
"Yes, I'm fine. I'm just enjoying being home," I replied, trying to reassure both him and myself.

"Okay, call me in the morning," he pleaded. I felt a pang of guilt in my heart; all three had been by my side through thick and thin. Even when I was a bitch towards them, they showed me nothing but love and support. Now, as I grappled with my inner demons, I felt like I was pushing them away, but I couldn't seem to stop myself.

"I will," I said, barely above a whisper, "Good night."

"Good night, Baby".

Hanging up the phone, I sighed and leaned against the kitchen counter. Guilt gnawed at me, knowing I was keeping secrets from the very people who cared about me the most. Yet, I wasn't ready to share my burden, not until I fully understood what was happening within me.

I haven't told my mother about them. She saw them once at the funeral, and even though I knew she wanted to ask me about them, she didn't.

Walking back into the living room, my mom wasn't there. "Mom," I called.

"I'm up here, sweetie," she replied. As I made my way up the stairs, I heard rustling in my old room. As I walked in, she was making the bed.

"What are you doing, Mom?"

"It is past 11, and you're exhausted. Do you think I will let you drive back to New York?"

Smiling, I said, "I can do that, Mom."

"I know you can, but I want to do it for you," she said warmly.

"Thanks, Mom," I said, giving her a sideways hug.

"You're welcome," she responded, "now go take a bath."

I walked into the bathroom and noticed the bathtub was filled with water, and there was a book on the side of it. I couldn't help but smile; my mom knew just how to make me feel better.

I took a long bath, lost in the world of the book my mom had left for me to read. It was a story of love, hope, and resilience, which seemed to resonate with my current emotions. When I finally emerged from the bathroom, feeling more relaxed than I had in weeks, I found a plate with a sandwich on it and a glass of warm milk with a note:

"I know you're hungry."

She knows me well. I sat on the edge of the bed, wearing one of my mom's comfortable pajamas, and enjoyed my sandwich. The heaviness in my heart seemed to lift, and for once in a long time, I went to bed feeling genuinely content.

As I snuggled under the covers, I couldn't help but feel grateful for my mother's love and care. Her presence and support were exactly what I needed at that moment, and I knew that no matter what secrets I was carrying, she would always be there for me.

Sleep took hold of me instantly, and my dreams were peaceful for the first time in a while. In the embrace of slumber, I found some solace and relief, knowing I had someone to lean on in this difficult time.

With my mother's love surrounding me, I finally drifted off to sleep, hoping that tomorrow would bring clarity and a way to navigate the complexities of my emotions and the secrets I held within.

CHAPTER 37

BRITTNEY

The following day, I called Leo as soon as I got up, determined to make today a good day. I felt wonderful, even though I knew there might be ups and downs. Right now, I want to ride this high.

"Good morning," I said, my voice sounding unusually cheerful.

"Well, you sound happy this morning, Cupcake," Leo remarked.

I truly was, and it was refreshing. "Yeah, I think it was the tea my mom gave me yesterday."

"What's the name of the tea? I'll buy you a truck full."

I laughed, genuinely amused. "I think it's her secret blend, but I do know it has oranges."

"That helps," he replied sarcastically. "What time are you leaving there?"

"After breakfast. What, you miss me already?" I teased.

"You have no idea."

"I should be back around noon, okay?"

"Drive safe."

"I will," I assured him. "I love you Leo."

"I love you too Cupcake."

I changed and went downstairs. The smell of coffee and bacon filled the air, and my stomach churned uncomfortably. Oh no, not again. I tried to hold it together, but thank heavens, I managed to reach the bathroom on time.

After cleaning up, I carefully headed downstairs again. This time, I had my hand on my nose, hoping to block out the overwhelming scent of bacon. I was grateful to see my mother preparing the outdoor table. At least the bacon smell wouldn't be as potent out there.

As a child, autumn held a special magic for me. I'd sit beneath the changing leaves in the backyard, feeling the air turn crisp and cool. It was a simple joy, watching nature's transformation unfold, each leaf a vibrant brushstroke in the fall masterpiece. The colors danced before my eyes, filling me with wonder and contentment. I felt truly alive in those moments, surrounded by the season's beauty.

We sat down to eat, though it was more of a struggle for me than I had anticipated. While she indulged in her meal, my stomach churned uncomfortably, threatening to betray my unease. I forced myself to maintain composure, concealing my discomfort as best I could. I discreetly passed the bacon from my plate to Max's eager mouth when she wasn't looking, relieved to rid myself of the source of my discomfort. Fortunately, I found solace in the simplicity of tea and toast, managing to consume them without much trouble,

A few hours later, I walked into the apartment I shared with the guys, but no one was there. Disappointment filled me because I wanted to see them. I knew they were probably busy, but I couldn't help feeling lonely.

Grabbing my phone, I called Leo. "Where are you?" I asked, trying to sound like him jokingly.

"We had some business to take care of," he replied.

"That sucks."

"Why? Are you okay?" he inquired with concern.

"Yes, I'm fine," I said, rolling my eyes playfully. "I just wanted you to make love to me. That's all," I said teasingly.

He was quiet for a few seconds, and I could sense a mix of surprise and excitement in his voice. "Fuck," he finally said, his tone deepening. "Are you serious, baby?" he asked, his voice now more husky.

A sly smile crept on my face as I played along, "Yes, I am serious. I want you, Leo."

'We're done here,' I heard him say to someone on his end. "I'll be home in 10 minutes," he said, his voice becoming more intense and seductive. Then he hung up.

My heart raced with anticipation as I knew what was about to happen. We hadn't been intimate since we came back from California, and today, I felt amazing and wanted to be with him, to feel close to him.

I went into his bathroom and ran myself a bath. His bathtub is enormous compared to my mother's; you can fit at least five people in here. Carefully lowering myself into the hot water, I felt my bones relax, and I let out a soft moan, thoroughly enjoying the feeling.

A few minutes later, the door swung open, and there stood Leo. As usual, he was wearing his three-piece suit; this one was blue with a white shirt, and he looked absolutely irresistible.

"You look relaxed," he said, taking off his coat.

"I am," I replied, laying back in the tub and closing my eyes.

"Good girl," he murmured, the endearment causing a tingle down my spine.

When I looked up again, he was only in his boxers, and my heart skipped a beat. I couldn't help but smile, "Coming in?" I asked, my eyes playfully inviting him to join me.

Leo's eyes darkened with desire as he stepped out of his boxers and slowly climbed into the bath behind me. His strong arms encircled my waist, pulling me closer to him until my back was pressed against his chest. The sensation of his warm, naked body against mine sent shivers of pleasure down my spine.

I sighed contentedly, feeling safe and loved in his embrace. He gently started massaging my shoulders and neck, skillfully relieving the tension. His tender and sensual touch, and I melted into his hands.

"You always know how to make me feel better," I whispered, slightly turning to look at him.

"I'll always take care of you, Cupcake."
His hand felt amazing on me; he was gentle, pulling my nipple softly. The sensation was electrifying, and I found myself arching my back, craving more of his touch. The pregnancy hormones must intensify every sensation, making me respond to his caresses in ways I never imagined.

Leo's fingers danced across my skin, carefully exploring every curve and contour. I felt a mixture of vulnerability and desire as he continued to tease and please me. Each stroke of his hand sent waves of pleasure through my body, building up an intense heat between my legs.
His lips found mine, and we kissed passionately, our bodies pressed tightly in the warm water. I could feel his desire for me, and it only fueled my arousal.

As his hand ventured lower once more, I stopped him again, this time guiding his hand back to my breasts. "Please," I whispered, my voice filled with need and longing.

Leo's eyes darkened with desire as he focused his attention on my breasts again. His touch was masterful, his fingers sending shivers down my spine. It felt incredible, and I couldn't believe how sensitive I had become.

Lost in the pleasure he was giving me, I arched my back, pushing my breasts further into his hands. The sensations were overwhelming, and I could feel myself inching closer and closer to the edge. Leo had to hold me still with his other arm because I was squirming about, thrashing water everywhere.

When I finally reached my climax, it hit me like a tidal wave. My entire body trembled with ecstasy, and I let out a soft moan of pleasure. Leo's eyes were locked on mine, and he looked pleased with himself. He gently held me close, his other hand still resting on my breast.

"Baby, did you just ... ."

"Maybe," I managed to say, cutting him off.

"Fuck, Brittney," he said, his voice filled with arousal. He rarely used my actual name, always opting for pet names. "You're so responsive."

My anxiety got the best of me, and I was hoping Leo didn't realize why I was so sensitive. But as he turned me around and kissed me, my nervousness washed away. His lips were soft and gentle against mine, and I could feel the warmth of his body pressed against mine. I melted into his embrace, savoring the feeling of being desired and wanted.

He took his time kissing me like he didn't want this moment to end, and I felt the same way. His hands explored my body, caressing and teasing me in all the right places. I couldn't help but let out a soft moan as his lips traveled down my neck, igniting a fire within me again.

He positioned himself between my legs, and with a swift, smooth motion, he entered me. A gasp escaped my lips as he filled me, and I clung to him tightly, my nails digging into his back. He began to move, setting a steady rhythm that sent me spiraling toward ecstasy.

"Cupcake, you feel fucking amazing," he said.

Each thrust was like a jolt of pleasure, and I couldn't control the moans that escaped my lips. Leo's movements were skilled and deliberate, and it was clear that he knew exactly how to please me. I surrendered myself entirely to him, lost in the sensations he was stirring.

"You look beautiful riding my dick."

As the water splashed and spilled onto the bathroom floor, Leo and I were too lost in each other to worry about the mess. His passion and desire overwhelmed us, and nothing else seemed to matter. The intensity of our connection was electrifying, making it hard to focus on anything else.

When I opened my eyes to steal a glance at this sexy man, I noticed he was staring at my breasts intently as they bounced in front of his face. A pang of nervousness crept in again, wondering if he saw any changes.

"What's wrong?" I asked, trying to hide my anxiety.

"Your boobs," he said, his breathing heavy with desire. "They look bigger."

Shit, he knows. What should I do? What should I say?

"Fuck," he added with a seductive smile, lunging for my breasts again. This time, he bit and sucked hard while continuing to fuck me with passion and intensity.

A few minutes later, I was overcome with pleasure, and my screams echoed in the bathroom as I tilted my head back, giving him a full view of our intimate connection.

Leo's fervor intensified, and he groaned, releasing himself inside me. We both rode out our climax, the waves of pleasure seeming never-ending.

He smiled and gently kissed me when we finally came down from our high. "You're spending the night with me," he said, holding me close.

The rest of the evening went smoothly. After Leo took his time washing me, he got a call and had to leave for a few hours with Sonny. So, after getting dressed, I went looking for Dom.

As I walked into Dom's room, I found him engrossed in something on his computer. I decided to surprise him and walked up to him silently, wrapping my arms around his neck from behind and kissing his cheek softly. He turned his head slightly and grinned, clearly pleased with the unexpected affection.

"What was that for?" he asked, a playful glint in his eyes.

"I just wanted to kiss you."

Dom pulled me closer with a playful grin and said, "Well, you can kiss me as much as you want, baby girl. My heart beats for you alone."

It seemed like just yesterday I was hesitant about being intimate with them, but now everything had changed.

I wanted them more than ever, and the desire was overwhelming. I leaned in closer, my lips grazing his ear as I whispered, "You have all of me, Dominic."

As I started to leave, he grabbed my hand and pulled me onto his lap, not letting me go so quickly. "Is that all I get?" he asked, his hands holding onto my waist.

I leaned close, my lips just inches from his ear, and whispered, "What do you want?"

His breath hitched, and I could feel the heat radiating from his body. "You," he murmured, his lips kissing mine passionately.

At that moment, I forgot about all the pain and worries that had been consuming me. Being with my men made me feel alive and desired, and for a brief moment, I allowed myself to get lost in his touch and forget about everything else.

My heart was pounding in my chest as I got down on my knees in front of him. His eyes darkened with desire as he watched me, knowing exactly what was on my mind. His intense gaze sent shivers down my spine, but I couldn't look away. I was drawn to him like a magnet, captivated by his presence and his exuded power.

I reached for his belt buckle and slowly undid it, feeling the moment's weight. I wanted to please him, to make him feel as good as he makes me feel. As I unzipped his pants, I could already see the bulge growing, and a surge of excitement washed over me.

"Are you sure about this, baby girl?" Dom's voice was husky, his eyes never leaving mine.

"Yes," I whispered, my voice barely audible, but he heard me clearly.

He lifted his hips, allowing me to slide his pants and boxers down. His hard length sprang free, and I licked my lips in anticipation. My hands wrapped around him, feeling his warmth and hardness in my grasp. I looked up at him, seeking approval.

"It's all yours baby."

I leaned in and kissed the tip of his shaft, earning a sharp intake of breath from Dom. Encouraged by his reaction, I took him into my mouth, sucking gently at first, then increasing my pace. As he guided me, his fingers entwined in my hair, setting the rhythm that drove him wild.

His groans filled the room, and I felt a sense of pride, knowing that I was the one pleasing him. My arousal grew with each passing second, but I focused on him, losing myself in the act of pleasuring him.

"Fuck, you're so good," Dom groaned, his hips moving in sync with my mouth. "Just like that, baby girl."

I picked up the pace, my movements becoming more urgent and desperate. I could feel him at the back of my throat; his impressive length and girth had me fighting back tears and trying not to choke, but I wanted to taste him, to feel him release in my mouth, and I knew he was close. His grip on my hair tightened, but it only spurred me on.

As I continued, I felt his body tense, and I knew he was on the brink of orgasm. "Baby, I'm... ."

With one final, deep groan, he released, and I eagerly swallowed, savoring the taste of him.

Afterward, Dom pulled me up into his arms, his eyes filled with tenderness and desire. "You're incredible," he whispered, kissing my lips softly.

"Dom," I said looking in his eyes, "fuck me."

Something in him shifted; he lifted me off my feet, threw me on his bed, and ripped off my dress.

His clothes were off him in the blink of an eye. My body surrendered to Dom's powerful desire. It was an intense and raw experience, but it felt like exactly what I needed. I moaned and gasped as he aligned himself by my entrance and thrust inside me with a primal intensity, his grunts mingling with my cries of pleasure.

"Is this what you want?" he asked, seeking affirmation, but I could not form words. I could only nod and let the overwhelming sensations consume me.

"Answer me, baby girl," he said with a deep voice.

"Yes, Yes," I screamed.

He smirked fucking me harder, lifting me slightly to reach my G-spot.

The next few hours were a blur of passion, desire, and connection. Dom explored every inch of my body, taking me to heights of pleasure I had never known before. He unleashed a side of himself that I had only glimpsed before, a side that was hungry for me, possessive and wild.

He left marks on my skin, both from his teeth and his insistent hands, marking me as his own. Each touch was electrifying, igniting a fire deep within me. He took me in ways that were both tender and demanding, and I surrendered to him completely, trusting him with my heart and body.

As he took me in my ass, I felt a mix of pain and pleasure, but it only served to intensify the connection between us. There was a sense of liberation in embracing our desire's rawness, letting go of any inhibitions, and just living in the moment.

Afterward, as we lay tangled in each other's arms, our bodies glistening with sweat, I felt an overwhelming sense of contentment and peace. The pain and sorrow that had weighed on me for months had been temporarily forgotten, replaced by a profound feeling of aliveness.

"Thank you," I whispered, my voice filled with emotion.

He kissed my forehead gently, his touch now tender and loving. "No, thank you," he said softly. "For trusting me, for letting me in, for allowing us to share this moment. You're the missing piece I never knew I needed, completing me in ways I never thought possible."

His words washed over me like a gentle tide, washing away any doubts or fears and leaving behind a sense of being loved unconditionally.

We stayed wrapped in each other's embrace, cherishing our shared intimacy and vulnerability. At that moment, it felt like we had transcended the physical act of sex and had connected on a deeper level, soul to soul.

My body tingled with the lingering sensation of pleasure as I sat in the kitchen, watching Dom prepare pasta. He looked incredibly sexy in his black boxers and an apron, and I couldn't help but feel a rush of desire for him again.
Before we could even start eating, Dom's intense gaze locked onto mine, and without a word, he pulled me back onto the kitchen island. His touch was possessive yet tender as he explored every inch of my body as if trying to imprint me with his love.

The contrast between the rough, intense sex we had just shared and this more gentle and intimate moment left me feeling emotionally charged. His fingers traced delicate patterns over my skin, and I closed my eyes, savoring the feel of him.

"Dom," I whispered, barely able to form words.

He silenced me with a passionate kiss, his lips demanding and hungry. My hands found their way to his chest, tracing the contours of his well-defined muscles. He growled in response, sending shivers down my spine.

The pasta was long forgotten as we lost ourselves in each other once again. Dom's hands were possessive yet gentle, and his touch ignited a fire within me. It was like rediscovering each other, exploring uncharted territories of pleasure and connection.

He lifted me effortlessly, and I wrapped my legs around his waist, pulling him closer. The kitchen island became our sanctuary, where time seemed to stand still, and the outside world ceased to exist.

Our lovemaking was a dance of desire, passion, and love. It was wild and tender, rough and gentle, all at once. The emotional connection between us heightened the pleasure, and I knew then that this was what I had been craving— this raw, unfiltered intimacy with the man I loved.

As we reached the pinnacle of ecstasy, we clung to each other, breathing heavily, hearts pounding in sync. Our bodies glistened with sweat, and I buried my face in the crook of his neck, inhaling his scent.

"I love you," he whispered, his voice filled with emotion.

"I love you too," I replied, my heart overflowing with love and gratitude.

We stayed wrapped in each other's arms, basking in the afterglow of our passion. I knew I had found my sanctuary and safe haven in Dom's love. No matter what challenges lay ahead, I had the strength and love to face them, hand in hand with the men who held my heart.

CHAPTER 38

BRITTNEY

The darkness was absolute, a suffocating blanket that hid even my hand before my face. Then, without warning, a scream shattered the silence, and lights blazed to life. The sudden brightness forced me to squint, my eyes struggling to adjust. As my vision cleared, a macabre scene unfolded before me.

Blood was everywhere – a crimson tide splashed across the walls, pooling on the floor and horrifyingly staining my clothes. Panic clawed at my throat, urging me to scream, to flee, but my body refused to obey. I inched backward, my movements hesitant, until a sudden obstruction made me tumble. My heart froze as I turned to see what I had tripped over.
Lying there, lifeless and pale, was a woman with hair like spun gold.
Francine.
Her eyes stared blankly at the ceiling, a dark bullet wound marring her forehead. Tears blurred my vision as I choked out her name, my voice a broken whisper. I reached for her, but her skin was icy, a chilling contrast to the warmth that once radiated from her. My body began to shiver uncontrollably, a cold dread seeping into my bones.
  "No, no, no," I murmured, cradling her lifeless form.
  "It should have been me," I whispered, a torrent of guilt and sorrow washing over me.
  "Francine, please," I begged, my voice rising in desperation. "Get up, wake up!"
But then, reality shifted. I was jolted awake, sitting upright in my bed, drenched in sweat and gasping for air. It was all a dream, a vivid nightmare that left me trembling. Beside me, Leo slept on, blissfully unaware of the turmoil that had gripped me.
  I slipped out of bed, seeking comfort in the quiet of the kitchen. As I poured myself a glass of water, the first light of dawn began to chase away the remnants of night. Yet, the echo of my dream lingered, haunting me.
  "It should have been me," I whispered into the silence, the weight of those words heavy in the air.
A haunting whisper echoed, "It should be me." The thought was a relentless echo, a reminder of my irreversible choice. If I hadn't met Francine for that fateful lunch, she would still be laughing, breathing, living. Leo had brought up the idea of involving her, and even though it gnawed at my conscience, I didn't voice my doubts. Now, her death weighed on me like a millstone, a constant reminder of my silence.

Tears blurred my vision as I stumbled towards the kitchen, my body wracked with sobs. The cold steel of a knife on the counter seemed to call out to me, promising an escape from the unbearable guilt.

"If I end it, I can be with her again," I thought, the blade now pressing against my skin, the pressure breaking through to draw blood. I watched, almost in a trance, as the crimson droplets formed, the pain a distant reality.

But then, a sound in the house's stillness jolted me back to the moment. My gaze snapped towards the noise, then back to the blood now dripping onto the floor. A wave of horror washed over me. "What am I doing?" I whispered, my voice laced with disbelief and fear. The knife clattered to the floor, the sound echoing in the empty room.

Memories of my mother, her gentle smile and unwavering support, flooded my mind. She had already lost so much; I couldn't bear to add to her pain.

And then there was the baby, a new life growing inside me, innocent and unaware. My hand instinctively caressed my stomach, a mix of fear and protectiveness welling up inside me.

I slid down against the wall, the cool tiles of the kitchen floor grounding me as I tried to steady my breathing. My wrist throbbed with each heartbeat, but the physical pain was nothing compared to the turmoil inside me. I was overwhelmed by my selfishness and the sheer stupidity of my actions.

Leo's voice, sharp with panic, broke through my haze. "What the fuck?" He stood there, his eyes wide with shock and fear. In his haste, he rummaged through drawers, finally finding a towel and pressing it against my wrist, his hands firm and steady.

Sonny and Dom appeared their expressions a mix of confusion and concern.

"What happened?" Sonny's voice was strained, filled with worry. Tears streamed down my face, unrestrained and raw. The sound of my crying was guttural, a manifestation of all the pain and guilt I had been carrying. Their stares, filled with concern and disbelief, seemed to pierce through me, making me feel even more exposed and vulnerable.

"I'm sorry," I whispered, my voice barely audible, drenched in regret. I was sorry for the chaos I had unleashed, for the pain I had inflicted on myself and those I cared about. At that moment, the depth of my despair was palpable, a desperate cry for redemption and healing.

Leo's eyes, filled with concern and disbelief, never left my wrist. "What were you thinking, Brittney?" he asked, his voice trembling slightly. Shaking his head, he repeated, "Why, Brittney?"

"It was an accident; I didn't mean to— " My voice broke, unable to complete the thought.

"A fucking accident?" Dom interjected, his voice laced with anger and disbelief. "You accidentally slit your wrist?" His tone rose, a crescendo of frustration and fear.

"WHY?" His voice was now a yell, echoing off the walls. Sonny stepped in, placing a calming hand on his shoulder, but it did little to quell his rage.

"I'm sorry, Dom," I stammered, tears streaming down my face. "All I think about is Francine. She's everywhere. I can't sleep, I can't eat. I just wanted it to stop."

"By killing yourself?" Dom's voice was a roar, his words slicing through the tense air.

I turned to Leo, seeking some semblance of understanding in his eyes, but he couldn't meet my gaze.

Dom stood before me, his presence overwhelming. "I'm sorry," I repeated, my voice a mere whisper.

"All you had to do was talk to us, Brittney," he said, his tone softening. "You could have talked to any one of us. I would have done anything for you, you know that." His words trailed off, laden with a sense of finality.

"You are fucking weak," he spat out, turning his back to me and walking away.

"Dom," I called out, but he didn't respond. "DOM!" My voice broke as he disappeared.

Shaking my head, I wished for a way to turn back time, to undo the irreversible.

"Come on," Leo finally said, his voice gentle yet distant. He helped me up, his hand supporting my waist.

As we passed Sonny, I paused. "Sonny," I said softly, "I'm sorry." His gaze was a turbulent mix of anger, disgust, and something akin to hatred. It was a look that chilled me to the bone, and I had to look away.

I reached out to him, but he pushed my hand away and walked to his room without a word.

Leo led me to his bathroom, where he silently tended to my wrist. The silence between us was heavy, laden with unspoken words and emotions. He carefully cleaned and bandaged the wound, his eyes never meeting mine.

When he was done, he guided me to the bedroom. "Come sit," he said, patting the edge of the bed.

"Have I ever told you how our mother died?" he asked suddenly. I was taken aback; they never spoke of her, so I never asked.

"No," I responded, my curiosity piqued despite the heaviness in my heart.

Leo's voice grew softer, almost distant, as he delved into the memory. "The night before... it was strangely beautiful, in a way. She seemed so happy, almost like her old self again. We even sat down together and played chess, my favorite game. It had been ages since we'd done that. I remember going to bed that night feeling this sense of safety, a warmth I hadn't felt in so long."

He paused, a sad smile flickering across his face. "She came into our room and read us a bedtime story. She used to do it all the time, but she had stopped. That night, she read one of my favorite books, and her voice was so gentle and full of love. My brothers and I were so happy; we didn't question it. We were just kids, basking in the moment, feeling loved and cared for."

His expression turned pensive, a shadow of regret passing over his features. "I was the eldest; I should have seen it... the sudden change. It was like a final burst of light before the darkness. But I didn't see it. I just felt grateful for that moment of peace, of normalcy."

Leo's eyes, now clouded with deep sorrow, fixed on a point in the distance as he continued.

"The next day, the garden, which had always been a place of life and growth, transformed into a scene of profound tragedy. We found her there with her beloved flowers, her wrists cut. It was a harrowing sight, utterly out of sync with the beauty surrounding her. The contrast was jarring, a peaceful setting marred by an act of despair."

He took a deep, steadying breath, his voice thick with emotion. "Seeing you in a similar state, Brittney, wasn't just a shock. It was a reliving of that terrible morning. Every fear, every moment of helplessness we felt as kids came rushing back. It's not just my pain. Dom, he saw it too. He's angry because that memory is a wound that never fully healed. We all dealt with it in our ways, but none of us ever got over it. He was only seven."

Leo's gaze finally met mine, filled with a pain that was both old and freshly awakened. "That's why Dom reacted the way he did. It's not just anger at what you did; it's the fear and the pain of that day reignited. We thought we had lost you, just like we lost her. And for Dom, for all of us, that's a reality too painful to face again."

Leo's words, filled with concern and tenderness, resonated deeply. "Brittney, what you did tonight wasn't just about you. It brought back a flood of painful memories we've all been trying to keep at bay. Our mother's death left scars, deep ones, and what happened tonight... it was like tearing them open all over again."

He squeezed my hand gently, his eyes never leaving mine. "I need you to understand something important. When we decided to stay here, it wasn't out of obligation. It was a choice made out of love and concern for you. We saw that you weren't ready to face everything back in California, and we wanted to be here for you, to support you through this."

His voice softened, "Brittney Elisa Wright, I love you more than words can express. I want to be there for you, to help you heal and find your way through this pain. But I can't do that if you shut me out, if you hide your struggles from me."

I was shocked by his confession, and at that moment, I realized I loved them, too. The depth of my feelings, long buried under layers of fear and uncertainty, suddenly appeared.

"I need you to be honest with me from now on. Do you understand?" Leo's voice pulled me back to the present.

All I could do was nod, tears streaming down my cheeks. They were tears of joy, hate, pain - a tumultuous mix of emotions that I couldn't fully comprehend.

"Is there anything you want to tell me now?" Leo asked, his gaze piercing into me.

He knows. Does he know? He knows.

"I'm... " My heart pounded in my chest. Should I tell him? How will he react?

"I'm... " Perhaps it's best to wait until all the men are gathered in the room.

Sighing, I mustered up my courage. "I do have something to share with you... with all of you."

I placed my hands on Leo's face and kissed him gently, then stood up to find Dom. I finally found him in his office; Sonny was there as well. But before I could tell the guys about my pregnancy, I knew I had to apologize.

"Dom, I am so-"

"Weak," he said, cutting me off. His voice was sharp, a clear indication that he wasn't going to let me off easy. And I didn't want him to.

"Dom," I said, my voice barely above a whisper, feeling the tears burning the back of my eyes, threatening to make another appearance.

"You are so fucking weak, Brittney," he said, standing up from behind his mahogany desk. His presence was imposing, his anger palpable.

"Damn, Dom, calm down," Sonny interjected, still seated on the sofa, placing his drink on the side table.

"I will not calm down, Sonny," Dom retorted, his fiery eyes never leaving mine. "We asked and practically begged you to let us in, but you didn't. You pretended to be fine, you lied to us, you lied to me."

"I know, and I was fine until this morning," I said, tears streaming down my cheeks.

Sighing, Dom asked, "How did Francine's death affect you?"

I already knew where he was taking this. I stayed quiet, not wanting to relive the moment I found her.

 "ANSWER ME," he spat, his voice raised in frustration and desperation.

The only time I had ever seen him so upset was when I went to see Jimmy. "It hurt," I screamed back, "It fucking hurt!"

He shook his head, now walking towards me. "And now you want to kill yourself, huh? Not thinking about us, about your mother? The pain you would cause? What the fuck is wrong with you?"

"Dom, please," I pleaded, shaking. I understood his point, but my turmoil overwhelmed me.

 "Get the fuck out," he said, now standing right in front of me, towering over me.

 "What?" I said, taken aback by the sudden change in his demeanor.

 "Get out of my office, Brittney," he repeated, his voice cold and unyielding. The intensity in his eyes was unrelenting, and I felt a chill run down my spine for a moment.

 Sonny stood up, his expression a mix of shock and concern. "Dom, come on, man. That's harsh. She's going through a lot."

Dom turned to Sonny, his jaw clenched. "And what about what we're going through, huh? She almost did something irreversible, Sonny. She didn't think about us, her family, anyone. I need space. She needs to leave."

I stood there, frozen, the harshness of his words cutting through me. The room felt smaller, the air thicker. I knew I had to leave to give Dom the space he demanded, but my heart felt heavy with unsaid words and unresolved pain.

Leo was in the room, almost unnoticed, until our eyes met. "It's okay, I'll talk to him. Just give us a minute," he said quietly, his voice a soft contrast to the tension that filled the space.

Despite his reassuring words, I felt despair wash over me. I couldn't stay there a moment longer. I needed to walk away, run away.

Turning swiftly, I left the room, my heart pounding with mixed emotions. I moved quickly through the loft; the early morning light began seeping through the windows, casting a soft glow over the luxurious space that now felt so distant from my troubled thoughts.

Choosing the stairs over the elevator, I descended the many flights from our lofty perch. The stairwell was quiet, my footsteps echoing in the empty space as I hurried downwards.

Stepping out into the early morning, the streets were quiet, the city still in the gentle hold of the pre-dawn hours. The air was cool and fresh, starkly contrasting to the oppressive atmosphere I had just escaped.

I turned left, wandering along the streets that bordered Central Park. The park was peaceful in the early morning light, its paths and benches deserted, a tranquil oasis amid the city's grandeur.

I began to walk, each step heavier than the last, as I wrestled with the notion that perhaps the men would be better off without me.

What Happens Next?

Brittney and the brothers' story isn't over……

You've just finished Shattered Secrets, but the next chapter in their journey is just beginning-and its about to get even more intense.

Something isn't right. The apartment is empty, and Brittney is nowhere to be found.

Turn the page for an exclusive sneak peek into **Book Two**, where Dom Sonny and Leo come face to face with their worst nightmare………

She's gone.

Keep reading.

SONNY

"Damn it, Dom! Why the hell did you have to go off on her like that?"

My voice was sharp, laced with frustration, but I didn't give a damn. Brittney had been barely holding on, teetering on the edge ever since Leo told her about our mother. And then Dom—fucking Dom—had pushed her too hard, too fast.

Leo said there had been regret in her eyes. That she'd hesitated. That there had been a moment of clarity before she—

I swallowed hard, the memory of that knife in her hand seared into my brain.

Dom exhaled, dragging a hand over his face. His usual cold control was slipping, and for once, he looked like he knew he'd fucked up. "Yeah, I... I might've gone too far."

"Might have?" I barked, pacing like a caged animal. "You *think*? She was already breaking, and you—" I stopped, pressing my fingers to my temples. "We need to fix this. *Now.*"

"We need to talk to her," I said again, softer this time. I hated the way my voice almost sounded like pleading, but I didn't care.

Leo's jaw was tight, his expression grim. He nodded. "If she'll listen to us now."

Our eyes landed on Dom, who was gripping his glass of McCullen like it might anchor him to reality. His jaw twitched, his knuckles white against the crystal. For a long, tense moment, he just sat there. Then, finally, he exhaled sharply, tilting his head up to meet my gaze. "Yeah, okay. Let's do it."

Without another word, I turned and strode toward Brittney's room. My gut twisted with every step, dread creeping into my bones. She *had* to be in there. She had to let us fix this.

I knocked softly. "Brittney?"

Silence.

I knocked again, firmer this time. "Princess, it's me."

Nothing.

A cold prickle ran down my spine. Something felt *off.*

I hesitated only a second before easing the door open. "Brittney?"

The room was empty.

Panic hit me like a wrecking ball.

I stepped inside, scanning every inch—bed rumpled, lamp slightly askew, but no Brittney. The bathroom door was ajar, empty. The closet—empty. I yanked open drawers, checked under the bed, behind the drapes—anywhere she might've curled up, hiding from us, from *him.*

Nothing.

"Brittney!" My voice came out sharp, urgent, the desperation bleeding through as I turned to Leo and Dom, who were now standing in the doorway. "She's gone."

Leo's face turned to stone. Dom set his glass down so hard it cracked against the wood.

Nothing.

Dom cursed under his breath. "Did you check everywhere?"

"Yes!" I snapped, unable to mask the edge of fear in my voice.

Leo tried to steady himself, pulling out his phone as if that small device could somehow anchor us.

"Maybe she went for a walk," he suggested, though he sounded far from convinced. He dialed her number, pressing the phone to his ear, and then we all heard it: a faint buzz from her room. We followed the sound, my heart sinking further as we found her phone lying abandoned on the bed.

"She left her phone," I murmured, feeling the sharp bite of reality closing in.

Leo's face hardened. He grabbed her purse, shoving in her essentials with tense efficiency. "Sonny, let's go. She can't be far."

Dom stood rooted, his expression stripped of its usual confidence, uncertainty apparent in his eyes. "What should I do?" he asked, voice low, almost a whisper.

"Stay here," I said firmly. "In case she comes back." Without waiting for an answer, I followed Leo out the door, each step laced with urgency and a raw, aching fear. We had to find her. Fast.

Three hours passed, each more torturous than the last. I'd combed through every street, store, and park within a twenty-mile radius, but Brittney was nowhere. My phone buzzed—Leo, calling to confirm what I feared: no sign of her on his end either. And Dom's terse text confirmed she hadn't returned. The dread settled deep, an oppressive weight I couldn't shake.

Back at the loft, Dom paced like a caged animal, his calm exterior completely shattered.

"I shouldn't have spoken to her like that," he muttered, voice thick with regret. He grabbed a vase, staring at it as if it might hold the answers, then hurled it against the wall where it shattered, fragments scattering across the floor like the pieces of our fractured state.

"Dom," I said, forcing calm into my voice, "that's not helping."

He looked at me, eyes wild. "What do you expect me to do? We need to fix this!" His voice cracked, and I saw the fear beneath his anger for the first time.

"We need to think, not break things," Leo said, his tone edged with restraint. "We have to focus on finding her."

Dom raked his hands through his hair. "She wouldn't just disappear. Not without—" He cut himself off, exhaling sharply. "What if something happened to her?"

Leo's gaze hardened. "Then we find out who made it happen."

We slumped onto the couch, the silence heavy and oppressive. Then, Brittney's phone rang from across the room, and Dom lunged for it, nearly tripping in his haste.

"Hello?"

His voice was sharp, edged with desperate hope.

"This is St. Auguste Clinic. May I speak to Brittney?" a woman's voice asked.

"You can speak to me, this is her—" Dom stopped himself, jaw tightening. "I'm a close friend."

"I'm sorry, we can only release this information to the patient directly."

Dom let out a slow, frustrated breath. "Listen, If this is about her health, we need to know."

"I understand, sir, but privacy laws prevent us from—"

"Put it on speaker," Leo cut in. Dom swiped at the screen and the woman's voice filled the room.

"We have important results for her, but we can only disclose them to—"

"Goddamn it," Dom growled, raking a hand through his hair. "Can you at least tell me if it's serious?"

A pause. Then, carefully: "I strongly suggest she contact us as soon as possible."

Dom exhaled sharply, gripping the phone as if he could will an answer out of her. "Thanks for nothing," he muttered before hanging up and tossing the phone onto the couch."Clinic in Connecticut," he muttered, rubbing his temples. "They had blood test results for her."

My mind whirred. Connecticut.

"She was at her mom's a few days ago," I muttered, standing and moving to my laptop. My fingers flew over the keys as I pulled up a list of all St. Auguste clinics near her mother's house, narrowing them down one by one. A few clicks later, I found her records. My heart pounded in my chest as I scanned the file.

I opened my mouth, but no sound came out. My throat closed, the weight of the truth pressing down on me.

Leo moved beside me, eyes narrowing at the screen. His face went pale.

He inhaled sharply. "She's… she's pregnant."

The words crashed through the room like thunder.

Dom went utterly still before grabbing a coffee mug and hurling it at the wall. The shattering sound felt final, like a door slamming shut.

"Goddamn it, Dom, stop throwing things!" Leo snapped, his patience fraying.

Dom's voice broke. "We have to find her. I have to make this right. I have to apologize."

245

Dear Readers,

As you turn the final pages of this book, I hope you've enjoyed the journey as much as I have enjoyed writing it. Your support and enthusiasm have meant the world to me, and I am incredibly grateful for each and every one of you who has picked up this book and embarked on this adventure.

While this story may be coming to a close, I'm thrilled to announce that the journey is far from over. The second book in this series is already in the works, and I can't wait to share it with you. Stay tuned for more updates and be sure to keep an eye out for its release!

Once again, thank you from the bottom of my heart for your support. Readers like you make all of this possible, and I am genuinely grateful for the opportunity to share my stories with you.

With warm regards,
Sophia.

Acknowledgments

Writing a novel is a labor of love, a creative endeavor that requires dedication, sacrifice, and a strong support system. I am immensely grateful to the extraordinary individuals who have been there for me every step of the way, offering their unwavering support, encouragement, and love.

First and foremost, I would like to express my deepest gratitude to my husband. Your patience, understanding, and unwavering belief in me have been a constant source of strength. Thank you for standing by my side, being my rock during challenging moments, and constantly reminding me of my potential. Your love and support have been instrumental in bringing this novel to fruition.

To my children, who have witnessed firsthand the ups and downs of the creative process, thank you for your endless patience and understanding. Your little acts of kindness, from leaving me quiet time to write to offering hugs during moments of self-doubt, have meant the world to me. I am so grateful to have you in my life.

A special mention goes to my oldest daughter. Your insightful feedback has been invaluable throughout this journey. Thank you for being my sounding board and for challenging me to think deeper. Your creative spirit inspires me every day.

I extend my heartfelt appreciation to my friends, who have provided support and encouragement throughout this writing process. Your belief in my abilities, willingness to listen to my ideas, and constant encouragement have been lifelines. Thank you for being there to celebrate the victories and offer a shoulder to lean on during the more challenging times. Your friendship means the world to me.

In conclusion, completing this novel would not have been possible without the unwavering support, love, and understanding of the incredible people in my life. I am forever indebted to you all, and I offer my heartfelt gratitude for joining me on this remarkable adventure.

With all my love and gratitude,

Xoxo

Sophia.

About the Author

Sophia is an aspiring author embarking on an exciting journey into the world of storytelling with their debut novel. As an avid reader, Sophia has always found solace and inspiration within the pages of books, immersing themselves in different worlds, diverse perspectives, and captivating narratives. This deep appreciation for literature has fueled their desire to craft stories and share them with the world.

When not lost in the realms of imagination, Sophia finds joy in nurturing life through gardening and planting. The beauty of nature serves as a wellspring of inspiration, influencing their writing with vivid descriptions and an appreciation for the natural world. The symbiotic relationship between creativity and the environment is a theme often found in Sophia's storytelling.

Family holds a special place in Sophia's heart. They draw inspiration from the bonds of love, support, and the dynamics that shape familial relationships. This profound connection informs the depth and authenticity of their characters' relationships, as they explore the intricate dynamics of families and the impact they have on their stories.

Traveling is another passion that has greatly influenced Sophia's writing. Exploring different cultures, discovering new landscapes, and immersing themselves in diverse experiences provide a wellspring of inspiration for their storytelling. The enriching encounters and perspectives gained through their travels are reflected in the tapestry of their narratives, adding depth and authenticity to the worlds they create.

With their debut novel, Sophia hopes to captivate readers with their love for literature, passion for storytelling, and their unique perspective on life. They aspire to create stories that touch hearts, transport readers to new and exciting worlds, and leave a lasting impression. Through their words, Sophia invites readers to embark on a journey of imagination, emotion, and self-discovery.